Across the Dark Stream

The Douglas Town Chronicles
~ Book Three ~

By Ginger G. Howard

Sequel to: **Beneath the Stairs**

First Edition

ISBN: 978-0-578-37935-7
Publisher: Gemini Pacific Publishing

For more information, visit: https://gingerhowardauthor.blogspot.com/
 Or https://www.facebook.com/g.howard.author/

Edited by: Angie Gia-Bennett and Paul Howard
Cover Design: Copyright© 2022 Riley M. Howard

Circled round a roaring flame
Their dancing figures can be seen
Within a clearing in the trees
Across the darkened stream.

Arms raised up unto the moon
They give themselves in offering
To ward off darkened winter nights
And bring the light of spring.

By: Ginger G. Howard

Poem title ~ *Solstice*
Written: Nov. 2021

Chapter One
After the Party

In the haze of coming into full consciousness, the huge candle in the center of the room was the first thing to come into focus. Drip after drip the wax oozed slowly down, becoming one with a dark-red, cooling mass - resembling a pool of blood.

The sight started synapses firing and created an urgency to get up from lying right side down. It was immediately apparent there was no feeling below the shoulders.

Why can't I move?

A female voice called out. "HELP!"

Why do I sound so strange?
Whose voice is that?

The line of sight shifted to allow for a visual assessment of all body parts... a female body.

It appeared that her arms were being held behind her back somehow, with ropes wrapped around the ankles, just above a pair of dirty tennis shoes.

Those aren't my shoes.

She tried to move her body back and forth but struggled against the lack of feeling in her extremities, as well as the restraint of the bindings.

"No!" I heard the girl yell out in frustration.

Hey, can you hear me?

"No, no, no, this can't be happening," she cried.

She made one last feeble attempt at freeing herself. Exhausted and confused she screamed out with the very last of her energy, "HELP!"

"No... no... no..."

I was pulled up and out of the dream, as I heard the sound of my own voice, and felt myself flailing against invisible bindings.

Someone was shaking me.

"Huh?" I panicked, as I opened my eyes, still caught up in my dream state. "Where am I?"

A quiet voice whispered in my ear, "Shhh, shhh... you're okay."

Through blurry, tired eyes, I could see light beginning to peek through the drapes across the room. As I allowed my eyes to adjust, the floor-to-ceiling brick fireplace of Cat's living room came into focus.

Russell pulled me closer into our 'spooning' position on the couch. "You must have been having a bad dream," he said quietly.

"That was so… real!" I responded.

I moved my legs, relieved to find they weren't bound.

Trying to sit up, I realized my arms and legs ached. My wrists and ankles actually hurt.

"You're shivering," Russell commented. "Here." He pulled the extra blanket up off the floor and wrapped it around my shoulders.

Pulling the blanket tighter around my torso, I noticed I was still fully dressed from the party. The scent of bonfire still clung to my hair.

"I can't believe I fell asleep."

"It was an eventful night," he replied, scooting back into the corner of the couch, pulling me towards him. "What was your dream about?"

"I'm not exactly sure where I was, but I was lying on a floor on my right side, staring at a candle… a red candle. I remember not being able to move my body, but I could lift my head up to look around. It was pretty dark, but I was able to make out that there were ropes tied around my ankles. I think my hands were tied around my back."

"That's really freaky."

"It was! When I realized I was tied up, I started to panic."

"I know! You were kicking me. That's why I woke you up."

"It was so real. I just can't shake it."

"You're okay, though," he reassured me. "It was just a dream."

"Yeah, I know." I shook my head trying to clear the images from my mind. "But it wasn't like any dream I've had before, though."

"Like the ones with people from the house?" he asked.

"Exactly! And there's something else…" I continued, still trying to piece it all together. "At the party, I bumped into someone while we were walking through the crowd. I had a vision of that same candle."

"Really?"

"Didn't *you* get a sense from someone in that crowd? Someone… *off* somehow?"

"*Off*?" he asked, chuckling quietly. "It was a party filled with teenagers on Halloween night. You'll have to be more specific."

"Someone, whose energy was dark and icky, you know, like they wanted to do something bad."

"*Icky*? Hmm… no," he answered, snickering a little.

"Don't laugh, I'm being serious."

"Okay, to be fair, I normally put up a mental barrier before I go into large groups like that, to block out everyone's thoughts and feelings. The only thing I was in-tune to, was *you*."

"I need to learn how to do that."

"What? Block people out?"

"Yeah… tonight was a lot to handle. There were too many people, and the vibes were all over the place. It never used to be like that."

"It can be overwhelming, I know."

"I also thought I heard a girl scream."

"I heard a lot of screams, and howls," he responded. "It was a rowdy party."

"I really feel like something bad happened," I murmured, feeling the need for sleep pulling me back in.

I wanted to close my eyes, just enjoy the feeling of snuggling against him. I didn't want to think about the nightmare anymore. I only wanted to focus on feeling his heartbeat against my back, our breathing in unison.

Just then, light, from the headlamps of a car, raced across the wood-paneled accent wall of the living room, followed by the sound of Janice's car pulling to a stop in the driveway.

She was arriving home from her graveyard shift at the diner.

Normally, I never heard her return when I spent the night, because I would be asleep on the floor in Cat's room. I just knew that every Sunday morning she prepared a big breakfast, then went to bed for a few hours. I guess our breakfast was *her* dinner.

"Oh crap!" I exclaimed, as I tried to push myself up to a sitting position out of Russell's arms. "What time IS it? Oh my god! Oh my god!"

I'd just managed to sit up straight when Janice opened the front door.

"Oh my god! Oh my god!" I repeated under my breath as I desperately tried to untangle my feet from inside the blankets.

"Calm down. I sleep over all the time. It's no big deal," he whispered.

I managed to scoot over to the far side of the couch, wrapped myself back up in the blanket, and tried to act naturally.

She walked from the front entrance past the living room area, noticing Russell first.

"Good morning."

"Hi, sorry. I tried to be as quiet as possible, I hope I didn't wake you," Janice responded quietly.

"No, I was already awake. How was your shift?" he asked politely. He was there so often with Mike that Janice acted as if he were another one of her children.

She smiled, and was about to respond when she noticed me, and did a double take. "Gwen!" She paused, glancing back and forth between us. "You're up, too?"

"Good morning," I greeted meekly, my brain scrambling for an explanation. "Yeah, I couldn't sleep. We've just been talking."

"Couldn't sleep?" she asked, eyeing us both in curiosity. "Is everything okay?"

"I had a nightmare. I guess it's from all the Halloween movies we've been watching."

"Well, you can go back to Cat's room, now," she directed, in a very parental tone. It was obvious she was not happy to find me there. "I'll let you know when breakfast is ready."

"Okay," I responded, relieved to flee the uncomfortable situation.

As I made my way from the living room to the hallway, I overheard Janice talking to Russell.

"I wasn't aware that you and Gwen were so… chummy." I could hear the disapproval in her voice, and my heart fell a little bit.

I shuffled down the hall into Cat's room, slightly deflated by the circumstances, and closed the door behind me. She had one socked foot sticking out from underneath her covers, and her sheet pulled up over her head.

I crawled over to my sleeping bag and slipped inside. It was freezing, and the hard floor felt like a sheet of ice. I laid there shivering for what seemed like an eternity, not tired in the least, worrying over what Janice would say when she saw me next.

I heard Russell make his way down the hall to the bathroom and heard the clinking of pots and pans from Janice in the kitchen. Eventually, I recognized the sound of coffee percolating on the stove, followed by the heavenly aroma of bacon.

Sometime later, Russell tapped lightly on the door and said, "Breakfast is ready, guys." I heard him then walk away from the door towards Mike's room.

Sitting up, I gently put my hand on the back of Cat's exposed leg and shook it back and forth.

"Hey sleepy head, breakfast is ready."

She didn't stir.

"Cat! Breakfast!" I said a little louder.

I heard a moan, but no movement. I crawled up onto my knees and rocked her back and forth a little more aggressively.

11

Eventually she lifted the sheet up and poked her head out. "What? Huh?" she mumbled. "What time is it?"

"I don't know. I can't see your clock from here."

Slowly Cat sat up and sniffed the air. "Mmm, bacon."

I stood up, stretched, and then searched around for my sweatshirt. When I glanced back over at the bed, Cat had pulled all the covers back over her, wrapping herself up like a cocoon.

I shook her again.

"Too early. Too cold," she grumbled.

"Bacon. *Bacon*! BACON!" I repeated, as I shook her again.

Finally, she responded, "Okay! Okay! I'm coming!"

I waited while she found her soft terry cloth robe to wrap herself up in, and then made an unsuccessful attempt at tamping down her hair with her hands.

Stretching and yawning, she took a good look at me for the first time, and her face scrunched up in confusion. "Are you still in the same clothes from last night?" she asked. "You are! Did you even go to sleep?"

"I fell asleep on the couch," I answered coyly, feeling a sudden flush of heat to my cheeks.

"What? With Russell?" she asked, as the situation took shape in her mind. "My mom didn't find you, did she?"

"She did..." I moaned with regret.

"Crap!"

"When she got home, we were just sitting on the couch. I was telling him about a nightmare I'd had. Nothing else was going on."

"Let's hope she believes that," Cat remarked, as we made our way down the hall.

When we walked into the kitchen, I was so embarrassed that I did my best to avoid eye contact.

Russell joined us a few minutes later, followed by a very sleepy Mike, who did not approve of the daylight.

"Well, *this* is a surprise!" Janice commented, as she poured orange juice into the glass where Mike usually sat. He was rubbing his temples and squinting against the light.

"Did you guys have a fun Halloween night?" Janice asked the group.

Russell made his way to the chair next to mine and smiled at me as he sat down.

"Yes! We had a great time," Russell responded.

Mike hadn't even made it to his chair when he groaned, "UGH! Must you all speak so loud?" He turned back around and began to shuffle away. "I can't do this," he announced. "I'm going back to bed. Russ, if you wake me again, I'll kill you."

"I'm amazed you actually got him to make it *that* far," Janice commented to Russell.

"It was worth a shot," he replied, and reached over to grab a piece of toast. "The breakfast looks great, by the way. Thank you!"

"Yes, thank you," I added.

"Mom, you always outdo yourself when it comes to Sunday breakfast!" Cat exclaimed cheerfully.

"Thank you, honey," she responded.

Despite her pleasant nature, she looked exhausted as she turned back around to scoop scrambled eggs from the pan to a large plate.

Russell leaned in close, bumping his shoulder affectionately against mine. "Can you pass the butter?" he asked sweetly. I felt a wave of tender emotions envelope me, causing a flush of heat in my cheeks.

"Behave," I scolded in a whisper.

Janice had turned back around, taking notice of the comfortable familiarity exchanged between us. She had a glint of suspicion in her eyes as she proceeded to place the plate down on the table.

"Anything I need to know about?" she asked bluntly, as she sat down, looking at each of us in turn.

Exchanging glances, we replied in unison, "Nothing," then diverted our attention back to our plates.

"Great bacon, Mom," Cat remarked.

"The eggs are perfect, Janice," Russell commented.

I kept my nose down, nibbled my toast, and wished I could somehow restart the morning.

Chapter Two
· Sunday Confrontations

Russell offered to drop me off on his way home, so I didn't have to walk while carrying all of my stuff. We thought it wise for him to stop a couple houses away, so as to not arouse suspicion.

As I entered in through the front door, I heard my mother call out, "Gwen? Is that you?"

"Yeah, mom!" I closed the door behind me and quickly headed for my room.

"Come here a minute," she said loudly. A sharpness to her tone, one usually reserved for my dad, sent a prickly sensation down my spine, and stopped me in my tracks. I turned around and slunk towards her voice.

"What's wrong?" I asked, as I came around the corner to the kitchen. She sat at the dining table with a cup of coffee in her hands, looking stressed out. My heart sank into my stomach.

"We need to talk," she replied sternly.

I had a sinking sensation of what was to come.

"I got a call from Janice a few minutes ago," she stated.

My stomach dropped.

"She said that Russell also stayed over last night," she continued, looking directly into my eyes, gauging my response.

"Yeah," I responded nonchalantly. I tried to act as if it was no big deal, but my heart was racing. "Apparently he crashed on the couch after he and Mike got back from the Halloween party."

I conveniently left out that Cat and I went to the same party.

"She said she found you on the couch with him when she got home this morning."

"Yeah, I was *sitting* on the couch with him," I corrected, unwilling to relinquish my deepest secrets, despite her Jedi Mother mind tricks. "And, like I explained to *her*, I had a nightmare, so I got up to go to the kitchen. I accidentally woke him up. We were just talking."

"So, you don't think you or Cat should have, at any point, mentioned to Janice that you and Russell were dating?" she asked.

"No," I responded without hesitation.

"Or that you should have told *me* that Russell spent the night over there on occasion? You don't think that is *at all* concerning?" Her voice rose in pitch with each question.

"I didn't think about it like *that*."

"Really?" she asked skeptically.

"I mean, I knew he was going to the party with Mike," I offered. "I just didn't know he'd be there in the morning. It was a nice surprise," I lied. "But, you're right! We should have told Janice we were seeing each other. It was just... well... awkward."

"You mean, wrong," she responded accusingly.

"No! Of course not," I snapped. "What was I supposed to say, 'Good morning, Janice. By the way, your son's best friend and I are dating. Thanks for breakfast'?"

"Don't get sassy with me, Gwen," she chided, insulted by my show of disrespect.

"Well, you're *totally* making this out to be a *big* deal!" I rallied back, as I stood up from the table.

"If it wasn't such a big deal, why'd you have Russell drop you off where you thought I couldn't see you?"

I didn't know how to respond to that, so decided to walk away instead.

"Sit down!" she yelled. "We're not done yet!"

Taken aback by her raised voice, I plopped back down in my seat.

"Listen to me, young lady, you are way too young for this sort of *behavior*."

"What kind of behavior is that?"

"You *know* what I mean! Russell was in the house with you... overnight... *unchaperoned*!"

"Mom, I was asleep. I don't need a chaperone to be *asleep*!"

"Don't be a smart ass! You know exactly what I mean!" she responded tightly, and then went quiet, staring at me.

I returned her stare.

After a few painful seconds elapsed, she asked, "Are you still a... a... *you* know?"

"A... *what*?" I asked. I knew what she meant, of course, I was just daring her to say "it" out loud. She hadn't even been able to talk to me about my first *period*. The more personal and candid the conversation needed to be, the more she shied away from the subject. So *this* subject was the last thing either one of us wanted to talk about.

"Elizabeth? What's all the fuss about?" my dad called out from the bedroom. He continued talking loudly as he made his way towards the kitchen. "I go to change my clothes, and apparently all hell breaks loose."

"Dad, it's nothing!" I yelled back.

He came around the corner fastening up the last of his buttons, then tucking his shirt into his belt. "It doesn't sound like nothing."

"How long has this *thing* been going on?" my mom continued, in a high-pitched voice, hyper-fixated on the subject at hand.

"What thing? There has been no '*thing*'!" I exclaimed.

"Has something happened?" my dad asked, looking back and forth at us with concern and confusion.

"*Nothing* has happened!" I protested loudly.

"Answer my question," she insisted.

"A *virgin*?" I asked, almost screaming. I saw her wince at the use of the word. "Yes, I *am*!"

My dad's face tightened. "Why wouldn't she be?" he asked curtly. "What the hell is going on?"

"Go to your room, Gwen! I'm not going to stand for you yelling at me! Your dad and I need to discuss this." She really had worked herself up into quite a lather, uncharacteristically becoming both the interrogator *and* enforcer.

"OH MY GOD! I can't believe this. There is nothing to discuss!" I yelled, as I stormed down the hallway to my room.

I rammed through the door and it slammed back against the wall, leaving a dent. I threw my bag across the room, before turning around and grabbing the door to slam it shut against my parents' raised voices.

Trying to tune them out, I closed my eyes, and pressed my hands up against my ears. I did my best to suppress a scream of rage building up within me. I could feel the blood pumping up my neck into my head, a swiftly flowing rapid. A strange buzz pulsed and throbbed in my inner ear. It grew in intensity until it blocked out my parents and overwhelmed everything.

Suddenly a sharp sting quickly extinguished my rage. I opened my eyes, to focus on the sensation. A long red streak across the top of my forearm shocked me so much, I completely forgot about everything else for a moment.

The house went silent. My parents' arguing had ceased.

"Gwen, *what* was that?" my father yelled.

I looked around me.

What just happened?

Colorful glass shards were everywhere. It was as if my desk lamp exploded.

Hurried feet dashed down the hall to my room.

It was only then that I registered what felt like ants crawling down my arm, and I glanced down to see the red streak had been a gash. Blood trickled and oozed out along its entire length. My stomach churned at the sight, my head swooned, and that's when the pain hit. I lifted my arm up, putting my opposite hand over the wound - the contact only making the pain intensify.

My mother arrived at the door first. I leaned against it as she tried to push it open.

"Let me in, Gwen!" she yelled, as she banged upon it.

"Okay, okay," I finally relented, realizing there was no way I could hide the mess. I stepped forward, and allowed her in.

She gasped.

"*What* happened?" she asked, immediately noticing the glass shards everywhere. "Why did you do that? I thought you loved that lamp!"

"I didn't do it!" I answered in a shaky voice. "I don't know what happened. Really!"

She turned towards me, noticing the blood leaking through my fingers and pooling on the floor at my feet. "I'll go get the first aid kit."

I couldn't tell if she was concerned or angry. It was as if she'd gone onto automatic pilot. She turned and dashed down the hall.

It reminded me of how she normally handled uncomfortable situations, by diverting attention to something else... something she *could* control.

I stood there, bleeding on the floor, gazing around at the mess.

Well, at least we're no longer talking about my virginity.

"Gwen, what the hell happened in here?" my dad asked in a raised voice, as he got a complete view of the room. "See, *this* is what happens when you slam the door! We've told you a million times not to do that."

"I know, but I don't think…"

"Elizabeth! Are you getting something to stop the bleeding?" he yelled.

"Yes! For goodness sake, Bob!" she yelled back.

He looked around my floor, picked up one of my discarded shirts, sat me down on the edge of the bed, and then used it to wrap around my forearm.

"Dad…" I pleaded in a meek voice, feeling confused and fragile.

He interrupted, "Just sit here, and apply direct pressure on it." He took my hand and placed it over the ever-widening bloody patch on my shirt.

"I liked that shirt," I moaned.

My mom came back in the room, avoided looking at the blood, and handed the kit to my dad to deal with.

"You need to get this room cleaned up," she fretted, walking back out.

"You'll be okay," my dad soothed, after unwrapping the shirt, to take a better look. "I don't think you'll need stitches." He applied some Iodine to a cotton ball and starting to clean it.

"OW! Dad!"

"Hey, that's how you know it's working! We need to make sure it's clean," he explained, concentrating on the task.

The tenderness and concern, from my father, was not a side of his personality I saw much of anymore, I was reminded of my younger days when he referred to me as "daddy's little girl." He used to make me feel like I was the most special person in the whole universe. It was very comforting.

After applying a liberal amount of Neosporin, and placing gauze over the gash, he wrapped white tape around my forearm to hold it all together. "There you go. Good as new."

"Thanks," I replied, wishing it hadn't taken a bleeding wound to see that side of him again.

We sat there in awkward silence, until my mom returned with a wet sponge, dustpan, and broom. She kept the sponge, and set down the other two, motioning that they were for me.

No sympathy from her, I guess.

Dad got up and quietly left the room, while I started cleaning up the pieces of glass.

"You know, your father and I were a little concerned at first about Russell being older than you," she started to say, as she bent over to wipe the blood up off the floor, "but he seemed like a good guy, so we gave him a chance. We know now that we were right to be concerned! Some things are going to change around here."

"What do you mean 'things are going to change'? You can't ground me from him! We've done nothing wrong!"

Just then, the phone rang, and I heard my dad answer it. He came down the hall and leaned into the room. "Elizabeth, it's Russell on the phone for Gwen. What should I tell him?"

"Russell?" I started to put down the dustpan.

My mom put her hand on my shoulder to keep me from leaving the room. "No. We'll handle it. You stay here."

"What? *No!*"

"I mean it. Stay in your room!" She pulled the door shut as she exited. I heard more arguing, as they walked back towards the kitchen.

I cracked the door just a bit and listened intently. After much debate, on how best to handle the situation, my father got back onto the phone. A series of words followed that I never wanted to hear.

"… I know, Russell, you're a nice kid and all, but she's not going to be able to talk to you on the phone for a while…"

My heart sank, not just into my stomach, but down below the foundations of the house, below the surface of the earth, into a dark abyss.

Not going to be able to talk to him on the phone for a while? NO!

I turned, leaned against the door, and slowly slumped to the floor.

Russell, just come get me! Take me away from this place!

There I sat, as the hours ticked by, lost in the darkest reaches of my psyche, staring into nothing.

The only time anything makes any sense, is when I'm with you.

Night had fallen when I heard raised voices coming from the kitchen, followed by my mom calling out for me to come eat.

I ignored her.

Then I heard the heavy thud of my father's footsteps coming down the hall, followed by a loud knock on the bedroom door.

I ignored him.

Gradually he pushed the door open, against my weight, pushing me along with it. He walked into my dark room and stood above me with his hands on his hips - his body illuminated by the light coming in from the hallway.

I refused to look up at him.

I guess I had unconsciously willed myself to no longer feel, and could tell, on some conscious level, that I was systematically shutting down.

I hadn't experienced anything like that before. I wasn't even registering his words, or maybe, more to the point, not caring what the combination of sounds meant in the formation of words, that then translated into meaningful images of association.

I don't care. I just want to be with Russell...

That was it - dissociation.

I had become separate and apart from myself and my surroundings - like an out-of-body experience - observing from an unfeeling and safe distance until I could figure out how to process what was happening.

They can't keep Russell and me apart. They just can't!

As I was watched and listened to my father babble unintelligible words, to my unresponsive form sitting on my bedroom floor, I had a funny thought... my internal answering machine.

'I'm sorry, Gwen isn't in right now, but if you leave your name and number, and a brief message, she will get back to you as soon as she is able.'

Chapter Three
Monday Blues

The candle burned down. The flame finally extinguished within a molten puddle, morphed into a mound without identifiable form or function. The sudden darkness offered a welcome relief from the strange graffiti that had found a life of its own in the shadow play from the flickering candlelight.

Without sight, all the other senses took over, reaching out, like tendrils, stretching and twining around anything they could find.

At first, it was the sense of smell, and the recognition of hay. There was also an earthy aroma below her, where she could hear scratching beneath the floorboards… a mouse?

Then she noticed the sound of an elongated squeak, like a slow draw across a violin string. It started a rhythmic cycle of repetition… a cricket perhaps?

Off in the distance yips and yowls started - the cheers from a pack of coyotes celebrating a kill. ·

The thought of them delighting in a kill was distressing. This brought about a renewed burst of energy at yet another futile struggle against the bindings, which then brought about another throbbing headache - the only body part that wasn't completely numb.

Then there came a startling sound of the click of a lock, the creak of a door swinging open, followed by a refreshing breeze that wafted through into the room. It was reminiscent of crisp mountain air.

"Who's there?"

The voice that came out was raspy, followed by the sensation of pain from a very dry throat.

In the dim light of dawn, a person's silhouette stood in the doorway - rows of trees visible behind.

"Thank God! Help me! Can you please untie me?"

The sound of footsteps grew louder, as the person made their way across the flooring.

"I'm so thirsty! I could really use some water."

The shadowy figure knelt, and there was a hint of something floral in the air.

"Help me, please!"

The figure came closer.

"Who are you? Why am I here? Where's Kenneth?"

There was a forceful prick to the neck, followed by a sting that then began to burn and burn...

"AAGH!" My eyes shot open, reflexively bringing my hand up to my neck. There was a lingering ache throughout my body, I was cold, and I was overwhelmed with thirst.

Reaching over to my nightstand, I grabbed the glass of water I always kept there and drank it down ravenously. It never tasted so good.

After my thirst was sated, I took note of the faint morning light just beginning to illuminate my window.

What day is it?

I could still recall the vivid image of the faint sun lighting upon the tips of trees out beyond the door.

It hit me. "Ah, crap. It's Monday!"

~~

Ding, ding, ding, ding, ding!

The repetitive metallic clang of the class bell caused me to jump out of my own skin.

Where did the time go? Was I asleep? Noo... there's no way I could have fallen asleep. I thought, as I lifted my head up off of my left hand that had been propped up by my elbow.

I looked around the room casually - making sure no one was staring at me - then checked the corners of my mouth for drool. Quickly I gathered my belongings, shoved them into my bag, and made my way from class towards the outdoor quad to have lunch.

When I pushed my way through the double doors, the sunlight lifted my spirits from being stuck inside a dark, depressing building all morning.

Looking around, it appeared as though this was the day when all the trees had decided to give up on life - shedding their leaves like a dog shaking water from its fur. A brisk wind swept through the quad, picking them up, and whirling them around in multicolored circles. It would have been a spectacular display to appreciate, if I hadn't been so distracted by the chill that penetrated my core, freezing me from the inside out. The sharp icy bite of the air hurt my lungs with every breath.

It's going to be a long hard winter.

I grabbed my scarf, unwound it from the strap of my book bag, and wrapped it around my neck to cover my mouth and nose. I pulled my coat tighter around myself and made my way to our usual table.

As I walked, I casually scanned the faces and forms of the upper classmen rushing back into the buildings to get to class, hoping to catch sight of Russell somewhere. He hadn't met me at the lockers before school, like normal, and I feared I'd somehow missed him before lunch as well.

When I went to sit down the bench felt like an ice block. I put my math textbook to good use - as a seat warmer.

One-by-one my friends joined me, each with a flimsy Styrofoam cup of hot watered-down cocoa in one hand, and something to eat in the other. It appeared we were the last holdouts - not driven into the cafeteria by the cold - determined to soak in the last short days of sunshine.

Cat arrived and handed me the extra cup she was holding. "I thought you might like one, since you weren't here yet, and we were all getting one."

"Aw, thanks!" I replied, gratefully accepting it. "Here, I wrote this last night. I forgot to give it to you in Art class."

"Yay! A letter!" she exclaimed, about to open it up.

"Can you read it later... by yourself?" I asked, pleading with my eyes to keep the contents private. It explained how her mom called mine, and why I got grounded. It also explained the vivid dreams, and the lamp exploding.

"Oh, totally!" she responded, nodding that she understood, and quickly tucked it in her bag.

Wrapping my hands around the cup of hot chocolate, I remarked, "I can't believe how cold it is already. *Why* did we think it was a good idea to not go into the cafeteria?"

"I don't know anymore," Cat responded, shivering against another burst of wind.

"Because it's a social madhouse in there, that's why," Jennifer responded.

"Very true," I responded.

"Oh my god, yes!" Cat confirmed.

"Did you guys have any trouble getting to school this morning?" Kelly asked, as she folded over her jacket to sit on. "The fog was so bad down where I live, that my mom practically had a panic attack driving me here."

"It wasn't that bad for us," Jennifer replied. "Maybe it's just certain parts of town."

"Yeah, I guess," Kelly, responded. "We got a flyer in the mail from school that had a bus schedule for 'fog delays'. Now I know why."

Still exhausted, hazy, and in an emotional funk, I was mesmerized by the lift and evaporation of the steam rising from the surface of my hot chocolate. I was only vaguely aware of Brian speaking, but did register him proclaim, "That party was totally awesome!"

"Your mix tape was killer, dude!" Drew responded, and everyone added words of agreement.

They started recalling fun details of their experiences. My thoughts bounced all over the place, from cuddling with Russell on the couch and waking up in his arms, to the fight I had with my parents and the fact that I wasn't going to be able to talk to him on the phone after school.

Russell, where are you? Why aren't you here today?

I sensed a shift in energy. The sudden change pulled my focus away from my cocoa. A wave of conflicting emotions poured across the table at me. I lifted my gaze and met Liz's piercing blue eyes, surrounded by thick black eyeliner, staring back at me.

When she spoke, I was still in a fugue state. At first, I fixated on the steam cloud each word formed, and then how the steam slowly dissipated into the cold air, becoming invisible.

As if on a delay, I heard the sounds her words made slowly come into focus, and then translate into something meaningful.

"So do you, like, totally buy into all that stuff now?" she asked, tightly clasping a large crucifix dangling from a long silver chain around her neck.

Has she always worn that?

"I'm sorry, what?" I asked.

"Witchcraft," she repeated, in complete seriousness.

"What are you talking about?" I asked, now very much focused on her words, feeling as if I'd been dropped into an ongoing conversation.

"The bonfire...." She threw her hands out in exasperation. "You and your boyfriend were spouting off some pretty crazy stuff."

"Hello... Halloween," Jennifer interjected. "Duh!"

"I thought it was rad!" Brian commented.

Was everyone listening to our conversation?

"You would," Craig teased.

"And w*hy* would he?" Drew asked, ever playing the intellectual. "That doesn't even make sense."

"I dunno… because he's a freak-a-zoid, that's why!" Craig exclaimed. Then he laughed alone at his own joke.

"I thought it was cool when we threw stuff into the fire, ya know, to like, get rid of the things that were bugging us, or whatever. It felt good," Brian offered in the way of explanation.

"It did feel good," Kelly chimed in. "But I don't think you'd call that *Witchcraft.* It was more like *symbolism.* You know… 'out with the old, in with the new'."

"Gwen, come on, what about the other things you guys threw in the fire… things from the house," Liz persisted. "You were chanting, like, some kind of ritual."

"Like Kelly said… it was just… *symbolic,*" I answered, feeling a little defensive, as if on trial for something.

"Okay," Liz replied, clearly unsatisfied. "It's just that, I didn't know you before this year, so I don't know if, like, talking to ghosts, or whatever, is just a *normal* day for you."

"No. It's **not** a *normal* day for me," I answered tightly, my anger rising, "and, **I** wasn't the only one who saw the ghosts."

"Liz… back off!" Cat growled.

"What's the problem?" Kevin asked, walking up to the table with Chris, perhaps noticing the tension building between us, and feeling the need to intercede.

"Hi, Gwen," Chris said, using his eyes to motion towards Liz and mouth the words: *What's going on?*

"Hi, guys," I responded, shaking my head, and rolling my eyes. "No problem, Kevin. Just a misunderstanding I think."

"About what?" he asked.

"Well, Liz was just asking if Witchcraft and talking to ghosts was a normal day for me. I'm not sure what's she's getting at though."

"Liz, we told you about what happened this summer," Kevin responded in my defense.

"Yeah, that's what you *told* us, but you didn't think we'd really believe that, do you?" Liz countered, still holding the crucifix tight in her hand as if she needed protection.

"You believe whatever you want! You weren't there. We were," Kevin responded, standing tall with his arms crossed, daring her to challenge him. "I know what I saw!"

She persisted, ignoring Kevin, and aggressively focusing her attention back on me. "Okay, *but...* what's up with you supposedly casting a *spell* on that doll?"

"Liz, back *off!*" Cat yelled, slamming her hands down on the table.

"Yeah, stop it." Jennifer added. "You sound like a cop interrogating a suspect. It's rude."

"So you guys are telling me," Liz challenged, as she looked around the group, "that you actually believe her story about the ghosts, and you're okay with her practicing

Witchcraft?" She appeared truly astounded at the thought that she was the only one being reasonable.

"Where did you even get that idea anyway?" I asked, trying to keep my blood pressure under control. I could feel my face getting hot and my hands starting to shake.

"It's all *anybody* is talking about right now," Liz responded flippantly. "I just wanted to hear it from *you*."

Cat looked at me questioningly, raising her eyebrows, "I wonder who this *anybody* could be?" Then she glared back at Liz.

"Gwen, you don't need to explain yourself to anyone," Chris interjected.

"Thank you," I said, turning to him in surprise. He smiled back, which gave me hope we'd turned a corner and were friends again. Perhaps never the same friends we once were, but still there for each other.

"And yeah, I *do* believe in ghosts now. I saw some really crazy shit," he said.

Kelly then addressed Liz, "Listen, we didn't know *you* before this year either, and we were willing to let you into our group. So stop with all this, 'holier than thou', attitude."

"Oh, I'm sorry... you LET me into your group?" Liz spat back.

"Yeah, so cut the crap," Jennifer warned. "You're being rude to my friends."

"So suddenly I'm NOT your friend?" Liz responded, clearly hurt by the counter offense.

"That's not what I meant..." Jennifer rolled her eyes and sighed.

"Okay! Okay! Stop it, you guys," I said loudly, looking at the three of them in turn, trying to break the tension. I put my hot chocolate on the table, took a deep breath, then calmly put my hands together and placed them on my lap.

Turning back to Liz I said, "You want to hear it from me? Fine..." I took a deep breath. Despite wanting so badly just to put the traumatizing events of the Victorian house behind me, I continued, "We ended up going back to the house again, before Halloween, because we needed to free the spirits that were trapped there."

"No way!" Drew exclaimed. "I bet that was so frickin' scary! I'd never go into that house!"

"I know," Jennifer responded. "Me neither."

"With spells?" Liz pressed, condescension curling at the corner of her mouth. Apparently, my statement had been a satisfying admission to some guilt.

"That's so punk rock!" Craig exclaimed.

"What do you know about punk rock? Look at yourself," Brian scoffed, and pointed at Craig's Flock of Seagulls' hairstyle and fashion statement.

I hesitated before answering, distracted for a moment by all the commentary, and then I looked back at Liz.

Before responding, I weighed each word carefully. "I was given *instructions* on how to release the spirits from the house."

"These, so called, *'instructions'*, you got them from Russell, right?" she asked.

"Yeah, so what," I replied. I felt my nails digging deeper into the palms of my cold hands.

"So does that make *him* a Witch?"

"No! Of course not," I protested, perhaps a little too defensively. "What's your damage? Why are you obsessing about Witchcraft?"

"How would you explain it then?"

Cat interjected tersely, "Like an exorcism."

"A what?" Liz asked, looking over to Cat in annoyance.

"Yeah, we cleared the house of evil spirits basically. So, like an *exorcism*," Cat repeated.

Cat, Kevin, Russell, and I had all agreed to keep quiet about what we'd learned from Brighid, and the Wiccan paraphernalia hidden behind the blue beaded curtain in the back half of her shop. Cat had her own reasons for not wanting anyone digging too deep into the subject of the supernatural, considering she was able to commune with the ghost of her dead father. We'd never really discussed what it all *meant* though; let alone how to name it.

"But, you performed rituals and cast spells," Liz stated again, this time with an insulted look on her face as if I was trying to lie to her, "like a... *Witch*."

The way she said that last word sent a shiver up my spine. She was starting to seem, more and more, like one of those girls that followed Erin around - someone with a hateful heart and a narrow mind, who would have thrown stones, or burnt down my house, because they believed I was evil.

"That's ridiculous!" I protested. "Do you even hear yourself right now?" I got up, grabbed my math book off the bench, put it back in my bag, and started to walk away.

"Really, Liz?" Cat scolded. "Gwen? Gwen, wait. Where are you going?" she asked.

"To go wait by my next class." Turning back around towards her, I said, "I'll just catch up with you later."

"Gwen, come back," Kelly and Jennifer both called out. I heard various affirmations mumbled around the table from Brian, Craig, Drew, and Chris as well.

"Yeah, Gwen, it's okay. You don't have to leave," Kevin offered. Then he turned towards Liz, "Seriously, what's your problem?"

"What's MY problem? You guys are the ones with a problem if you're okay with all of this!" Liz declared, clearly dumbfounded by their lack of concern.

Cat got up from the table and ran over to me. "Don't leave," she said, placing her hand on my arm. "You're going to have to talk about this eventually and help them all understand it."

"Why? *I* don't even understand *it*. You and Kevin were there… *you* explain it," I urged, feeling beyond fed up with it all. "I'm so tired of being called a freak and a psycho… now *this*? They used to burn people *accused* of being Witches. That's what she's doing right now - accusing me! You heard the way she said that word."

She held both of my hands out in front of her, so that I had to hold still and look her in the eyes. "Who cares!" Cat responded. "This *isn't* Salem."

"Yeah, but it's high school! That's almost just as bad!"

"You can handle it. Look at all you've faced over the last couple months. You can do this!"

"You think Erin knew about the doll binding?" I finally asked. "Is she the one talking about it? *How* could she have found out?"

"I don't know, but you need to own it. If Erin, or anyone else, comes at you with this Witch stuff, tell her you can turn her into a toad or something. Scare her so bad she'll have to leave you alone."

The thought made me laugh, despite my emotional fatigue, and I smiled. "Okay, I do like the idea of her being turned into a toad."

"See? There's my girl," Cat said, smiling back. "Now come back and finish your cocoa."

I relented, and returned to the table, taking back my seat. Kevin came around from the opposite side, sat down next to me, put his arm around my shoulders, and pulled me against him. Chris, still standing on the other side, offered a smile of reassurance.

"Liz, I really think you owe her an apology," Kevin said firmly.

"What for?" she replied in a sharp tone. "I just asked a simple question. It's a free country."

"She's been through some really gnarly shit over the last few months, and faced it like a frickin' superhero," Kevin stated.

"*The Greatest American Hero*," Chris quipped, knowing it would get a smile out of me.

"Cat and I were with her every step of the way," he continued earnestly. "I had her back. So, if that makes her a Witch, then it makes me one too."

"And me," Cat said as she came up behind us.

I felt tears well up in my eyes, as I leaned my head against Kevin's shoulder. I had been feeling especially alone since the blow up with my parents, so it was a wonderful reminder that these two had stood shoulder to shoulder with me through it all.

Cat put her arms around the two of us, and kissed Kevin on the cheek. I heard her whisper to him that she loved him. It made my heart ache.

I miss Russell.

"Whatever," Liz mumbled as she rolled her eyes at us.

"I don't even know how to wrap my head around it," I answered honestly. "It's been confusing... and hard." My words made her face soften a little, but there was still a hint of some dark thought behind her eyes.

"As a fellow Witch, I can attest to the fact that she can definitely make your head explode with just *one* thought," Jennifer chimed in out of nowhere.

"Oh, yeah! That's right," Kelly confirmed, catching on.

"That dude never knew what happened," Jennifer continued.

"I know, and it was so totally grody. Blood, like, everywhere," Kelly added.

"And brains... don't forget the brains," Jennifer concluded.

"Like *Scanners*," Brian interjected, and Jennifer snickered in response.

Liz looked between the three of them, unsure what to believe. She became more annoyed once it dawned on her that they were making fun of her.

"Toads," Cat added, trying to suppress a grin. "It's her specialty. So don't piss her off." She squeezed me again in her one arm hug, just as the bell clanged.

"Thank you, guys, for having my back," I said, as I watched Liz turn in a huff and walk away.

Everyone else gathered their belongings and started to head out.

"Well, if I didn't have your back before," Craig started to say, "I do now!"

As the three of them walked away, Brian stated, "I know, right? I wouldn't want to be turned into a toad." He looked around slowly for dramatic effect, and added, "I'd look just like Craig!"

"HA! Burn!" Drew exclaimed, and patted Craig on the back.

This got me laughing, and I felt a lot better. "Bye, weirdos!" I called out. The three of them turned back in response and waved.

"Talk to you later, Gwen," Kevin said, as he joined back up with Chris and they headed off in the opposite direction. Chris turned and waved. I waved back, and then glanced over to the lockers, hoping I would catch Russell last minute, just for a brief hello, if nothing else. He was still nowhere in sight.

Chapter Four
Missing Person

After walking the two blocks from the bus stop, I trudged up my driveway to the front door, and entered completely exhausted.

"Gwen?"

For crying out loud, what did I do now? I wondered as I hung up my coat, and dragged my book bag dramatically through the entryway in the living area. It weighed a ton.

"Yeah, mom?"

She came around the corner from the kitchen, wringing her hands, a worried look on her face.

"I just got a call from the 'parent phone tree' at your school."

"What's that?"

"It's a list of parent's phone numbers. One parent calls the next person down on the list, and then that person calls the next number down and so on. It's a way to get urgent information out to everyone."

"What's the emergency?"

"A girl from your school has gone missing!"

"Really? Who?"

"Suzanne Crawford. She's a junior. Do you know her?"

41

With a sense of relief, I answered, "No, the name doesn't ring a bell."

"Apparently, she'd gone out Saturday night, and by Sunday morning, still hadn't come home. Her parents called around to all her friends, thinking maybe she'd just spent the night somewhere, but nobody had seen her since some big bonfire party out at MacLean's Fields."

She was at the party!

"I would be out of my mind if something like that happened to you," she continued. "I can't even imagine what they must be going through."

Oh, so you do care!

"Did they call the cops?" I asked, worried more so about the possible trouble we could be in for being out there.

"Yeah, just as soon as they realized nobody had seen her since the party. The Sheriff said it was too soon to report her missing, though. Then, she didn't show up for school today, and no one has heard from her, so finally she's officially been listed a missing person. That's why the "phone tree' was activated."

"Oh! Okay," I replied.

"So, you haven't heard anything?"

"No. I could call Russell to see if he's heard anything!"

"Nice try! You're grounded, remember?"

"You said it was an emergency!"

"Yeah, that's why *I'm* going to use the phone now to call the next number down the list. After I'm done, you can call Cat, and find out if this party was the same one that Mike and Russell attended. *Mike* can call Russell."

"Fine," I grumbled.

I stomped down the hall to my room, dragging my bag behind me. After dropping it in the center of my floor, I kicked off my shoes, and plopped onto my bed. My tense muscles sang out in gratitude as I sank further and further into the soft comforter.

What a day! I thought - tempted to just close my eyes for a second.

∿

"Gwen, I'm off the phone! You can call Cat now!" she yelled.

"Okay!" I yelled back. Crawling off the bed, everything ached. All I wanted to do was turn off the lights, get under the covers, and call the day over.

Oh crap, I still have to do homework. Ugh! This sucks.

I shuffled out of my room and down the hall to the kitchen. My mom was busy grabbing things out of the fridge and getting things down out of the cupboards.

I picked up the receiver and dialed Cat's number. On the fourth ring, Cat answered, sounding winded.

"Hello?"

"Hey, Cat. It's me," I responded.

"Hey!"

"Why are you so out of breath?"

"I was just getting out of the bathroom. When I turned the water off in the sink I heard the phone ringing, so I had to run. I was actually just about to call *you*. After I read your note, I had so many questions!"

My mom turned around from the counter, where she was setting up vegetables to cut, looked at me questioningly, and urged me to get on with it.

"Okay, but before we get into that, I'm *supposed* to ask if you know a girl named Suzanne Crawford? She's a junior at our school."

"Suzanne Crawford?" she repeated slowly. "Hmm, no I don't think I've heard the name before. Why?"

I put my hand over the receiver. "No, she hasn't heard of her," I said.

My mom nodded, and then turned back around to resume preparing dinner.

"This girl was last seen at a party Saturday night. Apparently, there was a *bonfire* out in MacLean's fields.... *maybe* it's the same party Mike and Russell were at."

"Ohhh... *that* party... yeah, got ya," she answered. "Your mom's eavesdropping, isn't she?"

"My mom needs you to ask Mike if he knows anything. Then ask *him* to call Russell to find out the same thing."

"Well, Mike's at work, so I can't. Why don't *you* just call Russell?"

"I can't," I replied.

"Ohhh, that's right! You're grounded," she sympathized. "I can't believe my mom called! That's soooo bogus."

"Tell me about it," I answered.

I glanced over to see if my mom was still paying attention, before I quietly made my way down the hall, pulling the phone's extension cord along with me.

"Are you going to tell me what happened Sunday?" Cat asked impatiently.

"Yes," I stated, as I finally made it into my room.

"Well…"

"Hold on, hold on. I had to get down to my room," I replied, as I shut the door behind me. "Okay, where do you want me to start?"

"Duh! The dreams!" she exclaimed. "It can't just be a coincidence that you had these dreams, and then we find out a girl is missing. Do you think it means what I think it means?"

"No, I don't. These were different from the others. It was like being in real time," I explained.

"In real time?" she asked. "I don't get it. So… not a memory from a ghost then?"

"No. I don't think so."

Chapter Five
Reunited

Tuesday morning, Russell was waiting at the lockers. Once our eyes met, a relieved smile spread across his face. He walked towards me with his arms open. I quickened my pace, but the awkward weight of my books hampered my ability to run. He helped close the distance by walking faster. Eventually I just dropped my bag, and ran, throwing myself into his arms.

"I missed you," he cooed, pulling me in tightly and swaying us back and forth.

"I missed you too," I whispered into his chest, letting out a huge sigh. Once we touched, the burst of emotion that flooded back into me was like breathing fresh air after being submerged underwater for too long.

He rested his head atop mine, and we continued to just stand there, relishing the connection again.

"Where were you yesterday?" I asked.

"Well, I tried to call you… *again*… to explain, but your mom still wouldn't let me talk to you!" he said in frustration. "I've been going nuts!"

"Me, too!" I stated, recalling all the arguments over the last couple days. A bucket of tears threatened to pour out, as I voiced my deepest fear. "I think my parents aren't going to let us see each other anymore."

"What?" he exclaimed angrily, pushing us apart so that he could look directly into my eyes. "Why?"

I could feel his inner struggle to maintain control as he started to take in deep breaths to calm his emotions.

"Why would they do that? What's going on?" he asked more steadily.

"Janice called my mom," I grumbled.

"So what?" he replied, still struggling to understand.

"She told her that you *spent the night*."

"Okay. Again, so what? I spend the night over there a lot," he replied defensively.

"They didn't like the idea that we'd been there, while Janice was at work, unchaperoned! I think my mom wanted to have 'the talk'!"

" 'The talk '?" he asked.

"Yeah, you know…"

"*Ohhhhh*," he realized, "*that* talk." He sighed deeply, shook his head, and then sort of chuckled to himself.

"It's not funny," I chided, playfully socking him on the arm.

"Okay, okay!" he pulled back dramatically as if he were being brutalized.

"Seriously, they're worried you're too old for me. That you're going to take advantage of me, or something."

"It's not like I'm some creepy old geezer," he grumbled. "I just turned 17!"

"Yeah, I know. It's stupid."

Then he cocked his head to the side and looked at me inquisitively. "Something else happened, didn't it?"

"Well, yeah. My mom and I had a huge fight," I admitted. "I stormed off to my room. I was so angry that I slammed my door shut, and after I did, my lamp kind of, like, *exploded*." I held up my arm, pulling back my sleeve, to show him the bandage. "A piece of the glass flew from across the room and cut me."

"What?" He tenderly held my arm, looking at it. "Wow, are you okay?"

"My dad said it didn't look deep enough to need stitches, but it hurts."

"You said you got *angry*?" he questioned, staring down at my arm again, deep in thought.

"I've never been *so mad*."

"Do you think *you* had something to do with it?"

"With what?"

"The lamp exploding."

"You think that's possible?" I asked, trying to let that sink in. But the more I thought about it, the more tired I became. "Ugh, I don't even know what's going on anymore!" I leaned forward into his embrace, emotionally spent. All I wanted to do was run off with him, forget about everything else, and stay in his arms forever.

"Let's go find a place to sit down." He turned me gently in his arms, and led us to a section of the raised garden cement border that surrounded the quad.

When we sat down, it was even colder than the bench seats at the lunch table the day before. I put my legs up over his lap and curled into him as he wrapped his arms around me. We didn't speak for several minutes.

"Has anything like that happened to you before?" he asked, finally breaking the silence.

"No," I answered. "My dad tried to tell me it was because I slammed the door, and that's what caused the lamp to fall off my desk. But, if the lamp exploded when it hit the floor, wouldn't the glass have hit my leg? It shot out mid-air and cut my arm, so that just doesn't make any sense."

"No, it doesn't," he concurred.

After another several minutes of quiet he continued, "Do you want to know what I think happened?"

"Yeah, sure."

"I think, in your extreme emotional state, you caused a psychokinetic effect."

"A what?"

"The energy from your anger surged out of you like a wave, and then blasted into the lamp, causing it to explode."

"How *in the world* could I have done *that*?" I asked in disbelief.

"Obviously you didn't do it on purpose," he answered, with a little concern in his voice. "It was an unconscious emotional response - a new ability. It seems like things are accelerating, and you're getting stronger."

"So, what do I do?"

"You get a teacher! You need guidance, before you accidently hurt yourself."

"Or others…" I added morosely.

"Don't say that. You'd never hurt anyone on purpose," he said reassuringly, hugging me tighter against his chest. "I really think you need to come over to my house and spend some time with my mom and sisters. They can help you figure out what you're capable of - teach you to harness these abilities, and learn how to control them."

That just reminded me again about why I got so angry in the first place. "How am I ever supposed to do that, if my parents keep us apart?" I groaned, feeling the tears threatening again.

"Hey, it'll be okay. This is just a little bump in the road, not the end of the world," he reassured. "We'll just have to be on our best behavior. Get them to trust us again. Or we'll figure something else out. I won't let them keep us apart."

"You promise?"

"I do. I promise. Nothing will *ever* come between us," he asserted.

I wasn't sure how he could promise something like that, but it did make me feel better. "Good."

"You know how much I love you, right?"

"Yeah, I do," I sighed, feeling happy again for the first time in days. "I love you, too."

The bell rang. The first class of the day was about to start.

"Ugh," I groaned. "We never have enough time."

"I know! It sucks!" He helped me up, and gave me a quick kiss. "I'll see you before 4th period, okay?"

"Okay," I resigned, as he waved and headed off. "See you later!"

I turned to see Cat at the table, hurriedly waving me over, so we could walk together to class.

Oh damn, I forgot to ask him about the missing girl.

When I caught up with her, I asked, "Did you get a chance to talk to Mike?"

"No, I fell asleep before he got home. Did Russell know the girl?"

"It didn't come up," I replied, as we pushed through the double doors and headed down the hall.

"Didn't come up? How could it not come up?" She looked at me in astonishment. It was a big deal after all.

"There was a lot to catch up on," was my lame excuse.

When we were almost to my class she said, "Okay, well, remind me when we're in Art later, to show you what I found."

"Tell me now." I stopped in front of my class door, but she continued to her class down on the left. "What did you find?" I asked again.

"I'll show you later. Bye." She waved and disappeared through the door into the room, just as the tardy bell rang.

"Miss Evans, did you plan on joining us this morning?" Mr. Thatcher, my Algebra teacher, motioned to my empty seat as he held the door.

Chapter Six
Suspicion and Paranoia

Cat opened Mike's previous yearbook, and laid it atop my sketchpad. Flipping through the pages, she stopped at the sophomore section, and pointed to the picture of Suzanne Crawford.

"Get this... I do know her!" she declared. "I recognized her face from a group shot of Mike and Erik and their dates at Winter Formal."

"She was Mike's date?"

"No! She was Erik's!"

"Were they actually a thing, or was it just a date?"

"I don't know. Mike doesn't talk to me about this kind of stuff," she replied.

I placed my finger on her small black and white portrait, tracing the outline of her face, trying to get a sense of her.

"Are you picking up on anything?"

"No. I guess I would have to touch something that was hers."

"Did you have another dream vision thingy last night? Is there any new information to share?"

"No, now that you mention it, I didn't. Last night I had my first good night's sleep in days."

"You guys talking about the missing girl, Suzie?" a husky male voice asked from behind us.

Cat turned to answer, "If you mean Suzanne Crawford..." She stopped when she saw the shy punk rocker who normally sat in the back of class, standing directly behind us.

He wore black Doc Martin boots, torn up jeans, and a ratty Dead Kennedy's t-shirt under a long black jacket plastered with spray paint and patches. Because he kept so much to himself, our curiosity had been peaked, and this moment of contact was like encountering a rare endangered species for the first time.

"Then... um... yeah," she stuttered, clearly flustered. "Hi."

Smooth, Cat. Very smooth.

"Do you know her?" I asked, trying to hide my grin in response to how red Cat's face had gotten.

He nodded. The tall spikes in his hair did not waver, defying gravity. It was as if they were plastered upright with cement.

"Have you heard anything?" I persisted, trying to engage him in conversation.

He shrugged.

"What have you heard?" Cat asked.

Finally, he decided to rally the energy to speak. "Since Monday they've been quietly bringing people to the principal's office and asking questions about her."

"Did you get questioned?" she asked, nodding along to encourage him to keep speaking, hanging on his every word.

"Yeah, but, you know, there's not much to tell."

"Oh, right. Yeah, I get it," Cat responded, nodding up and down enthusiastically.

"She and Kenneth were at the party," he continued. "What else is there to say, you know?"

Kenneth.

My heart skipped a beat. "Kenneth, did you say?"

"Her boyfriend," he replied.

"Nick! Please take your seat and get to work!" Ms. Ogilvy called out loudly from her desk.

He threw his hands up and backed away dramatically down the aisle back to his desk.

We watched him return to his seat, slumping down loudly before hoisting his heavy boot ups, and plopping his leg down on his desk.

We turned back around, and Cat looked over at me. "What?"

"A man of few words," I whispered, "Isn't he?"

"Yeah, he is," she responded - her ears red, and her cheeks flushed

"What about *Kevin*?" I teased.

"What *about* Kevin?" she asked, fully aware of what I was implying, but deciding to play dumb. "*Anyways*... do you know Kenneth? Soon as he said the name, you got sort of pale... like something clicked or something."

"In my dream, the girl asked, 'Where's Kenneth?', before she felt the jab in her neck and it went dark."

"So the girl you were seeing through in 'real time' might *actually* have been Suzie," Cat concluded in awe. "How is that even possible?"

"I have no clue," I answered. Then in a whisper, I added, "How is talking to your father possible? How was *anything* we experienced in that house possible?"

"Yeah, you're right. Okay, so we just go with this... you were looking through Suzie's eyes, and she has been tied up somewhere for the last couple days. So what happened to Kenneth? Is he missing too?"

The commanding voice of Ms. Ogilvy rang out, "Ladies! Too much talking! You can't finish the assignment unless you work on it, right?"

"Right," we responded in unison. Cat closed the yearbook, and tucked it back in her bag, pulling out her sketchpad in its place.

After a few minutes, others in the room started whispering, so I felt it safe to lean over and pick up our conversation where we left off. "Do you remember hearing a scream at the party, right before everyone started howling at the moon?"

"Hmm... no. Why?"

"I'm thinking now it might have been Suzie... when she was taken."

"Makes sense," she whispered, trying to not look over and bring any attention to us from the teacher.

"What I didn't tell you was someone I bumped into at the party put a really disturbing image in my head, similar to what Suzie ended up seeing later. I didn't think too much about it at the time, until I heard that scream. I knew, *in my gut,* that something bad had happened."

"Oh, Gwen," she said, as she turned towards me, awash in sympathy. "Don't beat yourself up over this. What could you have done? I mean, like how on earth, could you know?"

"I don't know," I sighed. "It's like I'm picking up her SOS! I feel like I should be able to do something about it, but I have no idea what that is!"

"Picking up her signal? Like a radio wavelength or something?"

"Yeah, or something."

"Cat! Gwen! Stop talking and finish your project. Final warning!"

"Okay," we both replied, and went back to our sketches.

~

Later at lunch, as I passed by the crowded tables in the cafeteria, I realized the entire student body was abuzz with gossip about Suzie.

"I heard she ran away from home because her parents abused her."

"Maybe she's pregnant! They're just saying she ran away, but they're really hiding her somewhere until she can have the baby."

"No, the police have been asking questions. She really was reported missing."

"I heard her boyfriend hasn't been seen at school for the last two days."

"I bet he killed her, and ditched town."

"I heard he got hurt, and that he's in the hospital."

"Maybe she fought back!"

"Have you been to that farmhouse before? It's filled with some seriously creepy Satan worshiping kind of stuff."

"What did they do, sacrifice her?"

When I finally came up to Cat and Kevin, sitting off in the far corner by themselves, by brain felt like it was about to explode from all the energy bouncing around the room.

"Hi guys. Am I interrupting anything?"

"No, I'm catching him up on everything. We're discussing your visions and trying to figure them out."

"Have you heard the crap that people are saying about her?" I asked, gazing out over the sea of faces awash in a mixture of delight, excitement, dismay, and concern.

"That's why we're over here by ourselves," Cat replied. "It's awful."

"Cat said you mentioned it was like receiving a distress signal. So, you believe she was alive when you were receiving these images?" Kevin asked.

"I didn't know what to make of it at first," I answered. "But, yeah, I do now."

"Did you receive another image last night, or today?"

"No… nothing since Monday morning," I replied sadly.

"Ah, crap! That's not good," he groaned.

"No, it's not," Cat, confirmed.

"She was there at the party with us... We didn't even know this was happening. How could no one have seen anything?" he asked in dismay.

"Kenneth, her boyfriend, *must* have! Maybe you can get a reading off him?" Cat suggested. "If *he* saw her abductor's face, *you* would too!"

"Great idea!" Kevin remarked. "You're so smart!" He gave her a little hug. "So we just need to find this Kenneth dude."

"If what I just overheard is true, then he might have been hurt and is in the hospital."

"We could go to the hospital to visit him, that's easy enough," she suggested.

"He doesn't know us, and besides, aren't only family members allowed in?" Kevin pondered.

"I don't know. You're probably right."

Deflated, Cat responded, "Ohhh. Okay... well, never mind then. Scratch the Kenneth idea."

"Mike and Russell *must* know something," Kevin added.

I wanted to tell them what my heart was telling me, that it didn't matter and there was nothing we could do.

It's too late. I failed her.

"Yeah, maybe," I replied instead, trying to not let my own doubts get in the way of their hope.

～～

After I'd returned home from school, the phone rang. It was Cat, with an update. "It turns out Mike *was* one of the people called into the principal's office and questioned."

"What did they ask him?"

"They asked him if he knew Suzie - which of course he did. Then they asked him about Kenneth, but Mike only knows *of* him. They'd never hung out or anything. Then they asked about Erik."

"Really?" I asked. "Erik? Why?"

"They were wondering if Mike saw any sort of confrontation between Erik and Kenneth that night, or knew of any history of fights between them."

"Over Suzie?" I clarified. "I thought she and Erik were just dates to the formal."

"Apparently they went out for a while." Cat responded. "Something happened, and she broke it off. It turns out that Erik was pretty obsessed over her for a long while after that."

"What does that have to do with the party?"

"Well, Erik ended up going to the E.R. that night."

"No way!" I exclaimed. "Really?"

"Really!"

"Did Mike tell you what happened?"

"Erik told Mike that he was found unconscious, early Sunday morning, by one of the last people to leave the party," she explained. "They found him lying out in the field near where all the cars had been parked. They took him to the ER. Mike *was* supposed to be his ride home, but when it was time to go, Erik was nowhere to be seen. Mike just as-sumed he'd left with someone else. I guess that's not un-common, so he didn't think much of it."

"Why was he unconscious? Did Mike find out?"

"Erik told Mike that the doctors pumped his stomach, and drew blood, but didn't identify known drugs in his system. And it wasn't alcohol poisoning. He swears he doesn't remember taking anything. In fact, he has no mem-ory of the night at all."

I was amazed. "Nothing at all?"

"Well, nothing after arriving at the party and hanging out in the parking lot," she clarified.

"He seemed his usual sleazy self when we saw him there," I noted. "That's so weird!"

"I know, right? Oh, and get this, the rumors *are* true. Kenneth did get hurt. He's still in the hospital."

"What happened to *him*?"

"All Mike heard was that a couple went to the back side of the farmhouse to make-out, or something, and found him on the ground, underneath the back window. They tripped right over his body."

"Okay, so wait," I responded. "Why didn't we know any of this was going on when we were there?"

"It happened *after* we left."

"And that's when an ambulance came? Did the police show up? Why didn't anyone find Erik when all this was going on?"

"The party never got busted up, so the kids who found Kenneth must have taken him to the ER themselves," Cat answered. "Probably, so no one would get in trouble for drinking or anything."

"Okay, yeah, that makes sense."

"It's weird that two guys got hurt and ended up in the ER on the same night," Cat speculated, "with two things in common: they were both at the party, and they both dated Suzie."

"And we're no closer to understanding what happened to her," I bemoaned.

"I hope the police have more to go on then what Mike told us."

Despondently I responded, "Me too, because I feel like I've let her down somehow."

Cat sighed loudly, "You shouldn't. This has nothing to do with you."

"But it does! I was connected to her. And for all I know, I was with her when she *died*!"

"Jeez, Gwen!" Cat exclaimed. "Don't talk like that. She'll turn up."

"I wouldn't be so sure."

Chapter Seven
Catching Up

The next morning, as I was digging through my locker, someone startled me by sneaking up and whispering in my ear, "Well, hello there."

"Whaaa…!" I exclaimed, quickly turning, swinging my book bag around.

It caught Russell in the side, causing him to back up with his hands up. "Whoa! It's just me!"

Holding my hand to my chest, I tried to catch my breath. Of course, I was relieved, and happy to see him, but I'd been on edge since speaking with Cat the day before. I couldn't shake the feeling that bad news was going to drop any second, and it seemed as if my every last nerve was spring loaded.

"I thought you knew it was me!" he stated in concern. "I didn't mean to scare you."

"You didn't… well, okay, yeah, you did… kind of."

He stepped in closer, gesturing for me to lower my weapon. "What's got you so freaked out?"

"Sorry, I've just got a lot on my mind. There's a lot we need to catch up on."

"I tried to call you last night. Your mother shot me down… again!"

"Sorry."

"Here, let me take that for you. Get what you need, and let's go sit down." He grabbed my bag, while I closed my locker.

Looking out across the quad, I said, "It's drizzling, and too cold to sit at our usual spot."

"We could sit in the cafeteria with everyone else," he suggested.

"It's too noisy in there."

"Well, I guess here's as good a place as any, then - if you don't mind standing."

"That's fine. As long as we're together, it doesn't matter."

"Awww," he cooed, and then placed his backpack down by his feet, to free his arms. He pulled me towards him and held me against his chest. "So, tell me what's going on in that busy brain?"

"Suzie Crawford."

"Crazy, right?"

"Do you know her?"

"Yeah, she was dating Erik about the same time that I was dating Megan."

"Oh! I didn't know that." The mention of Megan was surprising. "You guys all hung out?"

"Sometimes we'd go on double dates, if that's what you mean."

This news further piqued my interest, so I decided to go fishing. "Cat mentioned that she saw a picture of Erik with Suzie at the Winter Formal."

"The professional 'couple' photo, or the group shot with all six of us?"

I didn't know he took her to the formal!

"Um…" I responded, feeling a twinge of jealousy, "the one with just Mike, Erik, and their dates."

"Ahhh…"

He didn't seem willing to divulge anything further, and the silence became awkward. Changing the subject, I asked, "So, were *you* asked into the office as well?"

"Me?"

"Duh! Yeah you! Who else?"

"Yes, I was."

"So, *what* did they ask you?"

"They asked me if I knew Suzie, how I knew her, and if I'd seen her that night at the party. Then they asked if I knew Erik, which of course I do, and if I knew Kenneth, which I don't. I mean, I know *of* him, because Suzie started going out with him after she broke it off with Erik."

"That's exactly what Mike said. Have you been able to talk to Erik?"

"I went over to his house after he was released from the hospital Sunday night, and we were all with him Monday when word got out that Suzie had gone missing. Judith took it really hard."

"Judith?" I asked in astonishment. "As in Judith… from the library?"

"Yeah. She'd really liked Suzie. She always commented on what a good influence she was on Erik."

"Why would Judith care about that? Why was she even there?"

"She's Erik's *mom*. I thought you knew that?"

His mom? Seems there's a lot I don't know.

"I'm sorry, I didn't mean to eavesdrop, but did you just say Judith is Erik's mom?" Cat asked, as she walked under the cover of the locker area, to join us.

The interruption startled me. "Dang it, Cat! Don't sneak up like that!" I exclaimed, holding my chest again.

"I thought you heard me. I yelled at you from the table."

"No, I didn't," I answered.

"And yeah, Judith is Erik's mom," Russell answered, as he shrugged his shoulders.

Then something dawned on me, I turned back to him and said, "You mentioned that Brighid and Judith were cousins."

"Oh, man!" Cat exclaimed, pointing at Russell. "That means you and Erik are related!"

"Yeah…" he replied, still not understanding why we were so shocked.

"Dude, the two of you couldn't be more different," she noted, shaking her head in awe.

"And thank God for that," I added.

"I take it you were questioned like Mike was?" Cat inquired.

"Gwen just asked that very same question."

"They think Erik had something to do with Suzie's disappearance?"

"Why would they?"

"Mike made it sound like they thought Erik and Kenneth might have had a fight over Suzie, or something."

"He swears he doesn't remember anything, and he was unconscious when they found him."

"That doesn't really answer the question. Is he a suspect?"

Annoyed by her persistence he answered, "I don't know about that, but what I do know is that he liked Suzie. He wouldn't have done anything to her."

Stepping in between them, to ease the mounting tension, I asked my own question, "Have you heard anything about Kenneth?"

"Just that he's in a medically induced coma, to help reduce the swelling in his head. Apparently, he was hit pretty hard. And *no*, Cat, I *don't* think Erik did that either," he answered tightly.

"Okay, okay. Chill out. I didn't mean to piss you off," Cat responded defensively. They stared at each other in a momentary standoff until Cat finally said, "Jeez! I guess I'll just go back to the table and leave you two alone."

"Cat, don't be like that. Russell's not mad," I declared, watching her walk away, and then turning to him and asked, "Are you?" I motioned with my head for him to say something to her so she wouldn't be hurt.

"Cat, no, I'm not *mad*," he called out. "I just don't believe he had anything to do with it, that's all. He's a victim too."

"Okay, cool," she mumbled, and continued to walk away dejected. "Whatever."

"Gwen, I'm sorry if I upset her… it's just that… well it's personal now, with Erik being family and all."

The annoying piercing clang of the first bell rang out.

Russell hoisted his backpack up on his shoulder, and we started walking out of the locker area together.

"Are you concerned about how he might fit in to all this?" I asked.

"We'll talk later," he responded, giving me a quick kiss.

I saw that Cat was waiting for me by the double doors.

"But…" I called out after him, watched him jog off in the opposite direction.

When I caught up with Cat she asked, "Sooo… how crazy is that news about Judith and Erik?"

"I know, right?"

Chapter Eight
After School

Later that day, when I headed out to lunch, Russell wasn't waiting at the end of the hall by the double doors like usual. Considering how unresolved our conversation was from earlier, it had taken an extreme amount of will power to focus on my classes and not dwell over his lack of concern at Erik's potential involvement.

He still didn't show after lunch period was over, so I went through the rest of the day obsessing over what could have happened to him. The ever-mounting anxiety, and feeling of dread that Suzie was already dead, had me bordering panic. By the time I got off the bus after school and made my way into my house, I was a bomb ready to explode.

My mom greeted me from the kitchen to ask how my day was, just as she usually did, and I almost bit her head off.

"UGH!" I groaned loudly. "Why do you always ask that? It was FINE!"

"That bad, huh?" a familiar male voice responded just out of sight.

My mom came around the corner from the kitchen. "Maybe this will cheer you up?" she responded, standing aside to reveal Russell standing behind her.

"What?" I was completely taken aback in surprise.

He stood there waving comically at me, with a grin spreading from ear to ear. "Hi!"

Before I could contain myself, I dropped my bag to the floor and ran to him, passing by my mom in a flash, and throwing myself into his open arms, the force of which had the effect of a football tackle.

He stumbled backwards toward the wall - one arm around me and one arm out to stop us from toppling over. After he managed to catch the wall with his hand and divert catastrophe, we started laughing.

"Gwen, really!" my mom exclaimed in exasperation. She sounded like she might as well have said, *that is not how a lady behaves!*

"What are you doing here?" I asked.

"Aren't you happy about that?" he asked, feigning insult.

"Of course I am!" I proclaimed, hugging him tighter.

"In my last class of the day, they gave us the option to use it as study time or leave early, so I thought I'd come over and surprise you. Your mom and I have been having a nice chat," he explained, as he stood us up straight, and tried to pry himself free of my bear hug.

It just felt so good to be in his arms, that I didn't want to let him go. I didn't like how we'd left things. Something just seemed *off*, and things around me felt chaotic.

I hated the feeling of chaos.

When I finally let him wriggle free, I looked back at my mom sitting at the table, her back to the kitchen. There were two half-empty teacups, and an empty plate in the center of the table.

"How long have you been here?" I asked as I walked to the cupboard to get myself a cup. I noticed my mom had actually opened up the special tin of shortbread.

"About an hour," my mom answered, taking another sip.

An hour? What could they possibly be talking about?

"Russell was telling me that you've already met his mother, which was news to me," she jabbed playfully. I could tell she was actually really annoyed, but she was putting on a polite air.

I poured hot water from the teapot on the stove carefully into my cup. "Yeah, I told you about the cool shop Cat and I discovered over at the Kilncroft Shopping Center, and the awesome Scottish lady we met."

"Yes, but you failed to tell me the shop owner was Russell's mother."

"Oh! I thought I had," I answered quietly, searching my memories for what information I had and had not shared.

A lot had happened since school had started. The previous summer's events, well, those might as well have been a lifetime ago. I was a completely different person than the one that hiked up the hillside with my friends, hid from the zoo train going by, and then snuck into an abandoned Victorian house in search of a ghost.

It was hard keeping track of all the secrets.

As I dunked the teabag into the steaming cup of water, I pondered what else they could have been talking about while I wasn't there. "I see you opened *the* tin of short-bread. It must be a special occasion," I teased. "Can I have one?"

"Yeah, go ahead. No need for a special occasion, I just knew he'd enjoy them."

"But…" I started before I thought better of it. It was all very uncharacteristic of her. First off, she never would let me have cookies after school. It was her normal response to say, "grab an apple, have some yogurt, or eat something healthy so you won't spoil your appetite." Secondly, every Christmas she received a special tin of Scottish shortbread from some relative, and then hoarded it like treasure.

What's going on with you today, mom?

With one hand full of cookies and the other holding the teacup, I turned back to the kitchen table to see Russell now sitting at the table across from my mom. He beamed at me, a proud twinkle in his hazel eyes, clearly satisfied with himself.

Oh, really? Do tell.

"My sisters have been pestering me for weeks to meet you, so my mom thought it'd be nice to have you all over to our house for dinner Friday," Russell responded.

"He was just telling me about their house and property. I had no idea such a place even existed in this town," she explained. "It sounds like something out of a fairy tale."

As I walked to the right side of the table, Russell pulled out the chair. "Thank you," I said, smiling warmly at him. He held my gaze, and it made me horribly self-conscious.

I looked slyly over at my mom out of the corner of my eye to see if she'd noticed. She was looking back and forth between the two of us, deep in thought.

I didn't get the sense that she was angry Russell that had come over. However, something was definitely on her mind.

"So…" she started.

Oh, no. Here it comes.

"As I was explaining to Russell, when we told him you couldn't talk on the phone with him for a while, it was because, well… we felt the two of you needed to take a break, you know… *to cool your heels.*"

"Mom!"

"Shhh. Let me say this," she stated in a balanced tone, clearly not wanting to get me agitated again and cause a scene in front of him.

"It's okay. We've been *'havin' a blether'*, as mum would say," Russell replied, putting his hand over the top of mine. Calm immediately replaced the spike in anxiety, and my blood pressure dropped. I felt two gentle squeezes from his hand and began to breathe normally again.

My mother noticed the immediate effect his touch had on me, and I thought I saw a slight purse of her brow as if trying to figure something out.

"Gwen, your dad and I have been talking about the two of you a lot this week…"

Ugh.

"…and we decided we'll lift your phone restriction."

Oh!

"That's awesome!" I exclaimed, as I squeezed his hand back, hopeful that it would all go back to the way it was. "Does that mean we can go over to his house Friday?"

"Let's not get too far ahead of ourselves," my mom responded. "First, I'm going to call his mom…"

How embarrassing! Can you humiliate me even more?

"You don't need to do that!" I insisted.

"It's okay. My mom is expecting her call," Russell explained.

I relaxed. "Oh, okay."

"Then I'll talk to your father about it when he gets home," she added. "I don't see anything wrong with our families getting to know each other, especially, if the two of you will be spending more time together."

"So, we *are* going to go over to his house?" I asked hopefully, trying to contain my excitement.

"We'll see," she replied, getting up from the table and taking her cup to the sink. "For now, I'll let the two of you visit while I'm finishing up the wash."

Russell gave my hand a squeeze again, and I looked over at him. That twinkle was back in his eye.

Don't give me that look.

I'll be good, I promise.

She turned back round, again taking us both in, as if debating whether or not we could be trusted.

"I'll just be down the hall," she reminded us.

"Thank you, Mrs. Evans," Russell responded, his charismatic personality on full display.

He did seem to have a *way* of persuading people. I remembered teasing him when we first met about him bewitching me.

"Elizabeth. You can call me Elizabeth. You know, it's a funny thing when someone calls me Mrs. Evans. It makes me think of Bob's mother. Just a different generation I guess..." she rambled on, as she walked past us down the hall.

"How?" I stammered, bewildered at the sudden turn of events. "Just... how?"

He responded impishly, "Ancient Chinese secret." Then put his finger up to his lips, stifling a laugh.

"This isn't a Calgon commercial, dork!" I whispered back, swatting him playfully on the arm. "Tell me."

I wondered how we were ever supposed to talk freely about anything. Someone was always within earshot. Even on the phone, we had to talk in whispers, or use code.

At least, when we hung out at Cat's house, we were free to be ourselves. I doubted if my parents would ever let me stay the night over there again, as long as Russell and I were seeing each other.

"Friday," Russell whispered, again eavesdropping inside my head.

I turned towards him, and whispered, "But we'll be there with your sisters and your parents. That's hardly being alone."

"I'll figure something out," he answered. "For now, let's just enjoy this time before your dad gets home."

"Do you want to go sit on the couch? It's more comfortable than these kitchen chairs, and we could see what's on TV?"

"Yes," he stated with enthusiasm, grabbing my hand and practically rushing us towards the living room. He threw himself onto the cushions as he pulled me along with him, landing us together in a heap.

I laughed too loud in response and heard my mom yell out asking if everything was okay.

"Fine, mom!" I yelled back, giggling sheepishly, as he rolled over on top of me and began to nibble at my neck and ears.

His mouth found my lips, and we stayed locked in a deep kiss for several moments. Then we heard the dryer door slam shut, followed by the sound of my mother's footsteps heading back towards the kitchen. Quietly, he slid off me, adjusting his hair and shirt, and pulled a pillow onto his lap.

I sat up and crossed my legs, leaning into the back corner of the couch. This was my usual go to position when watching TV, and I thought it would look the most natural if she looked in on us - which she did.

I *can't wait until we can finally have some privacy.*

Russell immediately swiveled his head to look at me and winked.

Me too.

I think I must have turned a thousand shades of red in that moment, because his grin got wider and wider.

"This is usually when my show comes on. Do you mind?" my mom asked, walking through the living room towards the television set to turn it on. "I can't miss finding out what happens with Luke and Laura."

So much for our visit.

"Her show?"

"General Hospital," I explained.

"Would it be okay with you if we went for a walk while you watch your show?" Russell asked.

"Just around the neighborhood, mom. We won't go far. Please?"

"It's really cold out there, are you sure you want to?"

"I'll put on an extra sweater," I offered, lighting up at the idea of getting away from the house.

"Okay, sure, but be back before your dad gets home."

Chapter Nine
Clearing the Air

Walking hand and hand down the street, I was finally able to relax for the first time in days. When I was with him, I felt more at peace within myself, as if everything was right again in the world. I was complete.

Right from our first dance, once I'd relaxed into his arms, and allowed the music to take us, I discovered a part of myself I never knew was missing.

"Been a hard week, huh?" he asked.

Coming out of my daydream, I replied with a smile, "It's better now."

"Good," he smiled back. A quiet contentment flowed between us, as we took in a deep breath of fresh air.

"Were you going to fill in more details about what happened to Erik?"

"I will, but *you* first. Something else is on your mind."

"Can't get anything past you, huh?"

He chuckled and replied, "No. Your mind is very noisy."

"Noisy? What does that mean?"

"Well, not like actual *sound*," he tried to explain. "Your brain is processing a lot of thoughts, and you're exuding a ton of energy trying to figure something out. I call busy thoughts, or energy, 'noisy'. Sorry, that's the only way I can explain it."

"Can you actually hear my thoughts like words, or do you see them like images?"

"No, I don't see them in my head like writing on a chalkboard or anything, if that's what you mean," he answered pensively. "Something will just occur to me, I'll hear my own voice telling me something, as if it was my *own* thought, until I realize it's someone else's. When it first started to happen, it took a while to get used to, and even longer to control it."

"That's what it's like for me, too. So that's why you put up your mental barrier... or protective shield... whatever it is you call it."

"I have to! Otherwise, the mental static can be overwhelming."

"I didn't realize it had that effect on you."

"It does... and I can't help it when *your* thoughts come across so clearly to me. I don't mean to invade your privacy or anything."

"That's good to know. What I don't get, though, is how come when I touch *you*, I don't get visions of your memories?"

"I don't know how it works," he answered. "I don't experience visions like you do."

"So, it's not because you're using your mental shield to block *me* out?"

"No, of course not!"

"Good! I don't know why I needed to hear that. I guess I've just been feeling insecure or something… like there's been too much distance between us, and we're losing our connection. I hate the way that makes me feel!"

Looking back over his shoulder, after stopping on the sidewalk under the branches of a giant tree, he answered sincerely, "You don't have to worry about that."

I followed his gaze and realized I could no longer see my house. I hadn't even noticed that we'd wandered into a different neighborhood.

He then led me off the sidewalk, under the shade of the tree, towards its trunk. He leaned me up against it. I glanced around, nervously making sure we were clear from view of any of the adjacent properties, and then relaxed. We were well hidden.

"It wasn't just you wishing we could get some privacy," he explained, leaning closer to my face, and looking me deep into the eyes. "I've missed you like crazy, and I couldn't wait to get you alone."

"Really?" I asked coyly, bringing my hands up his back, pulling him closer. "And why is that?"

He leaned in, and softly planted his lips against mine. They were cold from being outdoors, but once I opened my lips to allow our mouths to connect, the warmth ignited and continued to spread throughout my entire body.

Before I knew it, we were in the throes of a passionate kiss, his one arm cradling my head against the rough tree bark. The other hand found its way down below the back pocket of my jeans, and he lifted me to his level.

I wrapped my legs around his waist for support, with my arms around his neck, running my fingers through his hair, as he kissed my neck and nibbled cautiously.

The feel of his teeth against my skin sent surges of electricity to my loins, and I heard myself hum with pleasure.

This seemed to encourage him to put a little more force into the nibble. Instead of hurting, though, it heightened the enjoyment.

What am I doing?

"Whoa, whoa..." I finally managed to say, breathing heavily. I pushed back from him, using every ounce of self-control I could still muster.

"What's wrong?" he whispered, out of breath, repeatedly squeezing his hands into my thighs and butt, then running his hands up my jacket to touch my bare skin.

"Seriously! Russell! Look where we are!" I said a little louder, trying to break through to him, as much as I was trying to break through to myself.

We had to stop.

"Let them look. I don't care. I haven't been able to stop thinking about you lying there in my arms... waking up to feel your body next to mine..."

He went back to kissing my neck, trying to entice my lips back to his.

I turned my head away, and unceremoniously slid my legs back to the ground.

"What's wrong?" he groaned in disappointment.

"Nothing," I answered, trying to get my own breathing under control.

I understood his disappointment. My body was also on fire, and I ached with a need I'd never felt before. Every ounce of my being was begging to find a place where we could be alone to surrender to the moment. The acknowledgement of this need was both an exhilarating and frightening one.

I straightened my jacket and glanced around the neighborhood to make sure we hadn't brought about any unwanted attention. No one witnessed our stolen moment.

"I'm sorry," he whispered, having finally taken control of the carnal beast within him. "I don't know what happened. It's just what you do to me. I couldn't control myself."

I relished the idea that I had that sort of power over him, to drive him mad with physical desire, but I also understood it was something *beyond* just the physical. When we allowed ourselves that moment... where our brains started to shut off and something else took over... it was like opening a door into another realm of existing.

"No need to apologize. I almost lost myself as well."

After a minute of trying to gain our senses, and feeling slightly embarrassed, we started back down the sidewalk to continue our stroll.

"So, where were we?" he interjected awkwardly, which made me giggle, and the moment of embarrassment was over.

"My noisy brain," I laughed.

"Ah, yes."

"I kind of liked it when I *wasn't* thinking," I teased.

"Me too," he winked, and squeezed my hand. "No, really, go on."

"Now I hate to even go into it. It ruins the mood."

"That bad?"

"Yeah," I answered. "It's about the whole Suzie thing."

"It's a crappy situation. I hope they find her soon."

"But that's just it," I responded, hesitating while I desperately searched my mind for any other possible conclusion, and found none. The more I allowed myself to feel the reality of the situation, the more it rang true. It resonated throughout my entire being. I inhabited her body. I saw through her eyes. No matter how impossible or illogical it seemed, I'd been with her, experiencing her last moments.

Finally, I answered, "I don't think she's alive."

Russell stopped in his tracks, and turned to face me, the blood draining from his face. "*Why* do you think that?"

"I had a second dream Sunday night. It was even more detailed than the first, and it was as if, what I was witnessing, it was actually happening... to *me*. I tried to explain it to Cat. Like... Suzie sent out a distress signal, and I was the one who received it. It joined us together somehow, so that I shared her experience."

"So, the girl with her feet tied up, in your first dream... you think that was Suzie?"

I nodded. "And in the second dream, someone came into the room where she was still lying. She was thirsty and confused, and she was asking about Kenneth. They didn't respond, but they came up to her, bent down, and then poked her in the neck with something. After that, it went dark," I stated, involuntarily lifting my hand to the spot, feeling the sharp pricking. "I woke up and my neck hurt, I was dying of thirst, and there was still this lingering floral fragrance. I haven't had another dream since."

"Oh wow," he groaned, looking down at his feet, shaking his head in disbelief.

"I've had this sick feeling deep in my gut, that the last thing I witnessed was the last thing she experienced right before…"

"…she died," he finished, putting his hands up to his face and shaking his head again, as if trying to shake the image from his mind. Slowly he eased himself down to the curb, and sat down, sighing heavily.

I eased down next to him, feeling the wave of his guilt and anger envelope us both in a heavy cloak.

"I mean… I don't know for sure," I suddenly exclaimed, trying to make him feel better. I'd forgotten that he knew and had spent time with her. It was hitting him harder than I expected. "I could be wrong. She might show up."

"We were there. We were *right* there. You even said you felt something bad was going to happen. You said you thought you heard someone scream! I should have believed your intuition… I just didn't realize you'd reached that level yet! SHIT. I should have been able to do something."

"Weren't you just telling me you build a wall around yourself when you're going to be around people? That you are bombarded by too many thoughts and emotions, and it drives you insane? You can't go back and change the fact that something happened. Neither of us can. Trust me - I've been beating myself up enough for the both of us."

"Don't do that. It's not your fault."

"It's not yours either," I argued. "Besides I can't help it. She was alive when she was calling for help. I was the one who heard her. I was the one who didn't do anything about it. I don't know how to live with that..." I started to cry, as the rest of the words got stuck in my throat.

Russell lifted his head up out of his hands, in response to the timber in my voice, and then pulled me into a hug.

"Hey... hey... come here. It's okay," he soothed. "Really, there's nothing you could have done." He pushed me upright to look me in the eyes. "You didn't know what you were seeing, and, even if you did, you had no way of finding out where she was."

I turned my face away, as I wiped the tears from my cheeks, in embarrassment. I took a deep breath to get control over myself.

"I might have been able to find her if the clues made sense."

"And what clues were those?"

"It seemed like we were in some sort of barn, with rows of trees outside. Before the candle went out, I could see some stuff drawn on the walls."

"Like the graffiti at the farmhouse?"

"No, not stuff that kids spray paint. There were some crude hand drawn pictures – I've tried to block those out - but the symbols stuck with me. I'd seen something similar before, in the watercolor paintings at your mom's shop. You know the ones?"

"Ewan Blackwood has his watercolors on display," he answered.

"Blackwood! That's right. When we were checking everything out in the shop, Cat and I had been discussing him. We'd been wondering if he was connected to the Blackwood Estates. There was also another namesake, Carmichael, the wood carver."

"Yep, Fergus Carmichael, and you're right, they *are* connected to the names of places in town. They're actually descendants of the founding families."

"Really? So, why your mom's shop? Do the symbols have something to do with…"

"With what?" he interrupted defensively.

"The stuff… in the *back* of the shop," I continued.

For a split second, his body tightened.

That touched a nerve.

"Sorry, did I say something wrong?" I asked.

"No." He stood up and dusted off the back of his pants, and then he held out his hand to help me up. "It's just complicated."

"Then help me understand."

He didn't say anything for a minute or two as we started back down the sidewalk.

Finally, to break the silence, I blurted out, "Liz accused *me* of being a Witch, and the way she said the word… well it was like a slap in the face."

He slowed for a second, looking sideways at me. "I had no idea. Why didn't you tell me?"

"We haven't had the chance to really talk."

"True."

Another couple moments of silence, and he seemed no closer to explaining anything, so I continued to ramble, "When all this started, I just thought I had the ability to talk to ghosts - which took some getting used to. Then all of a sudden, I'm seeing people's memories when I touch them, binding a spirit to a doll, and then exploding a lamp. What am I supposed to call it? Is Liz right? Am I a Witch?"

I looked over at him out of the corner of my eye, and tried to get a sense, any sense of what he was thinking. It appeared as if he was struggling with something, at once looking as if he were going to respond, and then closing his mouth against it the next.

So I continued with my thoughts. "Your mom calls herself the High Priestess of the Circle of the Dark Stream, right? Does she consider herself an *actual* Witch, or is it just an interest, like a club or something?

"I hate that word."

"You mean *Witch*?" I asked. "Then *what* is the right word? Please explain it to me," I pleaded.

"When you come over for dinner, I'm sure my mom will be more than happy to answer these questions."

"Why can't you?"

"It's not up to me. It's not my place," he answered vaguely.

"What's that supposed to mean?" I looked up at him, trying to read his face.

"When you come over, we'll have more time, and my mom will help you make sense of it all. Let's just enjoy our walk for now," he suggested, and gave a slight squeeze to my hand. "It'll all make sense, I promise."

"Okay, but you've said that before."

"What?"

"You promised you'd explain everything," I grumbled.

"Okay, I double promise, pinky swears," he responded.

We circled back round the neighborhood, just as the streetlights started to come on. As we approached my house, from the opposite side of the street, I saw my dad's car parked in the driveway.

"Aw man! Dad's already home," I complained.

After we crossed the road and started to make our way up to the front door, we came to a stop at the sound of shouting coming from inside.

"It's just a dinner. We could meet his family and have the chance to get to know more about him."

"It's not about whether or not we like his family!"

"But, Bob!"

"I know... I know... she thinks she's so *in love*, but we agreed that she's too young and too naïve for this kind of relationship."

Russell and I just stood there, as my heart sank. I didn't quite know what to do.

"So much for a small bump in the road," I quipped, trying to make light of the situation, and not letting on how devastated I felt.

"Sorry I got you into trouble."

"*You* didn't do anything! My dad is the one being stupid."

"If I'd just driven home after dropping you and Cat off at her house, we wouldn't be in this mess."

"You were exhausted. We all were. You've got nothing to apologize for," I maintained.

"Is she still out there with him? Isn't she supposed to be back by now?" I heard my dad yell from inside, followed by his heavy footsteps on the foyer floor as he made his way to the front door. The front porch light snapped on.

"I guess that's my cue to leave," Russell stated, just about to lean in to kiss me good-bye.

"Yeah," I responded in kind.

The front door flew open. "Gwen! Get inside," my dad said sternly.

"FINE!" I replied in annoyance, letting go of Russell's hand. "I guess I'll see you tomorrow."

"Bye," he answered, and then he turned to walk down the drive to his car.

Turning back to face the house, I started, "Why…"

"Because you're grounded, remember?" he interrupted.

"But…"

"Just get in the house, this isn't open for discussion, and dinner is ready!"

Chapter Ten
The Satanic Panic

During lunch, Kevin spread out the morning's newspaper on the cafeteria table for all of us to see. The article recounted how two old fishermen had found the body of Suzie Crawford washed up on a river bend, just downstream from the farmhouse in MacLean's Fields - the last place she'd been seen.

I scoured the article in search of an answer about what had happened to her, but, according to the journalist, the police did not want to speculate on what may have been the cause of death until they heard back from the medical examiner. The police said they would release a statement when they had all the facts. At the time of the interview, it was just too soon to comment.

However, the journalist, who interviewed the two men who found the body, wrote that they saw markings *carved* into her skin. They didn't recognize what the carvings were, but one was quoted as saying, "they reminded me of markings of the Devil!"

The other fisherman went on to add, "If you ask me, it's those damn Goth kids, playing the Dungeons & Dragons and listening to that Satan worshiping rock music. We need to put a stop to this!"

The other fisherman agreed, and added, "It's just like that James Egbert '*Steam Tunnel Incident*' out of Michigan. He played Dungeons & Dragons and look what happened to him. It's the Devil's work."

The journalist wanted the reader to understand that these were just the opinions of the distressed men who found the girl. There was no evidence to suggest that the girl was a victim of Satan Worshipers, D&D participants, or Goths.

"What is it?" Cat asked. "Earth to Gwen!"

"Hey, space cadet," Kevin added. "What're you thinking about?"

It wasn't so much, *what* I was thinking, as it was *how* I was feeling. The depression from the weight of her death was crushing me.

How did the psychic connection with Suzie even occur? Am I just a radio receiver able to pick up random transmissions? How was I supposed to have helped her, if I didn't even understand what I was seeing?

"Gwen?" Kelly prodded. "You okay? You don't look like you're feeling too good."

Just then, I heard Russell's name being spoken aloud at a nearby table. I turned to see Liz sitting next to two "goody two shoes" type girls, and not in the sexy librarian kind of way depicted in the Adam Ant video. Liz was dressed conservatively, which was out of character from her usual Siouxsie and the Banshees style outfit and go-to dark eyeliner.

I leaned in to the group, and asked, "What's the deal with Liz? Who are those girls?"

"I guess she doesn't want to hang out with us anymore," Kelly remarked.

"Or she knows she pissed us off, and doesn't feel very welcome," Jennifer added.

"I know the one on the left," Cat answered. "Michelle. I have her in my math class. She's pretty quiet."

"The other one, to the right," Kelly added. "That's Julianne. I have her in history. She's bonkers."

"Why do you say that?" I asked.

"She's always talking about the crazy stuff her mother tells her."

"Like what?" Jennifer asked, leaning in – eager to take part in the gossip.

"Secret messages in rock music that command you to do bad things, like smoke marijuana or have sex." Kelly responded.

"Backmasking?" Kevin asked.

Jennifer's face scrunched up. "Back what?"

"You know…" he spun his finger one way, and then reversed direction." You play a record backwards, and there's supposed to be secret hidden messages. Some fundamentalist wackos claimed Zeppelin put Satanic messages on "Stairway to Heaven." You remember that, right?"

"So, is that why Liz was so weird the other day - when she was accusing me of practicing Witchcraft –because she's going to *that* kind of Church?" I asked.

"It's hard to understand how she's changed so dramatically," Jennifer mused. "She was cool to hang out with. We liked the same kind of music, movies... all kinds of stuff."

"I wonder what happened," Kelly pondered.

"What do you suppose they're talking about?" Cat mused, looking over at the table, as if the trio were an exotic exhibition of animals on display at the zoo.

"I overheard her say Russell's name, so I don't think I have to guess," I responded in disgust.

"Yeah," Kevin affirmed.

"Great," Cat grumbled.

The trio looked over at us when they realized we'd been staring. Julianne pulled a crucifix necklace out from under her sweater to display to us, then turned away and began whispering more urgently to Liz and Michelle. Finally, they made a dramatic display of rising in unison, and left the table, leaving the cafeteria.

"What the heck was that?" I laughed.

Kelly and Jennifer did a quiet golf clap. "Very impressive," Jennifer mused.

"Where's Chris when we need him? He'd definitely have the perfect movie quote for what we just witnessed," I remarked.

"Give me a second, I'm working on it!" Kevin exclaimed.

"You're just no good without your side kick," Cat teased.

"No, but seriously, where is Chris? Don't tell me he's hanging down the street now with the hard rockers?"

"Actually, he's got a new girlfriend," Kevin responded in a conspiratorial tone.

"Oh, do tell," Cat encouraged.

I leaned in, waiting to hear all the gossip.

"Oh, that's it," he announced, then sat back. "That's all I know."

"What? That's it?" Cat exclaimed, throwing her arms up in disgust.

"Well, if you know he has a girlfriend, then you know who it is," I concluded, trying to call his bluff.

"No, really, girls, I swear. I asked him where he's been lately, because we haven't hung out much on the weekends or anything. He said he's seeing someone. That's all he gave me."

"Right!" I scoffed.

"No, I swear!"

"Why all the secrecy?" Cat needled him. "What does he have to hide?"

"This!" Kevin swung his arms around our group, then pointed at Cat and I, smiling smugly. "*This* is why he won't tell me anything. He knew, that even if I swore to secrecy, Cat would beat it out of me, until I told her everything. Nothing is sacred anymore!"

"Don't be so dramatic!" Cat admonished, rolling her eyes at him. "He'd be right, though. I would have to beat it out of you."

"Promises, promises," Kevin purred.

"Ew!" I groaned. "Okay, listen up, you two, I'm going to the library."

No response. They were in a standoff.

"I'll catch you later, okay?"

"Uh huh, yeah, okay," Cat responded dismissively, as she then broke the accord and smacked Kevin in the triceps.

He pretended to like it.

She punched him harder, and he told her it felt like a feather tickling him. He called her a tease and began to laugh at the angry faces she was making. It was a comical match-up, like a Chihuahua verses a Great Dane.

Kelly leaned over to me, and asked, "What the heck is going on? What did we miss?"

"Yeah, what's going on?" Jennifer asked.

I was trying not to laugh, as I gathered my things. "I think it's a mating ritual," I mused, and then headed off to the library.

Chapter Eleven
Mind Games

The librarian had her back to me, her attention focused on something on the opposite counter.

"Excuse me, Mrs. Harrison!" I said. She didn't respond.

"Mrs. Harrison," I repeated a little louder.

"Yes?" she questioned, as she finally looked up, glancing over the top of her reading glasses. She placed her finger on the place where she'd left off, and then gave me her attention.

She was a plump woman, as old as my grandmother would have been, with snow-white hair that was so thin and fine that even tight curls couldn't hide the balding areas of her scalp. No matter how much powder she applied, she could not hide the large "liver spots" peppering her skin. The liberal amount of lipstick only accentuated how her jowls pulled down the edges of her mouth, causing an almost comical sad clown effect. But she had kind eyes, and a genuinely sweet and caring heart.

I couldn't imagine ever getting that old. My dad complained all the time about everything hurting. As he would stand up from a chair and groan, he liked to remind me that he was once an athlete in his younger days. Then he would walk across the room, and all I could hear was the snap, crackle, and pop of his knees.

"What can I help you with, dear?" Mrs. Harrison asked.

As she approached, the sound of her thick polyester pantsuit swooshed, and the strong scent of baby powder wafted towards me.

"I have to write an essay for English, and I was thinking about using the history of Douglas as my subject."

"What part of the history specifically?" she asked.

"Do you carry anything here about the founders? Not a history on when the town was built or anything, but more the personal stories of who they were, and what they went through to get here."

"You might have better luck at the main library downtown."

"I don't have time to go down there. Are you sure, you can't think of anything here? Like, maybe a biography on the descendants who still live in town?"

"There is one book here I could suggest. I'm not sure how detailed the information will be about the founders, but you can at least take a look."

"That would be great. Where can I find it?"

She wrote the call number down on a piece of scratch paper, as she made conversation. "It's just awful what happened to Suzie, isn't it? She was such a sweet girl. I remember her very well."

"Yes, it is," I responded.

Ugh! I can't seem to get away from this topic. I don't want to think about it anymore.

"She was a very bright girl. With her G.P.A. and her S.A.T. scores, she could have attended any school she chose."

"Really? I didn't know that," I responded, becoming more and more uncomfortable with the memories of Suzie's last moments flooding back into the forefront of my mind.

"You get to know a lot of people in my position," she continued. "It's always hard when my favorites graduate and go away, but this... well this is, just so, heartbreaking. She was so young and had so much ahead of her - tragic!"

"Yes. It really is," I was able to respond, before I started to back away towards the rows of bookshelves.

I was trying not to lose my patience with her, because she really was such a nice woman - always had been - but I had very limited time left during that lunch period to find the book.

"I'm going to go find the book now, okay? I'll be right back."

"Okay, dear."

I turned around, scanning the plaques on the end of each shelving unit, until I found the right section. I walked down the aisle reading each row, checking the numbers on the spine labels, until I found the right title: *Douglas Town - Then and Now.*

I opened to the table of contents to see if it had anything specific about the founding families, when a hushed male voice, behind me remarked, "Hey, Gwen! Coincidence, finding you here."

I turned to see Erik, sauntering his way down the aisle, as if he was God's gift to women.

"Well, I was just leaving, so…" I started, closing the book, and walking forward.

"What's your hurry? I just got here," he replied.

I shifted to the side to try and move around him. He slid over, placing himself in my way, then took a step closer.

Unconsciously, I felt myself back up. I couldn't remember if there was a way out around the shelving behind me, or if it was a dead end.

"You look good, by the way," he said, eyeballing me up and down, as if I was a steak and he was deciding which part to take a bite out of first.

"Uh, thanks," I responded lamely, looking behind me, as I took another step back.

It is. Damnit, it's a dead end! What am I going to do?

Then he leaned his arm against one of the shelves. I guess he thought it made him look more interesting or attractive. I never knew what he thought he achieved when posturing like that - he did it every time we ran into each other. Russell always laughed it off. "Erik's harmless" he assured me.

My gut said differently.

I wanted to get past him. I just wasn't sure how to accomplish that, without embarrassing myself, or causing a scene. I imagined I could pull a football maneuver - like a fake out - pretend to go left, and then duck and shoot around right. But the aisle between the bookshelves was too small for that.

"Do you mind moving?" I finally got up the nerve to ask, and tried not to sound too insulting or rude. I heard my voice echo back to me in the enclosed space, and it didn't sound very assertive; in fact, it sounded very small. "I still need to check this book out before the bell rings."

"You know, the Formal is coming up after winter break," he continued, ignoring my discomfort. He stood as tall as Russell, but bigger, heavier, more imposing. He knew he could intimidate when needed.

"Yeah, I've seen the handouts," I responded dismissively, looking for a way around him.

"Are you and Russell going?" he asked, taking another step forward.

"He hasn't asked me yet, so I don't know," I answered. I was getting very irritated. "Can you *please* step aside, Erik?"

"I thought he was your boyfriend," he continued, taking yet another step. "Wouldn't you know if you were going to be his date?"

"It hasn't come up in conversation yet. It's still pretty early," I responded, stepping back. "Erik, come on. Please move. The bell is going to ring."

"Oh, no, you've got to plan these things *way* ahead of time," he explained, as he continued to take in my face and glance down at my chest. "Maybe he just doesn't want to go with *you*."

"Well, I doubt that," I replied defensively, trying to sound strong, but my nerves were on edge, and everything felt wrong. The encounter felt, well… aggressive.

He took another step forward, as he continued, "I don't know, I heard he still tries to keep in contact with Megan. She broke his heart, you know, and he never got over it."

"He broke up with her," I countered, stepping back and feeling the wall with the edge of my heel.

I knew he was trying to get in my head. I understood this instinctually, but he succeeded at pushing all the right buttons.

"Is that what he told you?" he asked with a disgustingly perverted grin, still eyeing me up-and-down.

"Yeah, and I believe him!" I stood my ground, unfortunately easy, with the dead-end against my back.

"That's interesting," he sneered, "because Megan left him for me." He closed the distance even more, looming menacingly.

"For *you*?" The thought of it was laughable. "That's not what he said," I answered.

"And you believe that?"

"Yes," I responded again.

There had been no reason for Russell to lie. Why would he?

"So, let's just say, hypothetically speaking, if Russell and you hadn't gotten together, and he was going to the formal with Megan, would you be going with someone else?"

How can I get him to leave me alone? Why has no one else come back here? It's a busy library. Where is everyone?

"But that's not the case," I answered, trying desperately to figure out what his end game was, and how I could get him to move aside. "What are you getting at?"

"Just humor me," he hissed in a hushed voice, his force breaching the invisible barrier of personal space that no one was allowed through without permission.

His breath smelled of garlic and onions.

What did he have for lunch?

I was in shock.

"I don't know," I answered hesitantly. "I guess... if someone asked me."

I kept waiting for something to make sense.

My fight or flight instincts were kicking in.

Maybe if I shove him back, it will give me time to get past. But, what if that doesn't work, and I just make him angry? He wouldn't hurt me, would he? We're in the library; he wouldn't do anything... or would he?

"So, you're saying you would go with me, if I asked, and you weren't with Russell," he whispered, seductively moving himself in for a kiss.

Oh my god. Just get away from me.

"That's NOT what I said," I stared defiantly into his eyes.

"Mmm, you smell good," he murmured as he sniffed the air around my head. "Is that just you, or are you wearing perfume?"

I turned my face away from him, so he couldn't touch me.

"You feel that chemistry, don't you?" he whispered near my ear. "Why fight it?"

Revulsion rippled through my body. "When Russell finds out what you're doing right now," I hissed, "he's going to kill you! You know that, right?"

This strategy worked a little, because he paused for a second to consider what I'd said. Then he looked around at our surroundings as if finally realizing we were in a public space.

"And what exactly am I doing?" he asked, leaning away, relinquishing my personal space, and taking a step back. "We're just having a friendly conversation here."

"Then let me past… or I'm going to *scream*!" I declared loudly, with renewed confidence, stepping forward.

"Jeez, Gwen, what's gotten into *you*? There's nothing to scream about," he lifted his hands up and backed away a few steps, laughing as if I'd just told the best joke. "Are you sure you're *feeling* okay?"

"There's nothing wrong with *me*," I countered, infuriated at his attempts to twist the situation around. "*You're* the problem. Now just let me past," I repeated.

He continued to back up until he was almost out of the aisle leading to the main part of the library. "You do realize that he's just using you, right? It's all about getting you ready for the ceremony. He doesn't *actually* love you."

I stepped toward him quickly, knowing an escape was just a few seconds away, and willing to ram into him if I had to.

"Just stay the hell away from me from now on, Erik!" I said, with a newfound strength, and then charged forward.

As I brushed past him, we made brief contact, and a vision hit me...

I saw Suzie's face, through Erik's eyes, as she was looking up at him with an expression that reflected how I had just been feeling: scared and intimidated.

They were standing, he had her back pinned against a wall, and she was trying to push him back - squirming against him, saying no, and telling him to get off her. But her struggles to avoid kissing him only seemed to make him more excited - giving him an adrenaline rush.

The more she fought, the more of a challenge she was, which made the thought of her finally succumbing all the more enticing.

She enjoys the chase, he thought. She's been teasing me for so long. Now she's practically begging for it.

There were tears streaking down her face, reddened from efforts to push him off her.

'Can't you feel that chemistry, Suzie?' he asked. 'Don't fight it.'

Then, without warning, she dropped her hands to her side, and allowed her body to go slack and fall to the ground.

He fell forward from his own weight and momentum, allowing her time to crab crawl out from between his legs and escape...

"What the hell was that?" he exclaimed, pulling himself away in shock - trying to figure out what had just passed between us.

I wasn't sure what the sensation was like, from his perspective - to be "read" like that - but from his reaction, it wasn't pleasant. I suppose I was like a thief, in a way, invading a mind and stealing memories without permission.

But in my defense, I hadn't done it on purpose.

Welcome to the club, Erik. You were trying to take something from us without our permission too!

He reached out to grab hold of my shirt to pull me back into the privacy of the aisle. "Come back," he insisted. "We're not done with our little chat."

I reeled around to push him away, and we made contact again...

Music is blaring, and kids are crowding into the farmhouse, filtering around the keg to get their turn at the tap. He's pushing through the crowd, not paying attention to the curses and shoulder shoves that come as a response. He's focused only on one face. Suzie.

He saw her, from the parking lot, walking hand-in-hand with Kenneth into the throngs of partygoers. His anger and resentment were palpable. He could taste the bitterness of it.

How dare you bring him here, and flaunt him in front of me, he thought.

He pushed past the last few people in his way and grabbed Suzie by the shoulder. She spun around in surprise, her face hardening in recognition.

It felt like a gut punch, filling him with emotions he refused to acknowledge, which then manifested into anger.

"How dare you show up here with HIM!"

Suzie recoiled back.

"Hey, get away from her," Kenneth yelled, holding his hand out and stepping in between them to protect her.

"This is between us, low life. Now get out of the way or I'm going to kick your ass!"

"Good luck with that, loser!"

"What did you just call me?"

"You heard me."

The fury took a life of its own and he swung wildly, trying to knock the smug look off Kenneth's face.

The swing went wide. Kenneth dodged it effortlessly, but it made him step away from Suzie.

He focused on her face again, meaning to tell her something profound. His body just wasn't responding as quickly as he wanted, though. For a second he lost track of what was happening around him, trying to take stock of what he'd had that could make him so sluggish.

He saw Kenneth grab Suzie's hand, and tow her away from the front door, clogged with an influx of teenagers searching for the keg.

Kenneth dragged Suzie down a tight hallway lined with kids making out, or scribbling graffiti on the walls.

He followed, fast on their trail, but the world kept tilting. It took every bit of focus to keep upright.

Suzie looked back over her shoulder at him - fear in her eyes.

"It's all part of the chase with you, isn't it?" he yelled out at her, over the music.

They reached the end of the hall. Kenneth let himself out the back window. Suzie climbed up and sat on the window ledge, her arms outstretched, waiting for Kenneth to help her out.

"Who jumps out the back window? Kenneth, you're a coward! I'm coming for you!"

Recoiling once again, this time in anger, he growled, "Don't you *ever* do that to me again!"

"Mrs. Harrison!" I screamed, shaking myself free of his memories, and moving away from him as quickly as possible.

Oh my god, he's the one.

I saw the few students, that were studying quietly in their cubicles, turn around at my voice.

Oh, now you look! Where were you a couple minutes ago?

Refusing to look back at him, I quickly cleared the distance from the bookracks to the desk, and the welcoming sight of a friendly, responsible adult.

"Did you find what you were looking for?" Mrs. Harrison asked.

Shaking, and trying not to hyperventilate, I placed the book down on the counter.

Breathe. Remember to breathe. You're okay.

While I stood, slowly calming myself down, I saw Erik casually saunter his way behind me towards the library exit. We locked eyes, and I glared. A slight wave of fear crossed his face before it darkened. With a smirk, and a single finger wave he said, "I'll see you later," and then he walked out.

Was that a threat?

The librarian, noticing the obvious tension between us asked, "Miss Evans, are you okay?"

"Umm... yeah... everything is fine," I answered un-convincingly. I didn't know exactly what to tell her.

No, everything is not okay! That guy just tried to... What? What had he tried to do? How could I explain it to her?

"Are you sure? Did something happen?" she asked, and looked in the direction of Erik walking down the hall.

Her instincts were right on point.

The class bell rang out just then, startling me.

"You're shaking. Do I need to call a nurse?"

"No, I'll be okay."

She took the card from inside of the book, recorded my name and the due date on it to file, then replaced it with a stamped due date card. She gently closed the book and handed it back to me.

"Thank you." I was never so relieved to hear that bell, knowing I could seek sanctuary in my next class without seeing Erik in the hall.

"Be careful, dear," she responded. "I don't want any-thing happening to you, too."

Well, that's not ominous, or anything.

Chapter Twelve
Fall Out

After my second to last class of the day… it started. I noticed a trio of girls, who usually hung out with Erin, walking towards me down the hall. They stared and pointed, whispering to each other as they approached.

What are they doing here?

Up until that moment, I'd been able to avoid this gaggle of bullies by simply using alternative routes through campus.

When they came up beside me, they stopped.

Wow. This just isn't my day.

"I can't believe you'd do that to Erin, you skank!" Carol stated, venomously.

"What are you talking about?" I asked, genuinely confused, a nervous quaked through my extremities.

"Don't act stupid, Gwen," Tonya, replied.

This was no coincidence - they were looking for me!

"I'm not acting stupid," I responded, defiantly. "Seriously, what are you talking about?"

"You have your *own* boyfriend. That not enough for you? You have to make the moves on Erin's as well?" Stacey asked.

"I'm not making the moves on *anyone*. I don't even *know* who Erin's dating right now," I answered, my confusion and tremors intensifying.

"Russell will be *sooo* pissed when he finds out! I doubt she'll even have a boyfriend after that," Carol sneered to Stacey.

"You're right! I wonder if he already knows!" Stacey replied, clearly enjoying the idea of the pain this would cause me.

What in the hell are they talking about?

"I haven't done anything!" I exclaimed angrily, trying to understand what they were insinuating.

"You really aren't fooling anyone with your..." Tonya threw her hands out in angry disdain, "your... *I'm so innocent* act. Freak!"

Then it hit me. "Are you talking about Erik?" I asked.

Erin is going out with Erik?

"Oh, *now* she gets it!" Stacey exclaimed.

"Can't deny it anymore, can you *Witch*?" Carol jeered.

"I'm NOT a Witch!" I insisted.

" 'Me thinks, thou doth protest too much' !" Stacey mocked.

"If you're talking about the library, I didn't make any moves on *HIM*! He cornered *ME*!" I proclaimed.

"Yeah, right," Tonya responded.

"Liar!" Stacey hissed.

"He did!" I yelled. I shook, felt lightheaded, and my heart was beating out of my chest.

Why would he say that?

The warning bell for the last period rang out.

"Erin said to tell you, 'Stay the hell away from Erik, or else'," Carol spat, and then pushed me sideways.

Tonya leered as she and the other two walked past, "You know what they do to Witches, don't you?" she smiled grimly. "Don't say we didn't warn you."

Once I recovered, I turned around and yelled, "You tell Erin she can keep her *psycho* pervert boyfriend! They're made for each other! Oh, and you may want to warn her…"

"Shut up, skank!" Stacey yelled back, flipping me off.

… *that her boyfriend might be a killer!* I thought.

～～

That last period flew by in a blur. The events of the day had left me completely rattled. Every nerve in my body was on edge. So many questions spun through my mind.

I replayed the vision in my head…

Had Erik followed them out that window? Was he the one who hit Kenneth so hard, it sent him to the hospital? Holy smokes! Is Russell's cousin an actual murderer?

Russell… is he still hung-up on Megan? Why would Erik say he's just using me? What ceremony?

Thankfully, the last bell announced the end of the school day and broke through my erupting mental chaos.

When I rounded the corner to my locker, hurrying in fear of missing my bus, I saw Russell standing there. It was completely unexpected. His last class was on the other side of campus.

"Hi!" I greeted warmly, happy to see him. "This is a nice surprise."

I joined him next to my locker, expecting to see his arms open, inviting me in for a hug. When that didn't happen, the mood shifted quickly from one of happy reunion to that of prickly discomfort.

"What's up?" I asked hesitantly, trying not to appear hurt by the lack of physical contact. I turned towards the padlock on my locker and started rotating the dial.

"You know what's up," he answered evenly. I'd never heard that tone before. It felt like an icy cold knife in my heart.

After my confrontation with the girls in the hall, I should have expected the gossip to make its way to his ears... just not so fast.

"Yeah, I do," I responded in the same steely manner, turning back to confront him. The memory of my confrontation with Erik flooded back, and I shook with emotion. "Your *harmless* cousin *cornered* me in the back of the library today, during my lunch period. That's what's up!"

I met his eyes, my breathing unsteady, my heart racing, and I dared him to call me a liar. I tried to remain stoic, but I felt a well of tears threatening to surge up and spill over.

Not now!

His tense posturing slacked a little. I could see the conflict between what he sensed verses what he'd heard.

I didn't relent.

"Did *you* know he tried to molest Suzie? I do! I got a vision off him today – right from his own memories. AND...

you know what else? I saw him in a confrontation with her and Kenneth at the party! THAT'S the kind of person he is! THAT'S why I always feel uncomfortable around him!"

The effort of keeping it together until school was out, hoping to reach the safety and comfort of home before I completely lost it, collapsed. Tears streamed down my face, and I quickly buried my face in my open locker, trying not to sob.

"Gwen, hey, I'm sorry," he whispered, from behind, trying to wrap his arms around me. "It's just that all these people started coming up to me and saying shit about you and Erik. I should have known you wouldn't do anything like that."

I brushed his hands away angrily. "Yes! You should have! You *know* how I feel about you! How could you *even* believe that for a second?"

"I'm so sorry!" He spun me around, wrapped his arms and around me and held me tight to his chest.

"I told him if you knew what he'd been trying to do you'd kill him," I sniffled into his shirt, wiping the tears from my cheeks.

The muscles in his body tightened. "What exactly *did* he do?"

"Nothing… he didn't get the chance, because as soon as I threatened him with that, he backed off. Then he acted like I was over-reacting, that it was just one big misunderstanding."

"But it wasn't?"

"Hell, no!" I yelled, pushing back against Russell's chest, to look him in the eyes. "He *cornered* me, pushed me up against the back of the wall, and wouldn't let me past him. No one knew we were back there. He kept saying how there was *chemistry* between us. God, just the memory of it makes me feel sick to my stomach."

"Did he... touch you?" he asked hesitantly, not wanting to hear the answer.

"He was like, leaning in and *smelling* me, then was *going* to kiss me, if you want to know the truth, *but* like I said, I got him to back off!"

"I am... I'm going to kill him," he growled, my anger and pain now fueling his building rage.

"I touched him, by accident, trying to get away from him. That's when I saw his... memories. *Did* you know about that? That he tried to..." I hesitated, lowering my voice... "rape her?" I held his eyes, challenging him to continue defending his cousin.

"She'd accused him, but he denied everything."

"And you believed him?"

"He's family. I *had* to give him the benefit of the doubt." After a moment, shook his head in shame. He realized how awful his response sounded.

"You said you *saw* him having a confrontation with Suzie and Kenneth at the party?"

"Yes. I saw them almost come to blows. Then he chased them down the hallway. I *saw* them jump out the back window. He yelled he was going to get Kenneth. That's when our connection broke... didn't they *say* they found Kenneth unconscious below the back window?"

"No, that can't be right. Something happened to him that night as well."

"I saw it, clear as day, like watching a movie, through his eyes! I'm telling you what *he* remembers."

I could see Russell struggle, trying to think things through.

"Have *you* ever heard Erik's thoughts or sensed his emotions? Did you ever feel like he was lying? That something didn't make sense?"

"I've never been able to get *anything* from him - not once! And we've been around each other our whole lives."

"Huh. Ohhh. Oh, no! Crap!" I exclaimed, looking down at my watch. It hit me that even if I started running across campus at that moment, I would miss the bus home.

"What?"

"I missed the bus!" I stated. "I don't suppose you would mind giving me a ride home?"

"Of course not! I thought about offering a long time ago, but I assumed your parents would get mad."

"Well, today I've got a legitimate excuse. YOU made me miss my bus," I responded, a halfhearted smile touching my lips.

"Fair. It's my fault, I guess I'll take the heat," he smiled back. "Alright then, grab your things."

Chapter Thirteen
Shades of Gray

Once we pulled out of the parking lot behind the gym, Russell asked again about the encounter with Erik.

"He tried to get in my head about you."

"Really, like how?"

Just remembering it made me queasy, and I to concentrate to slow my breathing, to quell the rising nausea.

Finally, mustering my courage, I continued, "First off, he said you'd never gotten over Megan. That you were still in love with her."

"What?" He squeezed the steering wheel with his left hand so hard his knuckles went white. "No!"

"He tried to tell me Megan broke up with you because she wanted to be with *him*!"

He laughed involuntarily, and then said, "That's total bull crap! He asked her out *after* we broke up. She rejected him."

"He also mentioned Winter Formal, and how you were going to ask *her*."

"Jesus! Gwen… I haven't talked to her for months," he sighed. "Wow, he really was trying to get you to not trust me, wasn't he?"

"Yeah, but that's not all…" I hesitated, drew in a deep breath, and rallied some strength.

"There's more?"

It hurt to think about saying these next words aloud. "He told me you'd never loved me…"

"You *know* that's not true!" he interjected, this time taking his eyes off the road to make sure I felt the conviction of his words. He reached over and squeezed my hand. "I love you *very* much."

"…that you're just using me," I finished.

"What?" he asked, glancing at the road in front of us, then back in my direction. "What could I possibly be using you for?"

"Some ceremony," I responded.

"Ceremony?" The word rattled him. His protective shield faltered. It was only a second, but long enough to catch a wave of emotion.

Fear? Fear of what? The ceremony itself, what it meant, or me finding out?

I stared into his eyes, imploring him for an explanation. There were so many unanswered questions - too many.

We approached a stop sign, and he let go of my hand to shift gears. To my right was the entrance to the park where we'd kissed on the swings. That had been a much better moment than the present one.

We finally turned off Briarwood Avenue onto my street. He pulled up alongside the curb in front of my house and turned off the engine. Taking a deep breath, he leaned his head back against his seat.

I finally broke the silence by asking, "What ceremony was he talking about?"

He leaned forward, crossed his arms across the steering wheel, and laid his head on his arms.

"Considering I haven't been able to meet your sisters yet, or talk to your mom, and no one is helping me understand anything, the least you can do is answer this one simple question."

"I know," he relented, as he exhaled deeply.

"Tell me what's going on," I pleaded. I no longer felt it was a secret I needed to be let "in on", as much as it was a secret he needed to unburden himself *from.*

Russell lifted his head, as if he were going to speak, noticed something, and then motioned towards my house. I turned to see my mother standing in the doorway with her arms on her hips.

After I cranked down the passenger side window, I yelled out, "Mom, I missed the bus. Russell was nice enough to give me a ride home!"

"Oh, okay. Well don't sit out there all day." She motioned towards the sky, "Supposed to freeze tonight! They've predicted snow by Thanksgiving. Can you believe that?" she answered loud enough for the entire neighborhood to hear.

"Uh, huh," I nodded to her. "Be in just in a minute."

"Russell, you're welcome to come inside," she yelled.

I turned towards him and shrugged. "Do you want to?"

"Sure," he answered. Glancing back up at my mother, he smiled and waved. Seemingly satisfied she headed back inside.

Once we were also inside the house, she said, "Thank you for giving her a ride home, Russell." She turned to me. "It's a good thing he was there. I can't stand the thought of you waiting alone for me to come get you. What if someone had grabbed you?"

"Yep," I nodded, looking over at Russell fidgeting uncomfortably. We needed to continue our discussion, somehow. "Okay, well, I'm going to drop my stuff off in my room," I announced, motioning down the hallway.

"Did you need a snack?" my mother asked, looking around the kitchen area. "Russell, would you like something?"

"Um, no thank you. Maybe next time," he responded politely.

"Speaking of next time, I am looking forward to meeting your mother tomorrow. We had a lovely chat on the phone." She looked from Russell back to me. "I know your dad is being a big stick in the mud, but he'll come around."

"Yeah, I'm looking forward to it too," he answered - his usual charm flat - even my mom could tell that he wasn't acting the same.

"Is everything okay?" she asked, looking at me for an explanation.

"It's fine. I'm just going to put my things away. Is it okay if Russell comes back with me? We'll just be a minute."

"Um, sure," she replied, weighing the pros and cons of her decision, "just for a minute."

Once we entered my room, I closed the door as much as I thought I could get away with, dropped my bag on the floor, and then sat down on the edge of my bed.

Russell came over, sat down next to me, and placed his right hand on mine.

"So, first off," he nodded, "let's address the elephant in the room."

"Must be a pretty small elephant, because I didn't even know one lived in here," I quipped, and chuckled half-heartedly.

"No, really, I'm serious," he sighed, seeming determined to get something off his chest.

"Erik."

"Yes."

"You don't believe me? What I… saw?"

"No, I do. I believe you saw what you saw, so he *must* have…" He struggled. "She *had* been telling the truth."

"Yeah, she was… she did."

"But," he slowly shook his head, confused, "I don't believe he was responsible for what happened to her at the party. I just can't. Did you actually *see* him hurting either of them?"

"Well, no, he broke contact with me before it got to that, and he was really pissed off I'd seen those things."

"That could explain why he spread rumors about you, to deflect attention from what you saw!"

"Yeah, but he was already trying to get me to doubt you, our relationship, *before* any of that even happened. Why?"

"Maybe, it's like when we were kids. He always wanted what I had. As we grew older, he always fell for the same girls that I did, but he didn't get them. He's had this chip on his shoulder his whole life when it came to me, as if we were brothers."

"But he's your cousin, not your brother."

"Yeah, but we grew up together, and we're the same age. I think he's always felt like my house was his; therefore, my life should be equally his, or something. I've never been really sure what motivates him, because like I told you before, I can't read him."

"So, you're saying he's causing problems, because you got *me* and he didn't?" I asked, pondering the idea. "Okay, that's one motivation, but I have another - Erin."

"What does Erin have to do with anything?"

"I was accosted today in the hallway by some of her friends. They went out of their way to find me. They accused me of trying to steal Erin's *boyfriend* away from her, and gloated about how pissed you'd be when you found out."

"You think Erik is causing this drama because Erin put him up to it? Why? To break us up?"

"I don't know, but it's a pattern with her. Do you remember how she came after me over Chris? When he broke up with her, she probably blamed me for that as well. Her friends told me to stay away from Erik or else, and then one of them said, and I quote: 'you know what they do to Witches, don't you?'"

"What the hell is that supposed to mean?"

"It sounds like a threat," I stated. "And I just can't stop wondering how on earth Erin learned about the doll binding, and the ceremony at the bonfire? She wasn't there. But knowing now that she's Erik's girlfriend, it seems like he could have told her."

"Yeah, that makes sense."

"So, how did *he* know? Did you tell him about the ceremony at the house?" I asked.

"Yes," he nodded begrudgingly.

"Why?" I turned, exasperated, throwing my hands up. "Why would you tell him *anything* about what we were doing?"

"Because we're *family,* and…"

"Does he know about your abilities?" I asked.

"Yeah, of course."

I felt a sudden sense of dread. "Does he have any that I should know about?"

"None that I'm aware of. Despite being Judith's son, he doesn't seem to have inherited any of her gifts."

"Well that's a relief! I'm sorry, he may be your cousin, but there's something not right about him. I'd hate to think he had some sort of psychic powers or whatever. That's scary."

"I'm starting to get why you feel that way."

"So, is that how it happens? It's inherited?"

"In our family, yes."

121

"Is that what the Circle of the Dark Stream is then - just members of your extended family? Do they all have one sort of ability or another?"

"Well, no. Most are 'practicing' - trying to tap into whatever raw powers they may possess. And, no, not all the members are family. Do you remember me mentioning the history of the town?"

"Of course, yes! That's why I was at the library. I checked out a book today, because I thought I might do a little investigating on my own."

"You might learn some things, but not the whole story, and definitely not what's going on nowadays."

"What's that?"

"There are prominent people in town who are actually core members of the Circle. Their identities are kept secret, for many reasons. One reason, most importantly, is to avoid persecution and harassment – like you're getting a taste of right now. They can't let anyone know."

"How prominent? Like Mayor prominent, or principal of the school prominent?" I held my hand high and flat, then lowered it slowly, and lifted it again, wanting clarification.

"Prominent," he answered evasively.

"Are they part of the coven because they are trying to gain supernatural powers, or is there some other reason?"

"They seek guidance from the High Priestess, mostly, by participating in rituals during certain lunar cycles. Her guidance helps them become more successful – to gain power and influence in the community."

"If your mom is the one influencing their decisions, then doesn't that actually make her the most powerful person in this town?" I speculated. "Dang, she just seemed like a nice Scottish lady who owns a pretty cool store."

"Well, she *is* a nice Scottish lady who owns a cool store!" he confirmed with a smile. "But listen, you can't repeat this," he said in earnest. "You can't let on you know! I swore an oath to the coven, and to my family. I've already said too much. That's why I wanted you to ask my mom these questions. If she is going to bring you into the fold, and counsel you about your powers, then she can tell you what you need to know."

"What do you mean, 'bring me into the fold'? Does that mean, into the coven? As in make me a Witch?"

"Well, yes and no. No one can *make* you be anything. In the end, it's up to you. You have natural abilities that you can harness. You're more powerful than you realize."

"How do you know that?"

"I've witnessed it, for one. Plus, Judith saw it when she first met you. So did my mom. They mentioned being impressed by the raw power they felt within you. Each one of my sisters is powerful in their own right, but you have the potential to be like all three of them wrapped up into one."

"Really? They said that?"

"Yeah."

"Didn't *your* abilities come naturally to you, or did you have to learn how to tap into them?"

"It's both. It came naturally for my sisters and I, but we didn't display them at first. When we hit puberty, my mom saw hints of what each one of us might be capable of, so she started helping us focus. We had to practice. We had to learn to harness each gift and control it, instead of letting it control us."

"Like what happened to me," I added.

"Exactly! My mom hopes - if you can spend time at our house regularly - that she can help you figure it all out. She can provide you with a safe place to practice, so that you can reach your full potential."

"If it's inherited, has every generation of your family been like you and your sisters?"

"To some extent, however, there's such a thing as a *pure* bloodline, where the 'first daughters' inherit the strongest powers."

"And that would be your mother. That's why she's the High Priestess, right?"

"It's a complicated family tree. She'd have to explain it to you," he replied.

"If I have similar abilities, who did I inherit them from? Does it only come from the mother's side of the family? What about the father's side?" I asked. "I don't know anything about my mother's side, and if it were on my father's side, you'd think my grandmother would have said something. She and I were very close." I looked down at my wrist, to take in the warm memories her watch always brought to me.

Surely she would have said something to me if she'd come from a line of Witches and knew I would inherit her powers.

"My mom can explain it a lot better than I can."

The nagging suspicions Erik planted in my head started needling at me again. I hated them getting the better of me.

"You mentioned *my true potential*. Potential for what, exactly? Does that have something to do with 'the ceremony'?"

He stiffened, thought about his response, and then sighed in resignation, "Erik was probably just referring to *Imbolc*."

"What's that?"

"It's a festival held in February, halfway between the Winter Solstice and the Spring Equinox, when we honor Brighid, the Goddess of fire and fertility. The Christians refer to it as the feast day of Saint Brigit."

"A festival? That doesn't sound so bad. Why did he say you were *using me* for this?"

"I'm not using you for anything!" he bristled. "Let's get that straight."

"Okay! I believe you," I answered sincerely. I knew he was telling me the truth and was hurting at the thought he'd lost my trust. "What else happens at the festival?"

"We perform initiations into the coven or have rededication ceremonies."

"And…"

"And like I mentioned before, my mom and Judith both saw something significant within you. They both mentioned, 'welcoming you into the family'."

"And Erik thinks you're doing what? Acting as a secret agent to get me to sign up against my will?" I asked. "I don't get it. He made it sound so… scandalous."

"It's not! This is exactly why I hate the word *Witch*," he sighed. "When people think of a ceremony involving a coven, they think Devil worshipers and black magic. He was playing on your fear. And, I promise you, we're not part of a satanic cult or anything evil. He, of all people, knows better."

"No dark dungeons with medieval torture devices?" I asked playfully, trying to lighten the mood.

"And no human sacrifices," he replied seriously, but then sighed heavily again. "When a person wants to be part of the coven, it's not joining the country club, or a quilting circle. It's about dedicating yourself to a set of beliefs, and joining forces with others within the community, or 'family' as we refer to it."

"That's exactly the kind of pitch a cult leader would give," I teased.

"Gwen! I'm trying to be serious," he grumbled.

"Sorry. This is pretty heavy stuff," I responded. "A lot to take in, ya know?"

"Yeah… and just for the record, I'm not a secret agent!" he stated.

I tried not to giggle in response.

"I started falling in love with you the first time I saw you at Mike's," he asserted, looking deep into my eyes to make sure I felt his sincerity. "Everything else is just coincidence. I swear."

"Hmm… they say there are no such things as coincidences," I responded, lifting one eyebrow and trying to sound very knowledgeable.

"You just can't help yourself, can you?" he sighed, trying to suppress a grin. "Okay, I'll bite! Who says that?"

"Somebody... *important*, that's who," I answered, trying not to snicker.

"Right."

"Okay, so to be clear, you aren't a secret agent, and you don't throw virgins into a volcano or anything like that?"

"Not that I am aware of. But if it meant going to a tropical island for a vacation, I could be persuaded," he answered, grinning mischievously.

I punched him playfully on the shoulder. "Ha! Ha!"

"Hey!" he squawked, and rubbed his arm as if I'd actually hurt him. "Sooo... we good now?" He put his arm around my shoulders and pulled me closer so that I could lie against him.

"Yes," I sighed, happy to have resolved the tension. I scooted in, and he placed his head atop mine, while bringing his other arm around so that we could cuddle. "And just for the record, I love you too."

"Good," he whispered.

"I'm still concerned about Erik, though," I replied.

"Me too," he answered.

Chapter Fourteen
Cottage in the Woods

Trying to find a cute outfit to wear, I'd torn my closet apart. My mother insisted I wear a dress. I never wore dresses. It was too cold outside for one anyways, and there was no way I was going to put stockings on, as she suggested. I couldn't stand the feeling of wearing stockings - it was as if my skin couldn't breathe.

I opted, instead, for a pair of white corduroy pleated slacks and a pink angora three-quarter sleeve sweater. It had a fun neckline, high in the front, drooping low in the back. My mother didn't seem to mind as long as my bra strap didn't show.

After my father returned home from work, later than usual - delayed by Friday night traffic - we readied ourselves arrive at Russell's house by 6:00 p.m.

Once he double-checked everything was locked up tight, we walked in unison to the driveway, and piled into the car.

Pulling away from the house, we drove a couple blocks down my street and turned left onto Briarwood Avenue. A few minutes later, we took a right onto a road called Wild Hare.

"Cool name for a road," I remarked, as we drove up a small incline, passing through a tunnel of dark dense forest. "It's weird that I've lived here my whole life and never knew this road existed."

My dad caught my eyes in the rearview mirror and explained, "It's no wonder, you always head in the opposite direction towards school or the mall. There's a whole big world out here you haven't explored."

You have no idea.

As I continued to watch the trees pass, admiring the last remaining colors of fall, I remarked wistfully, "When I get my driver's license I'll be able to go anywhere I want!"

My mom groaned, "I don't even want to think about you driving yet."

"The novelty does wear off eventually," he chuckled.

We then drove slowly across a quaint wooden bridge. The rhythmic sound of the tires echoed throughout the car as we made our way across. Out my window, I could see the drop off down into the dark waters of the Douglas River streaming below us.

Once we reached the other side of the bridge, the pavement became gravel, and my dad had to drive much slower. Not too long after, my mother yelled, "Whoa!"

The car slid to a stop, throwing me slightly forward into the back of my mom's seat. "What is it?" my father yipped.

"Did we run something over?" I gasped.

"That was the turn back there," she explained, turning around, pointing back over her shoulder.

"Damnit! Don't scare me like that."

My father moved us slowly over to the far right, and then cranked the wheel all the way to the left to make a tight U-turn on the narrow road.

We came back to a concealed dirt road that cut through the dark forest. Only then did we see the carved wood sign that read:

White Stag Lane

"Ahh, there it is. Now I see it." My father shook his head, admiring the large tree that stood alongside the sign, resembling a deer with antlers.

I noticed the symbol. It was the same one from the coven flyer I'd gotten from Judith, and one I remembered from Ewan Blackwood's paintings.

We made our way along the road, winding up a hill, until the forest canopy fell away, opening onto a vast hillside covered in grass.

The dirt road gave way to a cobbled drive, bound on either side by columns of river rock, stacked a few feet tall, capped with softly glowing lamps. The rock pillars lit the way up to the top of the hill. There, silhouetted by the last rays of the setting sun behind the tree line, stood an incredible house.

With his mouth hanging open in awe, my father asked, "*This* is where they live?"

The house looked like an English stone cottage, ripped from the pages of a storybook, but on a grand scale.

"I had no idea they were rich!" my father exclaimed. "What is it you said his father does for a living?"

"He's a literature professor at Douglas University," I answered.

"Now, how in the heck can they afford this kind of house on a professor's wages?"

"Well, his mom does have the store," I added.

"Hmmm," he pondered, seemingly unsatisfied with my answers.

"It's positively enchanting," my mother cooed.

The house had several terraced levels cascading down the hillside. The multitude of windows were adorned with boxes of flowers. The steeply pitched rooflines, covered in dark stone tiles, looked almost thatched at a distance, complete with terracotta chimney pots.

When we made our way level with the property, parking next to the two-car garage, I was able to take in more detail.

The whole home was made of stone with accents of timbers, and stucco here and there. A courtyard at the entrance, under a gabled overhang, was lit with a rock pillar on either side. Surrounding each pillar, a garden area filled with a variety of flowers and herbs - some already withered from the drop in overnight temperatures. Beneath the courtyard roof, I looked up to see exposed timbers.

Everything about the place felt like it was at once both part of the forest and the surrounding hillside. With lit up accents included in the landscaping, it really did seem enchanted.

My father was just about to knock at one of the two large wooden doors, when it swung inward, and Russell stood there. He wore a dark blue wool sweater with a white oxford shirt sticking up above its collar, over a pair of tan khaki pants.

"Hello!" He stepped back and extended his arm into the foyer. "Come on in, I hope you didn't have any trouble with my directions."

"They were great," my father responded. "You were right, the tree does look like a deer with antlers."

"Thank you for having us," my mother nodded politely.

"You're welcome. My mother can't wait to meet you," Russell responded, closing the large double doors behind us.

Inside there was a partitioned area off to the right with a bay window looking back out into the front courtyard. The area served as a type of mudroom, with rows of mounted coat hooks along one wall, and a giant mirror in a dark wood frame mounted on the other. Below the mirror sat a matching wood bench with a variety of shoes camped underneath. Standing on the far end of the bench, tucked into the corner against the wall, was an umbrella stand.

Russell turned towards me and said quietly, "and my sisters can't wait to meet *you!*" I could smell his "only for special occasions" cologne, and breathed it in deeply, evoking the memory of our first dance.

I whispered back, "You keep saying that, but surely they've met one of your girlfriends before."

"I've never had a girl and her family over for dinner," he stated simply, as he gently scooped my hand up into his. "This is kind of a big deal."

I felt myself blush, and my heart fluttered a little. I knew he wanted to kiss me, and I wanted him to, but he was restraining himself in front of my parents.

"Oh, wow! No pressure."

He winked. "You have nothing to worry about."

"Should we leave our things here?" my mother asked.

"Yes. Oh, here, let me take those." Russell let go of my hand and gathered up our coats. He hung them up before escorting us through two stacked rock columns that defined the foyer, into a large open floor plan extending off to the left and right.

Immediately, I was awed by the high beamed ceiling over the living room area with its angled fireplace off to the left.

To the right, was a space sectioned off as the dining room. Down its center spanned a long wood table that could easily seat a family of twelve. The wall, at the end of this table, featured a bay window overlooking the long grassy slope.

From this space, an archway led to the kitchen, where we could hear pans clanking together, followed by a familiar lilting voice ring out, "Are they haur, Russell?"

"Yes, mum!"

Brighid skittered out of the kitchen, around the enormous dining room table, to join us at the edge of the living room. Unlike the new-age Woodstock-hippie style she donned while on the job at Shanachie, that night she wore a simple ankle length blue dress, with long sleeves, and a belted waistline. Her flowing red hair stood out in contrast, drawing attention to her beautiful white skin and green eyes.

"Gwen! My dear!" she opened up her arms and brought me in for an extended hug. "Sae lovely tae see ye agin. Ah'm sae happy ye could make it."

"Thank you for inviting us. It's good to see you too."

"GIRLS! Gwen's arrived!" she yelled down the wide hallway that led back through the center of the house. "Whaur are they?" Then she turned towards the living room and said, "Cameron, luik who's haur!"

I turned in that direction and saw a large male figure rise from a tall leather chair that faced the fireplace. He turned, displaying a gorgeous smile, and ambled towards us.

Russell's father had dark brown hair with streaks of gray forming at the temples, a neatly trimmed mustache, and a beard peppered with gray. He had on an off-white knit sweater with patterned stitching, paired with a set of dark tweed slacks. Tall, like Russell, with the same slender build, I could see some resemblance between the two, mostly through the nose and eyes.

Russell made the introductions. "Mom, dad, this is Elizabeth and Robert."

In a powerful bass tone, his father came over to my dad. "Hello, I'm Cameron. Welcome to our home."

He sounded exactly as I thought a professor should - filled with confidence and authority.

"Nice to meet you, Cameron. You can call me, Bob." My dad took Cameron's extended hand and shook it once. "This is Elizabeth."

"So wonderful to finally meet you both," he responded, taking her hand gently between both of his, slightly bowing his head.

Brighid came over and brought my mother into a hug. "Hullo! Ah'm Brighid! T'is truly wonderful tae finally meet ye in person!"

"Nice to meet you as well," my mom responded, accepting the embrace. "You have such a lovely home by the way!"

"Thank ye..." Brighid started, "Oh?" She pulled back from my mother slightly, looking questioningly into her eyes. I could tell this was making my mother uncomfortable, but she remained still, waiting politely for Brighid to disengage.

Then Brighid looked over at me with the same questioning face, before shaking her head, and stepping back. "Well, noo ah see whaur, um, Gwen gets it fae."

"I'm sorry, gets what from?" my mother asked, a little put off by Brighid's response.

"Oh, uh, her *beauty* o' course!" she exclaimed, replacing her questioning look with her usual warm smile.

My mother blushed and stammered, "Oh, my, how kind of you to say that."

"Please make yersel' at hame."

Brighid then brought my father in for a hug, which was definitely not his style. "Ah'm sae glad ye all could make it. Tea will be ready in a bit. Ah'll be right back."

I knew Brighid was covering for something she had discerned when reading my mom. Just like the first time when she hugged me, and instantly knew I was a "seer" into both worlds.

I felt Russell nudge me in the arm, and whisper "You saw that too?"

"Yeah, what's that about?"

"She's been trying to figure something out ever since she talked to your mom on the phone about tonight," he answered.

"Obviously it doesn't have to do with my mother's good looks," I remarked under my breath.

"Well, she's not wrong," he responded and gave a little wink. "I suspect it's something else though."

"Aw shucks," I tittered. "Now, don't go perving on my mom!" I teased, nudging him back.

Cameron then turned his attention towards me. "Hello, Gwen." He came up to me and gathered my hands up in the same manner as had with my mother, bowing slightly. "I've heard nothing but wonderful things about you."

Ohhh, this is where Russell gets his smooth moves from.

Russell snickered behind me, and when I looked over at him, he looked away, trying to hide his grin.

Oh, dang, can his dad hear my thoughts too?

"Thank you," I stammered, feeling the heat on my cheeks, wanting desperately to disappear into the background.

"Why don't you all come join me by the fire and get comfortable." Cameron pointed towards the giant soft cushioned couch that faced the roaring fireplace.

Russell whispered, "Don't go perving on my dad!"

"Stop it."

There were piles of big pillows tucked into the corner, and crocheted throws folded on the floor between the couch and Cameron's leather chair. It was cozy and inviting.

"Can I get you something to drink before dinner, Bob? Bourbon. Scotch, perhaps?"

My mom lingered in the foyer and called out, "Brighid, can I help you in the kitchen?

"Naw. Naw. Ye sit an enjoy the fire," she yelled back.

"Scotch, please. I've haven't had the good stuff in ages," my dad responded. "Elizabeth, you want anything?"

"No, thank you. I'll wait until dinner."

"Ghee," Cameron yelled out, "Really now, stop fussing! Come sit down and relax with us."

"Ye ken I cannae. Roast is nearly done, an' the'r a haip o' kettle pans cuikin," she answered back.

Cameron led my dad to the drink cabinet, making small talk about jobs and town politics, while Russell led us over to the couch.

"Can I get *you* something? A soda, some juice... or a glass of water?" Russell asked clumsily. He wasn't used to entertaining a guest in his house and didn't know quite what to do.

"No, I'm fine," I answered.

Just sit with me.

He immediately joined me on the soft cushions of the couch, scooped up my hand and held it on his knee.

Cameron brought his drink with him when he went to sit back down in his leather chair, my father sat in the other easy chair with his Scotch.

"Does Russell owe his talent for poetry to you?" I asked, and then tapped Russell's leg affectionately.

"I didn't know Russell *had* a talent for it," he responded, with an intrigued purse to his brow.

"Oh, I just thought because you taught literature that it was something you encouraged at home."

"Well poetry *is* in our blood. Duncan Ban MacIntyre is regarded as one of the finest Gaelic poets of the 18th century. But I suspect it may have more to do with Russell finding his muse."

"Muse?" I asked. "I don't understand."

"You inspire him," he explained, staring at the two of us. "I can see why."

I felt my face blush in response.

My mom cleared her throat, as a way to change the subject and asked, "Did Brighid make these?" She motioned towards the hand knit throw blanket nearest her at the end of the couch.

"No, that's Aileen's hobby," Russell responded. "Personally, I'm glad she settled on knitting blankets, instead of forcing me into itchy sweaters and snow hats."

"I heard that little brother!"

I turned at the sound, and saw a tall, slender young woman with long blondish-brown hair glide around the corner of a long hallway. She had hazel eyes like Russell. She wore a long-sleeve white blouse tucked into a pair of pleated black slacks. The blouse buttoned up the back, had a high lace neckline, with matching lace cuffs at the wrist. A long set of necklaces dangled down the front of her blouse.

A second girl, with long chestnut hair, like Russell's, and wide green eyes, like her mother's, came up from behind. She stood a couple inches shorter wearing a casual outfit of a blue and white plaid shirt that buttoned up the front, tucked into a pair of jeans.

A smile spread across her face as we made eye contact. "Hello! I am Roisin," she chimed, gracefully gliding towards me with her arms open. "But you can call me Rose." I stood up and accepted the hug.

"Hi, Rose. It's so good to finally meet you!"

I felt a warm heat begin within my core and radiate out into my limbs. She held me tightly until I relaxed and held her back, much in the same way Brighid had the first time we embraced.

"We dressed you up in more than just sweaters and snow hats, Russ," the blondish one teased, closing the distance between us. She shoved Rose to the side, "Get off of her, you goof, my turn! Hi, I'm Aileen."

"Hey! Don't break her. I need her back in one piece," Russell scolded.

I noticed my mom swivel her head his direction, a look of surprise on her face - perhaps due to his protective manner, or the assertion that I was his.

My father hadn't noticed at all. He was enjoying his Scotch and the small talk with Cameron.

"These are my two sisters Aileen and Rose," Russell said looking over at my mom and dad. "Girls, these are Gwen's parents, Elizabeth and Bob."

"Hi. Nice to meet you," they replied in unison.

"Where's Ciara?" I asked.

"Oh, she's just closing up the store. She'll be here in a little bit," Aileen responded.

Sitting back down next to Russell, I glanced at the sisters' faces then back over at Cameron. I couldn't really see a true resemblance of him in either of them. At best, they were perfectly proportioned in their features between both mother and father - each unique, and equally attractive.

Brighid came around the corner wiping her hands on an apron, stating, "If yiv nithin on yir peenie yir no daein it richt!" She laughed, untied it, and tossed it aside. "Tea is maistlins done. I hope ilka bodie is hungersome!"

"Starving!" Russell exclaimed.

"Yer ayewis hungersome!" she teased shaking her head at him.

Chapter Fifteen
Rumbledethumb

Ciara, finally made it home, entering in through the foyer. She had dark wavy shoulder length hair and dressed like Stevie Nicks from the album cover of Fleetwood Mac's, *Rumours.* She was taller than her two sisters were, and resembled Cameron more than Brighid.

"Hiya!" Brighid exclaimed. "Welcome hame!"

"Hello, everyone," Ciara waved at the lot of us gathered around the fire. She looked uncomfortable with everyone staring at her. "Excuse me while I go freshen up."

Brighid called out, "Girls! Want tae help me noo?"

"Coming, mum," Aileen and Rose responded.

"Alright, there's our cue," Cameron stated as he rose from his chair, still holding his drink. He waited, looking at Russell to follow his example.

Russell then rose, helping me up off the couch with him, and led the way from the living room area across to the dining room table. My mom and dad followed suit.

"Take a seat wherever you like," Cameron suggested, after he'd made his way to the furthest end, his back facing the exterior window.

It was dark now, and I could no longer see the hillside.

Russell sat to his father's left, facing the kitchen, and pulled a chair out for me next to him. My mother sat to my left, and my father took the last chair on that side.

Ciara returned, taking the seat opposite of Russell on her father's right.

Aileen and Rose emerged from the kitchen, holding a bowl in each hand. They placed a bowl in front of Cameron and Ciara then came around to our side. After which, they retreated back to the kitchen for more servings.

Aileen then served my mother and father, while Rose placed a bowl down for Aileen and herself. Then Brighid emerged, with her own bowl, and proceeded to take her seat at the "head of the table."

"Tae start," Brighid chimed, as she sat down. "T'is whit we call 'Tattie Soup' - a Scottish tradition."

The siblings all dipped their spoons into the warm, creamy broth. I took their cue and took my first taste.

It was thicker than a chicken soup, but thinner than traditional chowder. Visibly I could make out chunks of potatoes, and some carrots; however, there were some translucent bits I couldn't quite identify. Normally I wasn't a fan of vegetable soup, but my mother always said to try new things, and if I didn't like it, I didn't have to eat it again.

"This is delicious, Brighid. Potatoes and onions? I must get the recipe," my mother declared between bites.

"An' leeks. Thank ye. Ah will gladly share the recipes wi' ye."

"That would be wonderful! How long have you lived in the United States, may I ask?" my mother continued.

Cameron interjected, "We met in Scotland after I graduated Princeton. We married at her family's home, and then she came back with me to the states. That's when Ciara was born. So, what is that now?"

"I just turned 21, dad," Ciara grumbled, shaking her head.

"Whar does the time gae?" Brighid mused, looking fondly at her eldest daughter.

Addressing Brighid, my mother asked, "It's just that you still have such a strong accent."

"You think *this* is strong, you should hear it when anyone from the homeland comes to visit!" Rose exclaimed.

"Especially around the holidays," Aileen added, nodding excitedly as the two of them giggled.

"Oh? And what happens then?" she asked, further intrigued.

"Girls! Haud yer wheesht!" Brighid laughed.

"They put on their kilted skirts, bring out the traditional swords, and perform the Highland Sword Dance. By then they've had a lot to drink…" Russell chimed in.

"Just a wee dram tae ward off the winter chill," she interjected in her defense.

"And the brogue is so thick, you can't understand a word they're saying to each other," Cameron finished.

The whole family erupted in laughter.

"That sounds like a lot of fun!" I remarked.

"Well hopefully we can have you back with us then," Cameron responded, looking between my father and mother for approval.

Brighid rose, and without a word, all three sisters rose as well, clearing away our finished bowls. Aileen chimed, "Time for the next course," and followed her mother back through the archway to the kitchen.

After a few minutes, the four of them returned, each carrying a plate of food, placing it down in front of us.

"Ghee, you really out did yourself. It looks amazing," Cameron crowed.

My plate had a huge slice of Pork Roast with a healthy side of a cheesy potato concoction. The smell was delicious.

After Brighid sat down, she responded, "Thank ye! Ah ken hoo much ye enjoy the *Rumbledethumb*!"

Elbowing Russell gently, I asked quietly, "Rumbledethumb?"

Cameron answered my question first. "*Rumbled* is an old English word meaning, food that has been scrambled or mashed."

"Aye, t'is tatties, onions, an' cabbage, mixed aa' taegither wi' cheese, then baxtered until golden brown," Brighid interjected.

"It's very similar to the English dish *Bubble and Squeak*," Cameron continued.

I started to giggle. "I'm sorry. Bubble and Squeak?"

"It's the sound it makes. It bubbles up and squeaks while over the fire," he answered.

"Oh, that is fun!" my mother smiled, and cut into her roast.

"Mom, it tastes great," Russell added.

The table went quiet while everyone enjoyed each morsel, until finally my father let his curiosity get the better of him.

"So, Cameron, how did you go from graduating Princeton to living here in Douglas? Better yet, why?" he chuckled.

"An opportunity presented itself," Cameron answered matter-of-factly, as he took another bite of his roast. I saw the wheels in my father's brain spinning. I knew he wanted to ask how they could afford such a beautiful home.

Before he could continue, Brighid interjected with a question of her own. One I'd felt burning just beneath the surface.

"Elizabeth, may I ask, whaur yer family hails fae?"

I noticed Brighid acknowledge me out of the corner of her eye, and felt Russell adjust his legs beneath the table, as he sat up straighter in keen interest to how she would answer. He looked over and slid his hand under the table where he gently rested it on my knee. There was a peculiar expression on his face.

What is that? Anxiety? Anticipation?

Why would that question trigger such a response?

He ignored my mental inquiry and turned back in the direction of our mothers' conversation.

Swallowing her last bite, she wiped the corners of her mouth with her napkin. "Where does my family come from?" she asked.

Gazing around the table, she didn't look at all pleased that suddenly she was the center of attention. "I really don't know," she answered dismissively, going back for another bite.

Ugh, why does she always say that? She must know something.

I pretty much lost interest after her disappointing answer, and turned back to my plate, cutting into the tender roast.

Brighid persisted.

"Wiz yer paintin o' the cottage on the cliff handed doon through yer *mother's* side?"

My mother fumbled her fork. It clanked against the edge of the plate. "Yes," she stammered. "How did you know that?"

"Russell telt me, t'is hangin in yer livin room."

"Oh... that's right. I had no idea what it was until he told me about it."

"Iona," Brighid nodded.

"Yes. It was my mother's suggestion to give Gwen the middle name of Iona. It made so much more sense when I understood where the name came from." She nodded her gratitude towards Russell. He nodded back, smiling.

"So, your mother's family comes from Scotland? That's wonderful!" Cameron chimed in.

My mom responded vaguely, "Your guess would be as good as mine. All I ever knew of the painting was that it held some sort of sentiment, and they wanted me to have it."

"Dae ye ken, whit's yer grandmother's maiden name?" Brighid asked.

"Ghee, maybe we should just let the poor woman eat her meal in peace," Cameron chided gently.

"I dinnae mean tae neb. Ah'm the *shanachie* o' *my* family, so ah'm ayewis curious aboot such things."

"Oh, it's okay," my mother smiled. "Shanachie. Isn't that the name of your store? What does it mean?"

"It goes back to when each Clan had someone in charge of maintaining the family histories and traditions – the storyteller," Cameron interjected again.

My mother looked over to him, and responded, "Ahhh!" Then she looked back over to Brighid, and finally answered the question. "Her married name was MacDonald. I'm not completely sure what her maiden name was, but I remember hearing the name Cameron every now and then. I'm not sure to whom the name was in reference to though."

All the siblings' heads swiveled toward Brighid, their faces lighting up.

My mother hadn't noticed the response. She was chuckling to herself, and then turned to Russell's father and said, "That's a funny coincidence, since *your* name is Cameron."

She stopped, reading the faces around her, and asked, "What? Did I say something wrong?"

"Ah *kenned* ah felt somethin familiar aboot ye," Brighid stated, barely containing her excitement. "Yer kin!"

Russell's leg stirred against mine, and I realized his hand was no longer on my knee. He had his head down, making sure not to engage eye contact with my father.

What?

"I don't see how…" my mother started, looking around at the family as if hoping someone would crack a smile and let her know it was just a joke.

Brighid seemed to empathize with her discomfort and confusion, so she tried to make light of it. "Ye could throw a stone in Scotland an' hit a cousin," Brighid laughed. "So dinna fash yersel'!"

"Oh, okay," she sighed, and then laughed along.

"But mom," Rose interjected. "Nana's clan is Cameron."

"Oh jeez," Aileen exclaimed. "Russell… you and Gwen are kissing cousins!"

No!

"Shut up," Russell hissed. He cautiously glanced over at me.

You knew this the whole time?

He shook his head in response, pleading with his eyes for me to not overreact.

I feel sick.

My dad, into his second Scotch, didn't seem too phased by the news, and just laughed, "I'm sure it's just a coincidence."

"Can someone tell me where I can find the restroom?" I asked quietly, standing up and placing my napkin on my plate.

"I'll show you," Russell offered, standing up alongside me.

His adrenaline was buzzing so loud I could hear it, and his anxiety resonated within me.

"Uh, wait," my mother stammered, as she watched us rise.

"Dinnae fret Elizabeth, t'is awricht," Brighid cooed. "Whit cannae 'member frae yer childhood?"

He took my hand and began steering us down the long hallway to the heart of the house. I could still hear their voices behind us, coming from the table.

"Ghee, really, this isn't the time or place. Let's just finish our dinner," Cameron insisted.

"Well... umm... I never knew who my father was. I always thought her husband, Don, was my dad. It wasn't until much later when she confessed the truth..."

My father, speaking loudly over her, addressed Cameron. "You were saying that an opportunity arose to come to Douglas. Was that the teaching job at the University?"

Once Russell led us around the corner, out of view and out of earshot, he stopped and turned, holding both of my hands out in front of him.

"I know I promised you answers that I would explain everything, but I guess, first I need to confess something."

"You DID know!" I recoiled, as if punched in the gut. He held my hands firm to keep me from pulling away.

"Hold on! Just wait. Not exactly."

"What exactly then?"

"My mother told me something after she first met you, that day at the shop. I didn't think much of it at the time. I mean I did. But maybe I wasn't convinced."

"What did she tell you?"

"She heard a familiar *humming*."

"I don't remember humming."

"The way she reacted to hugging your mom," he went on, shaking his head, as if he couldn't really believe he was about to acknowledge something huge, "I know she heard it then too."

"What did she hear?"

"The 'old blood'."

Chapter Sixteen
Then and Now

After he showed me to the bathroom, I was able to have a moment to myself to collect my thoughts.

"Doing okay in there?" Russell asked, lightly tapping on the door.

"Yes, I'm coming," I sighed.

I took a deep breath to prepare myself for the rest of story, and then opened the door.

After I stepped forward, he took one look at me, and said, "Why don't we go outside. Maybe you just need some fresh air."

He led us through a set of French doors opening onto an uncovered deck overlooking terraced gardens below. I braced against the night air when it hit. It was much colder at his house than mine.

"You okay? You need a coat? We can go back inside," he offered.

"No. This is better. You were right - I just needed the fresh air." I inhaled deeply, gazing up at the stars.

"Well let me keep you warm at least," he said wrapping me in his arms. "Better?"

"Much."

For a long while, we just swayed back and forth, looking out into the darkening night.

Closing my eyes, I laid my head back against his chest, and tried to find his heartbeat by blocking everything else out. Once I could feel it, I focused, and allowed myself to be hypnotized by its rhythm.

"Why does everything have to be so hard?" I asked.

"I don't know."

"Everything is so chaotic."

"It's really not," he replied simply.

"It is," I countered. "I don't know what's real. I don't know what to think. I don't know what to do with myself."

"I know I love you," he whispered. "That's real. To me, that's all that matters."

"Yeah, that's real," I whispered back.

After a quiet moment, he added, "Kissin' cousins be damned."

Laughing, I responded, "Please assure me we are only distantly related. I don't want our children being mutants."

"Our children? Why Gwen, I hardly know you," he gasped.

I can't believe I just said that out loud. He doesn't need to know about my foolish fantasies.

"Uh… no… that's not what I meant. It was just a joke," I lied, pulling myself out of his arms, making sure he couldn't see the horrible embarrassment I felt.

"Speaking of cousins," he interjected, apparently happy to change the subject. He pivoted his attention back inside, "Come with me, I'm going to show you something."

We headed back through the French doors, then down the hall to a set of stairs. I followed him down two turns until we landed in a hallway on the second terraced level of the house. An additional set of stairs, just to our left, led down to the final level.

"These are our bedrooms on this floor," he explained.

There were two doors on either side of the open hall, one for each sibling, and at the far end was another set of French doors opening onto a covered porch.

"Which one is yours? Are you going to show me?"

He pointed. "That one. And, no, it's too messy." He tried to steer me away.

"Aw, come on. You've seen my room." I tried to pull him towards the door.

He pulled me back, laughing, "No. This way, come on! I wanted to show you something way more interesting. I swear!"

He headed towards yet another set of stairs.

"Do you mind if I ask how your parents can afford such an incredible house?"

"My mother sold one of her family's properties in Scotland when she married my dad."

"And *why* exactly did they come here? What was the opportunity your dad was talking about?"

"I think you'll get your answer in a few minutes," he teased, as we descended the steps.

"Is your parents' room on this bottom level?"

"No, they have the master suit on the main floor. This is where the coven meets," he answered.

"Is that why that symbol was carved into the road sign?"

"Yep," he confirmed as we reached the bottom level. "That's the Altar Room." He pointed. "This is the common area everyone congregates, and that room right there is where we're headed."

"Torture chamber?" I teased, trying to joke my way through apprehension.

"No, more like a library," he answered, chuckling at my question. "Really, Gwen, you HAVE to have realized by now that we aren't Satan worshipers, or some strange serial killing cult. And we don't like being called *Witches*."

"I'm not convinced of anything yet," I mumbled aloud, surprising even myself at the raw truth of the statement.

He looked hurt.

"Not even about my feelings for you?"

"No! That's not what I meant," I stammered, trying to fix my blunder. Diverting, I asked, "Did you ever tell your mom about the memories I received from Erik?"

He squirmed in discomfort. "Not yet, but I know I need to. She'll want to get to the bottom of it…" he paused, "in her own way."

"How is that exactly?"

Without answering, he opened the door to the room. It was actually only part-library with walls of books, and cozy chairs in a horseshoe shape around a large fireplace, and part-office, with a large wood desk and chair.

Between each of the four chairs facing the fireplace, were end tables with individual reading lamps. Russell led us past these, to a high table in the far corner next to a wall of tall windows. There he turned on the table light, which reflected off the windows, to reveal an oversized book bound in leather. He opened the book to a previously saved section.

It looks like he was planning to show this to me all along.

"What am I looking at?"

"*This* is the history of my family… I mean, *our* family."

The page unfolded once, then again, and finally once more, opening into a large scroll with a hand-written chart of names and dates going back hundreds of years.

"How can you even be sure we're related? What if this *humming* blood thing is something else?"

"Just like you're learning to trust your visions and the things you sense to be true… you need to trust that when my mom 'knows' something to be true, it is! She's the High Priestess for a reason."

Well, sorry I don't know how these things work.

"Come on now, I didn't mean it like that," he apologized. "Let me tell you how Douglas came to be, then how *we* ended up here – just like you're wondering."

"Okay, shoot."

"First… a little history lesson. The Witchcraft Act of 1563 declared that Witches were *real*, with actual magical powers, but they were powers attained through Satan. This Act made Witchcraft, the consulting of Witches, or hanging out with Witches, a capital crime. In Scotland, between the 16th and 18th centuries, an estimated 4-to- 6,000 people were tried for Witchcraft. More than 1,500 of those people, mostly women, were executed by strangling, then burning. The covens decided to go underground and draw as little attention to themselves as possible."

"Trials like in Salem?"

"Where do you think the people in Salem got the idea? Those Puritans were immigrants from England, and the Witch trials there resulted in about 1000 people being put to death – also, mostly women."

"Dang."

"Anyways, in 1735, a new Witchcraft Act went into effect. It reversed course, declaring there were no *real* Witches - no such thing as actual magical powers, and anybody claiming such things were cheaters, extorting money from gullible people. The covens still had to stay hidden, though, and a lot of them disbanded altogether. More people started to leave for the New World because of this sort of persecution."

"The founders of Douglas?" I asked.

"Hold your horses, don't skip ahead," he scolded lightly with a grin. "Fast forward to 1884, and the daughter of the High Priestess of our coven disappears. She had just come of age."

"What does that mean?" I asked.

"Our ancestors believed that the age 13 is representative of transition and change. The number 1 represents stepping into the divine path, and the number 3 represents the three Goddesses. Numerologists translate the number 13 to a whole number, to determine its significance. When you add

1 plus 3 you get 4, and 4 is the number of wholeness, or the full circle of life."

"Okay, wow. You lost me. I don't pay attention in math class," I chuckled. "It seems like the age 13 has something more to do with when a girl gets her first period! That makes more sense."

He sighed, "Can I continue?"

"Yes, by all means."

"And yes, during the old days, menstruation was considered a time of female energy - empowerment - a vital time for visioning. It was celebrated."

"I'm impressed. You said all that without laughing. Kevin never could have said any of that."

"I'm the youngest in a house of all girls. This isn't a taboo subject. If anything, it's a regular subject of conversation. *Anyways*, let me tell you about the ceremony. The Coming of Age rite is a way for the young adult, who has chosen to follow the path, to be accepted within the coven. Every culture has something similar - a welcome to adulthood kind of thing. You've heard of a Bar Mitzvah?"

"Yeah, I've heard of it, some sort of Jewish celebration. I don't know much about it, though."

"Okay, well, same basic thing, just different rituals. During *our* rite, the young adult chooses his or her identity, within the coven family, by announcing their magical name – a name known only to the circle. If that person was born into the coven, the parents may have already given them their magical name through a thing called, Paganing - like a Christening. In the Coming of Age rite they can choose to either retain their given magical name, or choose one that has more meaning to them."

"Do you have a magical name?"

"What do you think?"

"Let's see… your mom's the head of the coven, and you're telling me all this stuff, so, um, yeah," I answered, nodding my head. "Can you tell me what it is?"

"No," he shook his head apologetically. "It's known only to the circle."

"Really? Not even *me*? Wow. Okay, then if that's how you're going to be… back to the story then," I chafed. "Do you know why the High Priestess' daughter took off? Did she not want to go through the rite and be part of the coven?"

"That… or she didn't want to be married off in a couple of years."

"Married off? At 13?"

"No at 16. But sometimes there were… uh… arranged marriages within the coven."

"That's awful. No wonder she ran away. But wouldn't the High Priestess, with all her powers, have been able to find her daughter?"

"There were rumors the daughter had help escaping to the New World, and there were family members that had established residency on the West Coast."

"Ah ha! So, someone from one of the Douglas founding families was a relative!"

"Yep! The members who didn't want to live in secrecy constantly fearing persecution, just wanting to practice their beliefs freely… came here."

"Wouldn't the High Priestess be mad they left the coven?"

"Sister covens are created all the time, but, of course, only with the blessing of the High Priestess."

"So, she knew they were in Douglas? She gave them her blessing! Then she would have known if her daughter had ended up here with them, wouldn't she?"

"There were rumors, yes, but if she didn't' approve the husband the coven had chosen, maybe she helped hide her."

"Oh, the plot thickens! Okay, so I'm still wondering, how does *your* family fit into this story?"

"You mean *our* family."

"That's still not proven."

"Okay…" he sighed in frustration. "Anyway, *my* mother is a descendant of Ewan Cameron." He pointed to a name on the unfolded chart. "He decided to remain behind, with the main coven, when his sister, Isobel and her husband, Angus MacLean, left for a fresh start somewhere new." He slowly spread his hands out, implying *somewhere new* meant Douglas.

"Angus, the founder, got it."

He stepped away from the desk, walked over to the nearest shelf, and pulled out a thin book. Flipping through the pages, as he returned, he found what he was looking for and laid the book open on the desk.

"These are the five families," pointed to each name on the page. "Angus Maclean and his wife, Isobel Cameron; Ewan MacKinnon and his wife, Mary Cameron... that's Isobel and Ewan's sister; William Blackwood and his wife, Anne MacDougall; John Carmichael and his wife, Margaret MacGregor; Lachlan MacGregor, Margaret's brother, and his wife, Hellen MacDonald."

"MacLean, Blackwood, and Carmichael," I repeated the town's namesakes. "Were these people the original members of your coven?"

"No. Theirs was called '*Cobhan darach geal*' – Coven of the White Oak. Oh! Hold on!"

"What?"

"I just remembered hearing once, that for a while their Covenstead was a Victorian house high on a hill above the town."

I was shocked at this new revelation. "*The* Victorian?"

"I think so."

"And you didn't think to mention this before?"

"It only just occurred to me that it might be the same one they were referring to."

"Surely your mother must have known?"

"The house was abandoned long before my mom came to Douglas, and even if she knew it was once used as a meeting place for the old coven, I don't think she knew there were spirits trapped there. Not until you came to her."

"Is that who I saw sitting at the séance table with Tabitha? The old coven members?"

"I have absolutely no idea."

"What happened to the rest of them after Tabitha was killed, and everyone at the farm abandoned the place?"

"That's a good question. I don't know the specifics, just bits and pieces. My mom would know more about that for sure."

"I've always wondered why the stained glass wound up in library."

"Not just at the library. There are old Covenstead pieces placed throughout town, to…"

"To what?"

"Hmm…" he nodded, as if debating with himself, then shook his head no.

"Seriously? You've got to be kidding me. You've told me all this, but you can't explain that?"

"It's not my place."

"You can't explain any of it?"

"Well, I *can* finish explaining the family tree," he offered, changing the subject back to the book. "Where was I? Oh, yeah… more cousins of those original founding families came later, after the town was established, and formed yet another sister coven: The Circle of the Dark Stream." He tapped each name as read them out, "the MacIntyres, MacKinnons, MacNaughtons, MacQuaries, MacFies, Campbells, MacDougalls, MacGregors, and MacDonalds. All these families were from the Isle of Mull, and the surrounding area of Argyll, and Aryshire. Historically these clans had been feuding and intermarrying for hundreds of

161

years. That's why my mom joked about throwing a stone and hitting a cousin."

As Russell explained, his face lit up with each new tidbit of information. He loved this stuff!

"Is that how it is in Douglas now… filled with cousins?"

"It was, at least in the beginning."

"I guess there's no need to read the book I got from the library, then."

"I did tell you it wouldn't explain any of this."

"You mentioned your mom was descended from Ewan Cameron, the guy who stayed behind in Scotland. Does that mean that my mom is descended from him as well?"

"I don't think so. My mom referred to 'old blood'. The only time I've heard her use that phrase was in reference to the 'first daughters' and the direct blood line of the Great Gormshuil of Moy."

"Who and what is that?"

"Where, not what," he laughed, correcting my mistake. "Moy is a region in the Scottish Highlands, and the 'who' is, Gormshuil – considered one of the most powerful Witches in Scotland. It turned out that both Gormshuil's daughter and granddaughter wielded almost as much power as she did. That was the beginning of the bloodline of 'first daughters'."

"Witches… you said you hated that word, but you never told me how else to refer to them."

"Wicca is what we prefer. It's the Old Religion, meaning 'craft of the wise' or 'wise people'. The word also has come to mean a Sorcerer, Wizard, or Witch, but those are linked to dark magic, meant to do harm, thought to perform their supernatural powers in cooperation with evil spirits. That's not who we are. That's why I don't like that word, Witch."

"Do you remember when you said you were going to have your mother explain all this to me?" I asked. "Because you said she could do a better job than you?"

"Yeah," he eyed me skeptically, "that bad, huh?"

"No, just the opposite! In fact, you're doing a great job!" I exclaimed, glowing with pride. "Maybe *you* should become a professor of this kind of stuff."

"Thanks," he grinned.

"As I was saying, before being so sweetly interrupted," he continued, smiling down at me, "these 'first daughters' were groomed from birth - trained their entire lives in preparation to become the coven's next High Priestess."

He referred back to the chart, and pointed at a name, "This is the 11th heir of The Great Gormshuil, Evelyn MacKinnon. She was born around 1868, and became the High Priestess in 1905, after her mother died."

His hand moved down the tree, "and *her* first daughter, Elsbeth Cameron, was born about 1897. *She* was the one that disappeared in 1910, at age 13. Because she wasn't there to take over when Evelyn died in 1940, the daughter of her first-born son, William, became an eligible heir. The elders of the coven gave his daughter, Evelyn Cameron, their blessing. She's still the High Priestess to this day."

He moved his finger down the chart, and smiled, "and that's *my* grandmother, Evelyn Cameron."

"Wait, so your grandmother is currently the High Priestess? I thought Brighid was."

"Of *this* coven, yes, which is a sister coven to the main one in Scotland."

My brain hurt, but I held on, trying to keep all the details straight.

"Do you know if the missing heir…" I retraced the chart with my fingers, reaching the name, "Elsbeth, ever made it to Douglas?"

"No one knows what became of her. She truly did just disappear."

"And Elsbeth was 'old blood'.

"Right."

"And your mom says she heard that blood in me, and my mother?"

"Right."

"So, what you're saying is, you think my grandmother might be the 13th heir of the Great Gormshuil of Moy?"

He was just about to answer when a voice echoed through the stairwell calling out his name. We heard light feet descending the steps to our floor.

"Russell?"

It was Ciara.

"In here!"

"I've been looking all over for the two of you!" she announced sternly.

"Well, you found us," he answered, annoyed by being disturbed.

"What are you doing in mom's study?" Ciara scolded as she entered the room, and then gasped as she saw us leaning over the large book. "You're not supposed to be showing her that!"

Showing me what?

She ran over, folded up the scroll, and then slammed the book shut. "You know better!"

"It was just the family tree, nothing else."

She looked between us, eyes squinted, and gasped. "Russ! You told her!"

I forgot how good she was at that.

They exchanged looks, as if having a conversation beyond words.

I tried to pry.

I imagined her mind like a box from which I could pry the lid... if I could just find the right corner... get my fingers on the edge...

"Stop that. You are not welcome!" she growled, looking over at me.

Offended, I blurted out in defense, "Oh, but it's okay for *you* to reach inside of mine?"

"I don't need to *reach* inside. You project your thoughts onto a movie screen for all to see," she answered snidely. "Now come on, let's go! Mom's going to be so mad when she finds out."

"No, she won't."

"And how can you be so sure?"

"Because before you got here, she practically confirmed it when she was able to get close enough to Elizabeth."

"We'll see."

What a bitch.

"I heard that!"

Chapter Seventeen
Table Talk

The conversation shifted by the time Ciara, Russell, and I returned. I made eye contact with my mom as I approached. She looked annoyed. We'd been gone a long time.

I wonder if Brighid was able to pry any details loose from you, mother, while we were away.

"Thank ye, Ciara," Brighid smiled, as she watched us take our seats again. "Gwen, did ye get a tour o' the hoose?"

"Not the entire house, but most of it, yes," I answered politely. Out of the corner of my eye, I noticed Ciara's look of disapproval.

Waiting for Russell and I were bowls filled with mixed berries, topped with an oat crumble and cream.

"Rose is steward of our garden," Cameron boasted. "She had a bounty of berries this harvest. Aren't they delicious?" He smiled as he relished each spoonful.

"Aye," Brighid beamed, "An' whit she can manage wi' her plants in the greenhouse is pure deid brilliant!"

"Is that what you're going to school for?" my mother asked.

"I *am* studying Botany, yes, focusing mostly on the medicinal side of plant biology."

My dad looked impressed, then added, "Elie is the only one with a green thumb in our house. She can get anything to grow in our little patch of a backyard. Can't you, dear?"

"Oh, I don't know about that," she responded dismissively, clearly embarrassed. "This really *is* delicious," she deflected, with a smile, after having a bite.

"Our Ciara, here, she's almost got her Bachelor's in Literary Studies," Cameron interjected.

"Really? That *is* impressive! Do you plan on becoming a Literature Professor like your father?" my dad asked, trying to engage Ciara in conversation.

She looked over, then smiled uncomfortably back at her father, before responding, "I'm not sure yet. My Minor is in Philology, so I may go on to get my Master's in that."

"What is Philology?" my mom inquired.

"The historical study of languages and symbols," she answered dryly.

"Like Indiana Jones," Russell chuckled.

Ciara sat up straight, eyeing him darkly. "Hardly."

"Oh, listen tae ye twa. Ciara, pey nae attention tae 'is badderin'," Brighid stated.

Brighid and Ciara exchanged a quiet moment of eye contact, before Ciara relaxed, and went back to her dessert.

"Aileen is getting her degree in Animal Husbandry," Rose interjected, as if to break the tension.

"Really?" my dad responded, raising his eyebrows. "That sounds fun!"

"She can *talk* to them," Rose smiled, nodding enthusiastically.

Aileen elbowed her little sister. "Shush," she responded, and then looked uncomfortably over at my parents. "Oh, I wouldn't say that. They just like me, that's all."

"I know what you mean," my mother nodded. "I used to catch Gwen out in the yard talking to the gophers, trying to coax them out of their holes; having butterflies fly down to her fingertips; or chatting with the squirrels and somehow convincing them to come eat out of her hand. That's why she insisted we take her to the zoo each year, because…"

My father coughed, interrupting my mother's train of thought long enough for her to look over at him. Then she looked back down at her plate, and continued eating.

It took me a second to register my father's purposeful interruption of her commentary.

Ahh, that's right. We definitely don't want to talk about the zoo, do we?

Memories flooded into my mind of all the years they had accused me of having an overactive imagination, or of being a liar, for insisting that I saw a ghost in the forest.

Acknowledging those feelings of resentment took me even further through my memories. Before I could stop myself, I blurted out, "Mom, as I recall you used to tell me to stop doing that because the neighbors would think I was crazy. How was I supposed to know that animals weren't like *that* with everyone?"

My mother, ruffled from my sudden assertion, collected herself, and then dismissively responded with, "You were young and didn't know any better."

My father nodded in agreement.

"But, when I didn't care if people thought I was crazy, you started telling me they were going to bite me, just to get me to stop."

"Well, it's true, you could have got rabies or something," my dad rallied in my mom's defense.

Is communicating with animals another ability I didn't even know I had?

Frustrated, I looked across the table and noticed Rose and Aileen both smiling and nodding subtly.

Ciara was still focused on her berries, and not engaging.

"Well, in our family, walking barefoot in the garden, and telling the gophers to find their food elsewhere, is encouraged," Cameron declared jovially, keeping the mood light.

I hope I get to come back and spend more time here. I like it. I don't feel broken.

Brighid looked straight at me in that moment and stated quite clearly, "Yer welcome haur onie time ye like." Then she broke eye contact, smiled politely again, and deferred to my father, "I dae hope ye'll let her come o'er agin."

My father wiped the edge of his mouth, after stuffing in the last bite of his berries, "Oh, of course. Right, Elie?"

Aren't you the same guy that just the other day was yelling about how I was naïve and too young and still grounded?

My mom looked back at him in confusion. I wasn't sure if it was because she didn't agree or couldn't believe he'd caved so easily.

Maybe Brighid has crazy Jedi mind tricks of her own!

I heard Russell snicker quietly next to me. I glanced over to see him desperately trying not to laugh.

Russell? Anything you want to confess? Like, maybe you get that power of persuasion from your mom.

He blushed and turned his attention away.

"Well, of course… if Bob is fine with it," my mother responded, glancing again at my dad with her eyebrow raised.

"Wonderful," Brighid exclaimed, standing up from the table. The girls followed suit. They then began to clear the empty bowls.

Cameron rose from his chair, "Bob, you care for an after-dinner Scotch?"

My mom looked a little distraught by the prospect, "Bob! Really, we should go. It's dark, and we don't know the roads very well."

What? Already?

Russell's head dropped, and his smile faded.

I didn't get the sense that my mom was actually worried about the roads. It was more that she was uncomfortable and wanted to get away.

Why? Ugh, I wish I could read her. Why can't I ever get a vision off her for a change?

"Och, leaving sae soon? Ah hoped we'd have a blether," Brighid proclaimed.

I think that's what she's trying to avoid.

"Maybe another time," my mom replied.

"Could I pop o'er ane efternuin fer a cuppa tea?" Brighid persisted.

Put on the spot, she stuttered, "Yes, of course, that would be... lovely."

"Braw! Ah'll give ye a ring this week, an we'll set up a guid time," Brighid stated, leaving my mother no way to wiggle out of it.

"Well Bob, it was really nice getting to talk with you. We'll have to do this again soon," Cameron stated, extending his hand.

"Yes. We should," my dad replied, returning the handshake. "Brighid, again, the food was delicious. We can't thank you enough for your hospitality."

"Yer welcome!"

I hung back at the table, standing next to Russell, holding tightly to his hand. I didn't want to leave.

I watched as my mother slowly made her way back through the foyer, trying to make her escape look casual.

Cameron walked alongside my dad as he followed.

Brighid approached Russell and I and whispered, "Ah'm sae pleased this all worked oot tonight, an' that ye were able tae get more answers tae yer questions. The next gae, we'll have more time." She hugged me, and whispered, "An' just sae ye ken, ye arenae broken. Yer belter just the way ye are."

It was an eerie feeling to have such intimate fears heard so loudly. Her words of endearment nearly brought me to tears. I'd only ever wanted to be understood, accepted, and believed.

Rose and Aileen came over and took turns hugging me good-bye.

"We can't wait to spend more time with you," Aileen said.

"Come back soon," Rose smiled, hugging me again for good measure.

Ciara remained in the kitchen.

What's her problem? I really must have pissed her off.

Russell walked me to the door. "Don't worry about her. She's moody," he responded.

"Gwen, again, it was lovely to meet you," Cameron smiled, waiting at the open door. "Don't be a stranger."

My mom and dad were already walking through the lit courtyard out to the driveway.

"I won't. Thank you again for having us," I responded. "Bye, Russ. I'll talk to you tomorrow."

He leaned over quickly, out of sight of my parents and gave me a sweet soft kiss. "Yes, you will. Drive safe. Good night."

"Night," I waved back, as I followed my parents out to the car.

Chapter Eighteen
Pitch Black

In the first moment of consciousness, the odor of wet dog was overwhelming – an assault to the senses.

In the second moment, a pounding headache exploded as each eye opened and attempted to adjust to the faint light in the room. Immediately they shut, waiting for the sharp pangs within the skull to subside.

Slowly each eyelid opened again, blinking several times to help the vision adjust, but it didn't work. The light was too faint to focus on much of anything, except for one dim vertical line a ways away.

"Where am I? Hello?" The sound of a female voice called out into the darkness.

The smell of wet dog… or some other animal… grew stronger as full consciousness arrived.

The smell of hay?

"What's going on?" she yelled.

That's not my voice. Oh no! Not again.

To block out the smell, she thought of bringing a hand up to her nose, but nothing happened. The signal from her brain went out, but her hand didn't respond.

"Help!" *she screamed.*

I can help you - tell me where you are!

She continued to struggle.

HEY! Can you hear me?
Her futile struggle continued.

What is the last thing you remember?

Her struggles ceased, and she closed her eyes.
Suddenly, out of nowhere, a memory flashed through her
mind… walking through a park at night..

Oh! She heard me!

Foggy…
Public bathrooms…

Okay, great! That's great! Keep going!

A written sign… women.
Exterior lamp…
Dead moths…

Her eyes shot open, and the memories ceased. Instead, she fo-
cused on assessing her body's sensory inputs, or the lack thereof.

Her brain frantically sending out electric signals throughout her body, like searcher ants tasked with a reconnaissance mission.

Wait, what happened? No, go back!

Their orders were to report back any physical sensations. Her brain then taking inventory of each report:
Hips? Check.
Stomach? Check.
Chest? Check.

Hey! Can you still hear me?

Neck? Check.
Head? Check.
Arms? Missing...

What else can you remember? I need more to go on if I'm going to help you!

She then focused her mind on only the muscles of her core, flexing and contracting anything she could, until she could feel her body moving around on the ground.
The ground. She realized she was lying on very musty wood flooring.
Slowly moving her body back and forth, she shifted the weight in her hips and thighs, until she managed to roll over. A heavy lifeless piece of flesh fell down across her chest.
"What the hell?" she cried out in terror.

Oh, damn! What was that?

It took a few seconds for the blood flow to return to her arm.

Once she recognized the thing laying on her as being part of her own body, she sighed in relief.

"Oh, thank God."

She continued to take inventory:

Legs? Nothing.

A sudden panic spiked her adrenaline and she uncontrollably thrashed and bucked against unseen bonds.

I don't know if you can still hear me, but it's okay. Don't freak out! Just focus.

Feet? Hmm...

Toes?

Thinking only of her toes, she imagined watching them moving back and forth to gauge whether or not she could feel anything.

There. Just a twinge. At least that meant they still existed.

That's good. Keep moving!

Back and forth, back and forth... she continued this mental exercise, imagining her feet flexing until she could feel a sensation there as well.

Then she began to rock her body back and forth, trying to roll into a different position, even if for a minute, to start the whole circulatory system working again.

In all the time that she'd been trying to reacquaint herself with her own body, she'd failed to acknowledge that along with the absence of light, there was an absence of sound.

She stopped her fruitless fidgeting and took a second to listen. After several minutes, she finally heard the faint echo of what sounded like water hitting the ground.

Okay. We can work with that. Where's the sound coming from?

She focused and waited, until she heard it again.
A dull thud?

No, it sounded more like a "plop".

Dirt?
Mud?
Wet wood?

Is it raining? Is there a leak in the roof?

If it had been rain dripping into a puddle, she thought, it would have made more of a "doll – oop" sound.

She wasted several minutes trying to solve this puzzle when she suddenly remembered her real predicament. "

"Why am I here?" She screamed. "What do you want with me?"

She was alone in the darkness with nothing but the sound of dripping water, and the fear that she had been left there to die.

You're not alone. I'm here. But you need to try and get up.

Several minutes later, she heard rattling, followed by the slow squeal of hinges. There was movement above the dim vertical line. She realized then it only looked vertical because she was lying down. The band of light was the space beneath the door.

Oh, no!

"Hello! Is someone there?" she asked hopefully.
Her throat felt dry, and the words came out raspy and unclear. She cleared her throat and tried again louder, "Is someone there? Can you help me?"

IF you can hear me, you have to GET OUT of there. RUN!

Soft footfalls approached from the direction of the squeaky door. A cold breeze swept over her, bringing with it a fresh and pleasantly familiar odor... the smell of hiking in the hills.

PLEASE hear me! GET UP!

Whoever it was, did not answer, but the sound of their approach grew louder.
"Who are you?"

The person knelt down close to her face, and she could smell a hint of something floral, like the gardenias in her mother's garden.

Get away from her!

"Why are you doing this? Please don't hurt me!" she begged.
The only answer was a sharp prick to the neck, followed by a horrible burning sensation.

NO!

Then all went pitch black.

I awoke in a jolt, sitting straight up, rubbing my neck, and taking in my surroundings. Looking over to my window, I could see light filtering through the curtains from the streetlamp outside.

It was the first thing that brought me calm, when waking like that. The window had become a consistent tether to the real world, pulling me out of the dream state, and away from its horrors.

What exactly just happened? I think I was in that girl's mind. She seemed to respond to me. I don't think I imagined that. No, she heard me that one time. She showed me what she remembered.

Getting my bearings, and assured I was within my own body inside of my room, I jumped out of bed to my desk, where I quickly jotted down every detail while still clear in my head.

Nighttime... foggy... a park setting... women's restrooms...

Why did the bathrooms look so familiar? I feel like I've seen them before.

I knew there was no way I was going to be able to go back to sleep.

Hmmm... what else? Hay... water dripping...

Finally, I made my way out to the kitchen, poured a bowl of Fruit Loops, and settled down at the coffee table in the living room to watch T.V.

I wonder if Erik had anything to do with this new girl.

It was too early for Saturday morning cartoons - they didn't start until 8:00 a.m. I was just killing time until I thought Cat was awake to call her.

I can't believe I was actually co-existing inside of this girl... like a hitchhiker... no, a dream rider. Yeah, that's cool.

Hours later, when the Bugs Bunny and Roadrunner show was about to start, I couldn't stand it anymore, and went into the kitchen to give her a call.

I was surprised when she answered immediately.

"Hello?" she asked, sounding irritated.

"You're up!"

"Yeah, I'm sitting on my floor next to the radio waiting for the cue to call in."

"Call in to what?"

"The contest to win tickets to see Adam Ant, in Portland, Oregon, on December 12th, that's what."

"Portland? How are you supposed to get way up there?"

"I don't know yet. But that doesn't matter. I just need to be the 59th caller. I'm waiting to hear the secret word or phrase, which will be the cue to start calling. If I hang up suddenly then you'll know why."

"Uh, okay. Hmm... does that mean you won't be available to go on a bike ride with me?"

"That depends on when you want to go."

"I want to go now, but it's still really cold out. Probably better to wait until the sun's been up longer. An hour, maybe?"

"An hour? I don't know. If I have to, I'm going to sit here all day to win these damn tickets! I'm serious!"

"You are definitely 'Desperate, but NOT Serious'!"

Cat pretended to laugh, before responding in sarcasm. "Hardy har har. Dork!"

"Well then you better win, because I don't want to go by myself."

"Go where exactly?"

"To the park, to investigate a clue I got from a dream I had last night," I explained. "I'm pretty sure another girl has been taken!"

"Oh shit. You should have told me that to begin with!" Cat exclaimed in surprise. Then she paused, and grumbled, "Dangit, I really wanted to win those tickets!"

"Maybe you still can. It won't take all day. I promise!"

"Alright, come on over when you're ready then."

"Cool. See ya soon."

Chapter Nineteen
Saturday at the Park

C at peeked out through the kitchen window curtains, and what seemed like only a second later was at the front door waving me inside.

"The DJ hinted the cue to call's coming up soon. This'll be my third try!"

"Dang, how long you been up?"

"I have no idea. Okay hold on, the song's ending! I need to pay attention." She leaned into the speaker of her Boom Box.

"You've just been listening to the newest number one hit by Culture Club entitled, Do You Really Want to Hurt Me? But, the real question is, are you... Friend or Foe?"

"That's it! FRIEND OR FOE! FRIEND OR FOE!"

The song started, as Cat frantically started dialing. I could hear the beep of a busy signal before she pushed down the tab to disconnect and started redialing.

After each busy signal, she muttered a slew of curse words followed by an exasperated sigh, and then her finger went back to work frantically punching in the memorized sequence of numbers.

"OH MY GOD! It's ringing! Hello? Hello?"

"You're caller 33, try again." Click.

"WHAT?" She slammed the handset back into its cradle as she hung up. "NOOOO!"

"Whoa, Cat. It's not the end of the world."

She redialed, hung up, cursed, and then redialed again. This continued until the song ended, and the DJ came back on air.

"We have our winner! Who is this?"

"Hi! Did I get through? Am I caller 59?"

"Yes, you are! Congratulations! Now who is it that I'm I speaking with?"

"This is Amber."

"Well Amber, guess what?"

"What?"

"You're going to see Adam Ant in Portland, on December 12th! What do you think about that?"

"SQUEEL!" Incoherent screaming. *"MOM! MOM! I won!"*

Cat turned the radio off angrily. "BITCH!" She yelled, clenching her fists, and stomping her feet.

"Aw, come on now. Be a good sport. You'll get it next time."

She glared at me, as if somehow I was to blame. Then she wagged her finger and proclaimed, "I better, or I'm going over to Amber's house and stealing those tickets."

I laughed, amazed by the hissy fit. "You don't even know her."

"Oh, I'll find her," she responded ominously. "You mark my words."

"Whoa now! No need to get yourself worked up! You eat your Wheaties today?"

"Wheaties?" she asked, completely confused. I might as well have been speaking in a foreign language. "What are you talking about?"

"The 'Breakfast of Champions', ya know?"

She groaned, rolled her eyes, and growled, "Gwen, stop it. I'm not in the mood."

"Not a morning person, I get it! Would you rather just stay here then?" I asked, throwing my hands up in surrender to her foul mood. "I can go without you."

"Ugh. No," she answered, sighing deeply. "Hold on, let me get my shoes."

"Your 'Goody Two Shoes'?" I teased.

～

We flew down the sidewalk of Briarwood Avenue on our bikes, coasting mostly, concentrating more on hiding our faces beneath our scarves away from the cold. The high-level clouds occluded the sunlight, and a dark line grew fatter along the horizon, devouring more of the sky with each passing moment.

A storm was coming.

Cat pedaled off the sidewalk, her 10-speed making a *chunk* sound as each wheel hit the street and reverberated off the metal mudguards and started crossing the avenue. She didn't even look or slow down but managed to clear the distance before a car sped by.

I slowed down and stopped, putting one foot on the ground, then spinning the pedal up to my other foot, ready to get a good push off when the coast was clear.

She was already heading over the grass into the park area, by the time I was half-way across the avenue. A faint foggy layer was still hovering above the ground.

"Hey, wait up!" I yelled, pedaling as fast as I could on my trusty silver 3-speed. I thumped off the other sidewalk onto the wet grass and had to stand up to keep momentum over the damp terrain.

Up ahead, Cat stopped to stare at the crowd amassed in the parking lot. I saw men in blue uniforms, with notepads open, talking to small groups of teenagers.

"Aren't those guys on our football team?" I asked Cat, as I pulled up alongside her.

"Yeah, and those are some of the cheerleaders. I wonder what they're doing here."

My view of the park looked eerily similar to the memory I'd been shown.

"Let's head over to the restrooms. I need to check something out."

"What do you hope to find there?" she asked.

"I think I was shown flashes from the girl's memories, and I'm pretty sure those bathrooms were what I saw. Maybe there's something down there that will tell us where she was taken. I don't know... I'm kind of figuring this out as I go."

"Still. That's so cool!"

We kicked off and started to pedal, making a wide arc away from the crowd and police officers, to circle round to the public restrooms. Once the building was in sight, I realized we weren't going to be alone.

Dang it.

I slowed to a stop as Cat skidded up behind me.

"Are you two with the search party?" the police officer asked. "They're gathering over there." He pointed to the parking lot, and the gathering crowd. "The other police officers will assign you to a specific grid in the search perimeter."

"Oh, yeah. Um, we are, but I really needed to go pee first. Is it open yet?" I asked pointing to the sign that said "Women".

That's it. That's the sign from her memory.

He glanced over at the sign, realized he was standing in front of it, and in embarrassment moved aside. "Of course. Go ahead."

We parked the bikes against the brick building and stepped around the corner into the women's bathroom. It was like walking into a freezer.

"Are you really going to sit on one of those toilets?" Cat whispered.

"I don't really *have* to 'go'," I whispered back. "I'm just trying to bide us some time. Maybe he'll move away."

She went back towards the entrance and peeked around the corner, then shook her head. "He's still there. What exactly are we looking for?"

"I don't know."

"Wait a second. You specifically said that you *had a clue*," she responded in disbelief, not hiding how irritated she had become.

"I asked her to remember something that would help me find her. She showed me these restrooms."

Cat did a double take. "Wait, you actually spoke to her? I thought you said it was a dream."

"Dream riding," I smiled, liking the sound of it out loud. "It's like I was hitchhiking in her mind, seeing through her eyes, and experiencing things as she was."

"But this time you were able to *speak* to the girl you were traveling with?" Cat was growing ever more frustrated that I couldn't explain it better.

"Kind of. I don't think she was *consciously* aware of where the request for information was coming from, but it seemed to work. She remembered being here, right before she was taken."

"Okay, yeah, that's really cool, actually. *Dream rider*?" She seemed to be mulling the word over.

"*Dream weaver*?" I laughed.

"*Dream catcher*?" she offered with a "why not" kind of shrug.

"Anything is better than *dream hitchhiker*, right?"

"Yeah, that doesn't have the right ring to it," she nodded. "So... *anyways*, did you see anything that made you think she was taken to the same place as Suzie?"

"Maybe. I'm not totally sure."

"*Not totally sure*," she sighed, shaking her head. "So then, how *exactly* did you think this was going to help?" she asked tersely.

"Cat, I'm just trying to trust intuition and hope it pays off. You want to help this girl, or not?" I replied curtly.

"*How* am I supposed to help?" she asked, throwing her hands up in frustration. "And what if it's already too late?"

It might be. But there's still a chance.

I thought about it for a second, then responded, "You could distract the cop out there long enough for me to check the side of the building I saw."

"UGH! Fine!" she grumbled. She walked out through the doorway, calling out loudly, "Hey, Mr. Officer Sir!"

"Yes? Is everything okay?"

"Yeah, I was just wondering if you could show me where I'm supposed to go to help with the search."

"Well, like I was saying before..."

"Over... where? There?" she questioned dramatically. "Which part of the parking lot were you referring to *exactly*?"

"Okay, follow me."

I took my chance and crept around to the side of the building facing the open park. That side, hidden from the view of the parking lot, was a perfect blind spot, especially at night.

I closed my eyes and tried to recall the scene just as the girl remembered. When I opened my eyes, I glanced up to the overhead lamp covered in dead bugs and spider webs.

Lamp... dead moths. Check.

Then I glanced down to the small evergreen hedges below, where I noticed a faint glint of something on the ground - a silver hook with dangling beads attached to one end.

An earring.

As soon as my fingers pinched the hook of the earring to pick it up, a flurry of memories hit me so hard that they knocked me backward onto the ground.

The varsity football game…

Stadium lights…

Bus ride back to the school with the team…

They'd lost, and the guys were feeling pretty low, so she and the other cheerleaders were trying to lift their spirits with stupid songs.

Tailgate party…

Parking lot lights barely cutting through the thick fog…

Realizing she had to pee…

"Amy, you need me to go with you?" A girl asked from the back of a pick-up truck, cuddled under a blanket with her boyfriend.

"Nah, I'm good, Rach!"

"You sure you don't need any help?" one of the football players heckled, as he leaned against his car with a beer in hand. His teammates snickered and made rude innuendos.

"I think I can handle it, Thomas," she replied, flipping him off.

After walking away from the glow of the parking lot lights, into the enveloping fog, it got really dark.

She questioned her decision to go alone.

Glancing around continuously, she maintained her path to-wards the light atop the roof of the outbuilding, like a lighthouse, a welcoming beacon in a sea of darkness, where the restrooms were.

She quickened her pace, focusing on the sign that read WOMEN with an arrow aiming toward a door.

When she finally reached it, and tried the handle, she found it locked.

"Darn it!" she exclaimed. "Now what?"

She walked around the building to the other side, glancing at the bushes planted around the exterior, then stared out into the fog that was as thick as pea soup.

She wondered if she had the courage to take care of her business out away from building, or if she should risk the chance of someone walking up on her as she squatted behind the bushes.

Before she could decide, she heard footsteps approaching from out in the fog, and heard a muffled voice. "You know... the buddy system is always safest."

Putting her hand over her brows to shield her eyes from the light of the overhead lamp, she tried to see the origin of the voice and couldn't tell if it was male or female - the fog had a way of dampening and distorting sound somehow.

"Thomas, is that you? Ha, ha! Very funny!" she called out, trying to sound brave even though she could feel panic rising. "Don't be a creep, okay?"

The footsteps moved closer, closing the distance.

"Nope, not Thomas," a voice replied right behind her, not at all where she was expecting the person to be.

Practically jumping out of her skin, she squeaked, "Wha…" before whirling around. "Who's there?"

A dark figure stood in the shadow of the building.

She had no time to react before a hand reached around from behind and covered her mouth, while another arm snaked around the opposite side, fingertips tracing her throat, slowly clamping tight, tugging her back against a solid male form.

She struggled in vain against the height and strength of the attacker.

The figure, cloaked in black, then emerged from the shadows.

Despite fighting and kicking back at the person strangling her, she was losing her ability to focus. A firework display went off behind her closing eyelids – her brain deprived of oxygen.

Then it all went dark.

∽

"Miss, are you okay?"

I was sitting in the dirt, just off the edge of the cement surrounding the restrooms.

"Here, let me help you up." The police officer extended his hand and pulled me to my feet.

Feeling the earring still in my hand, as I rose, I dropped it back behind me.

"You have to watch where you're going." He pointed to the edge of the walkway where it rose several inches above ground level.

"Yeah, you're right. I must have tripped."

"Your friend is back at the parking lot getting her assignment for the search grid. I thought I'd come back here to check up on you."

"Thank you. I appreciate that."

"I'm not going to have any more girls go missing on my watch."

He walked with me over to our bikes. He grabbed Cat's, pushing back the kickstand with his boot, and the two of us pushed them over to the parking lot.

A lot of people had gathered to help, and I recognized nearly all of them from school, mostly upperclassmen that I'd seen walking the halls in their uniforms or jerseys. They looked exhausted.

It suddenly dawned on me that our friend, Andrea, had practiced with these girls during cheerleading camp over the summer. That she might even hang out with them socially. If she had been hanging out with them during the tailgate, the missing girl could have just as easily been her. It was a sobering thought.

Surveying the crowd, I noticed Cat loitering awkwardly off to one side. "Cat!" I waved to get her attention.

"Gwen!" She jogged over and thanked the officer for retrieving her bike.

Satisfied we'd been the last stragglers, he headed away.

"The missing girl's name is Amy," I whispered.

"*Doi*!"

"What?"

"That's who they're looking for! Amy Harcourt."

"Oh!" I responded, looking around at the coordination happening to begin the search. "Of course."

"The team has been here all night looking for her. Her best friend, the one over there crying against her mother,

Rachel something, is the one who called the police. I guess that's Amy's parents next to them. From what I've gathered, Amy was supposed to go back to Rachel's house after the game, but they all detoured here for a little party instead. At some point, Amy went to the bathroom, and never came back."

"Yeah," I nodded. All the events were lining up with what I saw.

Ahh, 'Rach' is Rachel.

"That guy next to Rachel is Adam, her boyfriend."

Oh, that's the kid that was under the blanket with her, in the back of the pick-up truck.

Just then, the officer in charge put his arms up above his head to draw attention to himself. "Okay, everyone, listen up!" he yelled out. "We've set you up in teams of four and assigned each team to an officer. You will work your section of the park, heading in a clockwise direction, and meet back up here. Anything, and I mean *anything*, out of place or interesting, bring it to your officer's attention. I don't care how small or insignificant you think it is… it could lead us to Amy, so keep your eyes peeled. Again, thank you, and good luck everybody."

"Gwen," Cat whispered, leaning over, "Do you think this is going to be of any help? I mean, what if it's already too late?"

"You're right," I replied with remorse.

"Wait… does that mean you actually know that… it *is* already too late?"

"I'm not totally sure," I shrugged. "If we help search, we might come across something one of the abductors touched. Maybe I can get something of substance, some proof, to lead the police in the right direction."

"Do you have an idea of where that might be?"

"Somewhere with hay and a musty old wood floor... maybe a barn? Oh, and a squeaky door! Also, in both dreams, I didn't hear cars, or people, or anything. It was really quiet... like out in the middle of nowhere. I could smell the mountains. And, when the door opened, there were rows of trees outside."

"Okay, wow! That's actually a lot of clues; but you're right, nothing specific enough."

"Oh, and one more thing - there were two of them – a male and a female. He's tall and buff. She smells like flowers."

"So, what you're saying is, we have a lot, and yet nothing at all," Cat concluded. In resignation, she slumped her shoulders forward and sighed, "We need to search the park."

Gaining our attention, the officer in charge of our search team yelled, "Girls, please stay in a straight line next to these two gentlemen. Keep your eyes to the ground, and scan evenly back and forth... and all four of you, keep an even pace with one another - move slow. Like the Sergeant said, *anything* at all unusual, let me know!"

After we stepped back into formation, and our group leader's attention was averted, I leaned back over to Cat and whispered, "By the way, I got to go to Russell's house last night for dinner."

"By yourself?"

"No, with my parents."

"Was it weird?"

"No, not really… not until the end, at least. But the house was amazing, and Brighid's food was delicious."

"Did you talk to Russell about Erik?"

"Yeah. He's having a hard time believing Erik would have done anything to Suzie. But now… with Amy? I'm not too sure what Erik's connection would be."

"It could be another case of rejection," she speculated.

"Maybe, but he's with Erin now," I offered. Then a thought struck me, "I wonder if *she* wears a floral perfume?"

"Ohhh! Now that's an interesting scenario!" She made a face as if she were deep in thought. "As much as just the sound of her name makes me want to punch something, I can't imagine her having truly gone to the 'dark side'."

"Can't you? I already think she's there."

We walked in quiet contemplation for a few steps, before she added, "I keep waiting to hear that Russell bashed Erik's nose in for what he did to you, though."

"Me, too!"

"If he doesn't, I will."

"Thanks."

We finished the first grid and found nothing. Our officer moved us to a new section and started the process again.

Callous as it seems, we both wondered when we'd be able to break away to go home.

"Cat, we know Suzie is dead, and Amy might be as well... so maybe it's time we bring in the big guns?"

"The *big guns*?" she asked.

"Your dad," I stated, as if it were the most obvious thing in the world.

"Oh! Huh?" She looked down at her feet as she walked, deep in thought.

"You don't think it would work?"

"I'm not really sure. This isn't the same as before. He was protecting me then, and got all tangled up with the other spirits because of it."

"Hmm..." I relented. "It was just a thought."

Chapter Twenty
Amy

The pages of Monday mornings paper were spread out across the lunch table in the cafeteria, the gang crowding around, vying for better views of the article.

Kevin shared the paper with Cat and I earlier in the day, so during lunch we sat quietly, ruminating over what it all meant.

The search at the park yielded nothing, which hadn't surprised me. I guess the only thing positive I took away from the weekend's events was that I *was* somewhat able to interact with Amy through the vision.

"The last time anybody saw her was when she left the parking lot to go to the restrooms!" Kelly recounted aloud to the group.

"Practically the whole football team was at that party. They looked for her for hours," Brian commented.

"I heard that her friend Rachel is absolutely inconsolable." Jennifer's voice cut through my train of thought.

"I bet! Those two were attached at the hip," Kelly responded.

"What are the chances that it's the same person who got Suzie?" Jennifer asked.

"Well, if Amy washes up on a bank of the river like Suzie did, then we'll have our answer," Craig stated bluntly.

"That's awful!" Jennifer exclaimed.

"What? It's true, isn't it?" he shrugged.

"Do you guys think there is someone actually hunting girls from our school?" Drew asked.

"I overheard a teacher saying someone from the police department will be speaking at the assembly later this week," Craig divulged.

"About what?" Kelly asked.

"Safety probably," Jennifer speculated.

"On how to *not* get abducted by a satanic cult," Brian asserted.

"Stranger danger!" Craig quipped.

"You joke, but my dad and I were watching a segment on CBS's *Evening News,* and they said like 50,000 kids are kidnapped by strangers… every year!" Drew explained excitedly. "And that's just in America!"

"I wonder if Amy's face will be the next one on the back of a milk carton," Craig mused.

"You really think we're in danger?" Jennifer asked in concern.

"Why don't we wait until the assembly and hear what the cops have to say before we start jumping to conclusions," Kevin chimed in.

The group looked up from the table, acknowledging Kevin. Only then did our non- involvement in the conversation stand out.

Kelly's eyes squinted at us suspiciously. "You three are awfully quiet about all this," she stated.

Cat chirped, from her oasis beneath Kevin's arm, "Yeah, because it's depressing as hell! Gwen and I helped with the search on Saturday. I guess I just don't want to think about it, or talk about it, anymore."

Jennifer's eyes opened wide as she expressed her amazement, "Wow! What was that like?"

Kelly's face softened, "Dudes, why didn't you say anything?"

"What Cat said," I sighed.

"Daang!" Brian exclaimed. "That's some heavy shit."

"What was it like to be part of a search team? You guys find any clues?" Drew inquired.

"You must have heard something! I mean, I hate to be that guy, but I'm getting the distinct feeling you know more about this than you're telling us," Craig theorized.

"What could they know that the article didn't tell us?" Drew wondered aloud, hesitating as he thought harder. A dawning of understanding washed across his features. "Oh, you think, because of the stuff that happened with the *ghosts*, maybe Gwen has access to some *hoobajoo* info that the police don't."

"Yeah," Craig nodded, "that sort of thing."

"Well," Kelly asked me directly, "do you?"

I looked over at Cat for help. She shrugged at me, not knowing how to stop this particular train from rolling down the tracks.

"I'd think if she had something, she would have told the police. Right?" Brian nodded to me.

"*Do* you know what happened to Suzie? Was it a Satanic Cult, like those fishermen said? Did Amy get taken by the same people?" Jennifer pushed, leaning towards me with her eyes wide open, desperate for answers.

"Um, well…" I started, looking to Kevin for help. He appeared as interested in my answers, as the rest of the group.

"Crap!" Cat suddenly exclaimed. "You guys, I totally forgot… I won tickets to Adam Ant!"

"What?" Kelly screamed back in excitement. "You actually managed to get through? When? I was trying to all day."

"Yeah, I got through late Saturday night! They're holding them for me down at the radio station!"

"Oh, cool!" Brian reacted loudly. "Congrats!"

Thank you, Cat!

"Question is…" she added, a grin forming on her face, ever widening like the Cheshire Cat, "which one of you retards am I going to bring with me?" She rubbed her hands together as if she was concocting an evil plan.

Oh, that's cruel. But at least the distraction's working.

Kevin caught on to her manipulation tactic, and played along, "Well, clearly I'm the obvious choice."

"Why? I've known her longer than you, and I like Adam Ant more!" Kelly challenged.

"To be clear, I think we all met at the same school at the same time, so your argument is moot," Kevin asserted, in his best lawyer tone. "We all know I'm the winner!"

"Yeah, right!" Brian declared. "The game's rigged! Gwen will totally be her choice. No contest!"

I took the opportunity to keep steering the conversation further off topic. "I can't go. It's the same night as Andrea's Christmas Party."

Cat deflated. "But... it's *Adam Ant*!" Then she got angry. "Wait! You got an invite to her party... already?"

"You didn't?" I asked hesitantly.

Oops.

"I *used* to get invited," she grumbled.

"Maybe it hasn't come in the mail yet," I offered, shrugging my shoulders.

"Awkward..." Brian sighed.

Craig started singing under his breath, "...square pegs..."

Jennifer joined in, "...where's the party, and how come we weren't invited?"

Drew and Kelly sang along, "...square... pegs!"

"The Waitresses would be a great show. I wonder if they'll ever come through town." Brian mused.

"To Douglas? Keep dreaming," Craig scoffed.

"I *totally* love the TV show. I can't wait for next week's episode," Jennifer exclaimed.

"*Fer sure*," Kelly added.

Kevin gasped dramatically, and drew back from Cat in mock disgust, "Wait, so you were going to take *her* and not *me*?"

He playfully pushed Cat down the bench with his foot.

"What? Wait. Kev, come on. Be fair...." she stuttered and pleaded, as he continued to push her closer towards me.

"You're sleeping in the doghouse tonight!" he stated in exaggeration, suppressing a grin.

"But Kev, we don't even own a dog!" she responded.

The antics worked, everyone was distracted, deep in discussion about TV sitcoms or concerts they'd been to or wished to attend.

～

Two days later, an elderly couple, while hiking with their dog, made a most unfortunate discovery. The dog, while following a scent, bound off trail and then went berserk. They followed the barking and found him freaking out next to a young woman's body washed up along the bank of the Douglas River. Amy had been found.

The news crew and newspaper journalists, swooped down on the scene like vultures, and interviewed the shaken couple. They said that they noticed strange markings carved into her skin, just like Suzie. They described one of the symbols as a simple triangle, while another was more like a circle with a maze in it.

～

Hot off the presses Thursday morning, the very same newspaper journalist who'd interviewed the fishermen, dropped the scoop of the century: Amy wasn't the second missing girl to be found dead in recent months... but the fourth. The first two were from Glenview, the town on the other side of the hills.

Chapter Twenty-One
Fear and Speculation

Two weeks later, on the Monday before Thanksgiving break, I sat at the kitchen table across from my mother, eating buttered toast. I hadn't had any more incidents of dream riding, and there were no further reports of missing girls. That week's mid-term exams were the only thing the kids were focused on. I, on the other hand, was mulling over tactics to get my mother to talk.

"Mom?"

She looked up from spreading some strawberry jam over her own piece of toast.

"Yes?"

"If you won't let me go hang out at Russell's house, will you at least let me visit him at work during break? I can take the bus."

"Not by yourself," she answered, picking up her pencil and starting on that day's crossword puzzle.

"I've taken the bus by myself before, and you've never had a problem with it."

"That's before four girls were found dead. We have some sort of serial killer loose in Douglas, and I need you to be careful. Russell can always just come here."

Ugh! I can't learn anything new by hanging out at my house.

Along with not letting me go to Russell's house - despite the open invitation - she kept making excuses to not have tea with Brighid and refused to discuss the possible family connections with me.

Every day, I tried new, and increasingly roundabout, ways to start a conversation, without once divulging a thing about the 'old blood', or our possible lineage to a great Witch of Scotland and the old coven. But nothing worked. She was an immovable mountain.

I hated thinking she may have known her true bloodline the whole time. That would imply she had powers. It also implied she would have known I'd likely inherited them from her as well. So, if she did know, why would she ignore them, and more importantly, why would she refuse to acknowledge what was happening to me? I couldn't imagine her being so cruel, allowing me to struggle with so much for so long, feeling alone and overwhelmed.

Did she truly not know, or was she just avoiding something? Time to try again.

"Speaking of Shanachie, have you had a chance to check it out, and visit with Brighid?"

"No, I haven't," she answered mid chew – her attention focused on the puzzle.

"Ah that's too bad, because the shop has some really cool things."

"Hmm," she hummed, as she kept chewing, reading the clues for the puzzle, and sipping her tea.

"Did you know there are paintings and wood sculptures in her store that are by descendants of the original settlers of Douglas?"

She still didn't look up from the puzzle, as she responded listlessly, "No, I didn't know that."

"The Blackwood Estates, where Kevin lives, they are named after a descendant as well."

"Uh, huh."

"Same with Carmichael High School. John Carmichael and his wife Margaret MacGregor were one of the founding families."

"That's fascinating."

"Did you know that the clans of the founding families intermarried for hundreds of years before those five families made their way to America?"

She took another nibble of toast, followed by a sip of tea, "Is that so?"

"It is. Then after they came here, their children and grandchildren intermarried. So, that means, if their descendants are still living here, then they're all cousins!"

"Hmm…"

"Kind of like what Brighid said… you know, about throwing a stone," I fished.

She finally putting her pen down and pursed her brow. "What exactly are you getting at?"

"Oh! So you *were* listening."

"Of course!" she replied. "I can listen and drink tea at the same time."

"Okay then… is it possible?"

"Is what possible?"

Don't pretend you don't know what I'm talking about.

"That you and Brighid come from the same family! Don't you want to find out more? You've said you don't know anything, but surely, you must have *some* memories of conversations from when your grandmother was alive? Maybe talking to Brighid could help jog some of those free. She has a lot of books about her family at their house. Russell showed me..."

"Stop it," she interrupted coldly. "There is nothing to this theory of hers, and to be honest I don't appreciate how... well, I feel like it's an invasion of my privacy."

"What do you mean?"

"She asks so many questions. It's none of her business."

"Okay, so you don't want her prying into your family history, but why can't I go over to his house to hang out?"

"I just don't think it's a good idea."

"Why?"

Why has she purposely kept me from their house?

She stood up and brought her plate and cup up to the sink, keeping her back to me.

"Do you not want me going over there, because I might find proof that our families are related? Is that it?"

"No, that's not..."

I interrupted before she could finish, "Did you know?"

"Gwen," she sighed, staring down into the sink. "Please just drop it." Then she looked over at the wall clock. "Your bus will be at the stop in a few minutes. You better get going."

"Did you know?" I asked again, standing up from the table.

I was furious by the possible implications. My entire childhood, she made me feel ashamed of my behavior. If she knew we were... different, that we might have powers, she could have helped me. She could have been there for me, just as Brighid was, for her children. But, no - instead, she was embarrassed.

She shook her head, but still refused to look at me.

I dragged my book bag to the front door, put on my coat and gloves, and started to turn the doorknob. I was so angry.

"Mom," I called out, shaking with emotion. "I'm going to open *all* the closet doors, letting out *every* skeleton there is, until I find out..."

"Gwen!" I heard her gasp. "No, wait!" I heard her quickly coming around the corner just as I exited out onto the front stoop.

"...who I am!" I yelled, running down the steps.

I heard her coming through the house after me and turned to see her marching towards the open front door.

I snapped! "*NO MORE* stupid secrets!"

The door whipped close between us, slamming hard.

She yelled in surprise. "Gwen!"

I hoisted my book bag over my shoulder, walking quickly towards the bus stop.

That was no gust of wind.

I felt much better, suddenly, having let off some steam.

What was Russell saying about that? Kinetic energy or something.

I ignored her pleas from the front doorstep, as she called after me, "Gwen! Please just let it go!"

～

Exams came and went. Throughout the week, my mom and I simply avoided one another, and dad just continued to be dad – never really fine-tuned to the subtle nuances of the female spat.

Thanksgiving was lame. We went to my dad's brother's house. He was on his third wife, and they had no children. Boring.

I brought a book to read while the men watched football, and the women did whatever women do while waiting for the turkey to cook. It was an excruciatingly long day. What I would have given for a sibling or cousin to hang out with, which is ironic, considering the only highlight of the day was getting home to talk to Russell on the phone.

Kissin' cousins.

"So what time are you going to come by?" he asked.

"Cat and Kevin are going to swing by around 10:45. We'll catch the 11:00 bus, so I should be there around 11:30."

"Okay, cool. Are you and your mom still not talking?"

"Well, it's not a complete standoff. We say words," I responded.

He chuckled.

"Okay, but not words with any significance behind them?" he asked.

"No. And I don't get it, I can't I get a reading off her!" I complained. "I've tried being sly about brushing against her while putting dishes in the sink, and stuff like that. But I get nothing! Why?"

"Well, so far your visions from direct contact have never been from you soliciting them. Usually it's been when you were in a heightened emotional state."

"Ah, yeah, that again - like the door slamming shut. That was pretty cool, actually."

"Be careful," he warned.

"I know, I know. Try to control it. But that's easier said than done, isn't it? When I'm upset, not thinking straight, how do I control some weird telekinetic burst?"

He sighed. I could tell he was sad I hadn't been able to spend time at his house. "I wish my mom and sisters could help you."

"Why don't you just stop saying that, and help me yourself?" I asked frustrated. "Like, what did your mom tell *you* the first time you had an outburst like that?"

"Hmm, okay… let's see… we spent months focusing on breathing, settling my blood pressure, and I guess just learning to meditate. And then she'd have me remember the 'spark' that happened right before the incident, and focus on exactly what it felt like."

"What do you mean 'spark'?"

"Right before the door whipped close, did you feel like a… gas bubble forming inside of you?"

"Are you asking me if I had gas?" I snickered.

"No! The spark! The spark feels almost like that moment right before you burp - you don't know quite what it is - it's uncomfortable and foreign - then it rises up, and out it goes. And then there's sometimes when a burp just sneaks up on you, and comes out without you even knowing it was there."

I started to laugh, imagining the shutting door, or exploding lamp, as being a result of a burp. "Quite the belching connoisseur, aren't we?"

"Gwen, come on. Work with me here," he sighed. "You want me to help you or not?"

"Yes. Okay, so that kinetic spark is like a gas bubble. Go on."

"Right! Once you start to recognize what a gas bubble *feels* like, you can force it out, and burp at will."

"Okay, I getcha! I can remember as a little kid having horrible indigestion. It hurt so bad I thought I was dying. My mom patted me on the back, telling me it was just like when I was a baby. I burped, and the pain went away. From that moment on I knew what indigestion felt like, and it didn't freak me out."

"Exactly. So, if you can remember what that bubble of energy felt like, right before the door whipped close, you can start to visualize it…"

"You mean, like imagine what it *looks* like?"

"Yeah, give it an image, name it - whatever works - and when you recognize the bubble start to build up again, do some deep breathing exercises to calm yourself down. Visualize the bubble getting smaller, until it disappears or evaporates - that's the kinetic power dissipating."

"Okay, cool. I can try that." Then I thought about it some more, and couldn't help asking, "What if I *want* to do it on purpose?"

"Why would you want to do that?" he asked cautiously.

"Well, you may not realize this, but I remember something about our night out skating."

He didn't respond, but I could still hear his steady breathing through the receiver.

"Remember, after Erin tripped? You grinned. You seemed pretty satisfied with yourself in that moment. I've always wondered about that. Were you satisfied because you saw it? Or because you did it?"

I heard a long exhale. "Okay, yes, you got me. I'm actually not very proud of that. I totally let her get to me. I *know* better!"

"So, *your* emotional response isn't totally under control either?"

"Of course not! No one ever gets absolute control. That's why they call it 'practicing magic'. I'm still working on it. It takes a long time to become a master of your craft."

"But you've mastered it enough to effect things around you on purpose?"

"Yes, *but…* with magic there are rules. The biggest one is 'do no harm'. The second is to understand that when we're using our powers we must accept responsibility for what happens. It's referred to as the *Law of Threefold Return*."

"What's that mean?"

"Whatever one does to another person or thing, it returns in triple force."

"Wow. So that could be really bad, if you're up to no good, huh?"

"I think the rule is in place to *prevent* you from doing bad things."

"Sort of like the Bible's *Golden Rule*, then."

"Exactly."

"I'm glad that your mom's cool with you sharing all this with me now."

"Well… to be honest… I'm still sharing *way* more than I should. This kind of information is supposed to be *only* for coven members."

"But your mom was fine with you sharing the family tree? You didn't get in trouble, like Ciara threatened, did you?"

"Nah. Ciara likes to act like the boss, and she wants the rest of us siblings to fall in line. Being around her these last couple months has been especially difficult. There might be problems with her boyfriend, Toby. I don't know."

"But, of course, you'd never be able to find out what."

"No way! She's really strong when it comes to mind reading, but even stronger when it comes to keeping people out of *her* head."

"Is she as strong as your mom?"

"Not yet."

"Is she supposed to become the next High Priestess when your mother retires, or whatever?"

"Well… I hope my mother lives a long life, but, if the day comes, then… yeah, it will fall to her as the first daughter. But…"

"But, what?"

"It's just that things have changed."

"Why is that?"

"If we can prove that your mother is the legitimate first daughter of the old bloodline, then that may change the entire dynamic of the old coven, *and* this one. I don't know how it would all shake out."

"I'm sorry… I'm confused. How would *what* shake out? My mom would never have anything to do with this *stuff*. Any of it!"

"You don't think so?"

"No way! She may not be a religious person, but I get the distinct impression she wouldn't be into becoming part of a Wiccan coven. You're talking about inheriting Brighid's position, right?"

"Or the coven decides to elevate Elizabeth up to the position ahead of time."

"You mean, replace your mom with mine?"

"I don't know… maybe. It's really complicated! Like I said, I really don't know what would happen."

"But my mom would've had to have mastered her abilities, and I've never witnessed anything."

"Nothing, huh?"

"Not a thing."

"Well… you know… in the end then, it might all come down to you."

"Me? You're kidding, right?"

"Not in the slightest."

"No, really… you're joking right now."

"No."

"What if I want no part of it? What if I just want to go back to being a normal teenager, and forget you even told me about this bloodline?"

"You can't."

"What do you mean, I can't?"

"*Forget* about it, I mean. You can't run from yourself, or your powers that seem to keep growing each day."

"I'll bet this is *exactly* why the heiress disappeared!"

"What do you mean?"

"*This*," I sighed heavily. "It's *too* big!"

"So, you don't think she disappeared? She ran away to deny her legacy - who she was, and what she could do?"

"Exactly! Then she kept it from her children, so they could have normal lives."

"Do you think your mom went through the same things, and her mom treated her the way she's treating you?"

"That's a better explanation than the alternative."

"Which is?"

"That she's a closet Witch, and has been lying to me my whole life."

Chapter Twenty-Two
Symbols

The following day, Cat, Kevin, and I took the bus downtown to the library. That is to say, Cat and Kevin went to look through the library, and I dashed across the street to the shopping center.

To be fair, I didn't ride the bus alone. You're welcome, mom.

As I crossed the parking lot, I caught sight of Russell standing under the awning out in front of the store. He was waving, hurrying me over. I started to jog.

He quickly scooted me inside - as I arrived slightly out of breath - and immediately swept me up in his arms.

"Finally, I have you all to myself," he laughed as he spun me around, my feet swinging wildly and nearly kicking over a book display.

"Until a customer comes in," I added.

"Don't worry, it's not like the weekends, Monday through Friday, it only picks up after lunch."

After a flurry of kisses, and continued spinning, I begged, "Okay, okay, enough! You're making me dizzy. Put me down!"

"Alright, down you go," he set me softly back on the floor.

After my equilibrium returned I asked, "Okay, what were you so eager to show me?"

He grabbed my hand, and led me to the sales counter. "This is one of the books my mom sells in the back of the shop." He picked it up, displaying it to me. "I've been thinking a lot about what the article in the paper said, about the witnesses seeing a triangle carved onto Amy's body."

"Yeah. What does it mean?"

He flipped through the pages, stopping at one of interest, and pointed, "These are the Wiccan symbols for the four elements."

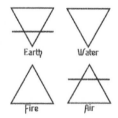

I read the text quietly to myself, as he looked over my shoulder.

"Earth symbolizes constancy and stability. This element grounds the magical workings in the here and now. The power of the Earth lies in its unchanging nature.

Water symbolizes quiet strength and perseverance. Water represents a power that builds over time.

Fire symbolizes passion and intensity. This element drives desire. Fire consumes wildly and quickly.

Air symbolizes the lifting of consciousness into a place where mystical wisdom can be transmitted. This element connects us to the realm of the spirit world."

"So, you think the carving might represent one of these four elements?"

"Perhaps."

Noticing an eerily familiar one, I asked, "What about this one?"

"That's a Pentacle. Each point on the star represents an element, the fifth one being spirit. It's a Wiccan symbol for protection."

"Protection? Funny, I always thought it was a symbol for the Devil."

"The Pentacle has been used as a religious symbol for a long, long time. There are records of it being used during the time of King Solomon, around 970 BC. Later, Christians adopted it to represent the five wounds of Christ. What *you're* thinking of is the version that's turned upside down, like this."

He rotated the book around.

"This became a thing in the late 1960s, when the Church of Satan used the inverted Pentacle with a drawing of a goat's head for their logo. The problem is nowadays everyone believes the Pentacle itself is the symbol for the Devil, when its origins are the exact opposite."

I closed my eyes and pictured the image from the earlier dream. "There was something like that on the wall in Suzie's vision."

"Really? Which version?"

I clenched my eyes tighter, tried to focus on the details. "I'm not sure which way it was facing - she was lying on her side."

"Hmm… well, I can't imagine a protection symbol being placed on the walls of a place where murders would be taking place."

"Are you aware of anyone practicing… bad magic? Are there other covens?"

Russell slightly stiffened.

I continued, "Everyone at school has been spreading around a Satanic Cult theory, but maybe there's something to it?"

"Yes, there are other covens, but if anyone is dabbling in *black magic*, I don't think that's something they'd want people to know about. Especially us."

Thinking back on the images from my dream, a thought occurred to me, "The color of the candle matters, doesn't it?"

"Yeah, it does. Why?"

"Remember me telling you about how I saw a red candle?"

Nodding his head, he responded, "Hold on." He walked back to the bookshelf, glanced around at the titles then brought down another book. After thumbing through the pages he said, "Here's the examples of colors and what they mean."

I scanned the page, closing my eyes again, to bring the image clearer in my mind. "Okay, now that I'm looking at these colors, I guess the candle I saw wasn't really a true red."

"None of these?"

"No, it was a darker, deeper red... almost, but not quite, purple."

"There *can* be blended colors. It all depends on intent. Purple's historically linked to the mystical arts, especially if the user is trying to improve their psychic power - divination, gaining knowledge, those sorts of things. Red taps into the power of Mars for physical strength and endurance. Combining the purple with a red candle *would* increase the potency of the spell."

"So, what I've been witnessing in these visions IS Wiccan magic!"

Russell crossed his arms, in response, standing defiantly straight. "We believe in respecting all living things! Remember, *do no harm*?"

"Okay, sure, but if it is Wiccan magic being used by bad people, would the carving of symbols into the skin, before killing them, be part of some sort of ritual? Some kind of… sacrifice?"

"Again, just to be clear, in Wiccan culture, when sacrifice is required, as part of observing a Sabbat, it means offerings of bread, fruit, wine, flowers… not human life. Blood magic is part of a *very* ancient time."

"It seems to me like it might not be so ancient."

"Well yeah, but…"

I paced, working through the details as they went pinging around my head. "Okay, let's just *suppose* someone *is* doing this kind of blood magic. What's it used for?"

Russell drew a long slow breath, his expression darkened. "Ancient Sorcerers used blood in their rituals and spell castings to…" he gazed away searching for the right word, "*intensify* the power of them."

We stood silent, the ominous possibilities swirling through both our thoughts.

"Okay, so, someone is carving symbols into their victim's skin, then putting symbols on the walls around the victim, burning the candles, and killing them for their blood."

"Seems like it."

"And, you're saying, the blood is probably used to intensify the *power* of the spell… What spell?"

"I have no idea."

"Nothing comes to mind?" I frowned. "Nothing at all?"

He shook his head, and shrugged. "If you could see more symbols, then we might be able to understand their motives better. Putting a combination of symbols together creates a sigil. It's a design that represents what you want to manifest..." he worked invisible forms in the air, pantomiming the process to help explain. "It's like putting together words to form a sentence, but in a drawing. This is then charged with the will of the person who created it, releasing the energy into the Universe to do the work."

"Hmmm... maybe that explains the peculiar images I saw," I speculated. "But, we don't know the intention of the spell, unless we know all the words of the sentence, right?"

"Exactly. Ciara would be a lot of help if you could give her details of all the symbols you've seen. This is her forte. Didn't you say you've been writing down what you remember, in your dream journal?"

"Yeah, but only after I realized what was going on. I didn't record anything from the first vision with Suzie. Can we go back to the first book with the random thingamajigs, maybe something will jump out at me?"

"Thingamajig, is that kind of like a Whatchamacallit?"

"No, but if you have one, I'll take it. I skipped breakfast."

He smiled, shaking his head, "Sorry, I don't."

Slowly thumbing through the pages covered in moon glyphs, and rune alphabets, we finally landed at a page covered in Celtic Pagan symbols. I stood up straight, and tapped my finger on one particular drawing.

"I recognize that one. What's it called?"

"The Triple Moon - It represents the Triple Goddess, Brighid, as the Maiden, the Mother, and the Crone in a lunar cycle," he answered as he tapped each figure in turn, "the waxing, full, and waning moon."

I pointed further down the page. "And this one?"

"That was in the center of the moon on the flyer Judith handed me, right?" I asked.

"Yeah, the Triquetra, also referred to as the Trinity Knot. We use it as a protection symbol. It represents a few things - one as another representation of the Triple Goddess - the others as life, death, and rebirth, or as land, sea, and sky."

Towards the very bottom of the same page, another one stood out. "Didn't that newspaper article mention something about one of the carvings in Amy's skin being something like a circle with a maze in it?"

"Come to think of it, yeah."

"Well doesn't this one look like a maze?" I replied pointing to the symbol.

"That's Hecate's Wheel."

"Who's Hecate?"

"A Goddess said to have power over the heavens, earth, and sea. In Greek legend, she is the guardian of the crossroads between the living and the dead." He traced his finger around the image, "Her labyrinth spirals around like a serpent, representing the power of knowledge and life. She eventually evolved into a Goddess of magic and sorcery. Those that still worship her, honor her in… just a couple of days, as a matter of fact."

"And exactly, how do these worshipers honor her?"

Russell shrugged, "I'm not sure. What I *do* know about her is that she was known as being capable of doing good *and* evil."

"Okay, so not such a *good* Goddess then?" I interjected.

He continued, "She was associated with necromancy, and creatures of the night."

"What exactly is necromancy?"

He smiled awkwardly, "Well… um, it's actually something you know a little about."

"Me? What?"

"Communicating with the dead, you know, like talking to ghosts."

"And that's considered something only *evil* people do?"

"No! Of course not! But when Sorcerers used black magic to manipulate spirits, it was never for good intentions. It was always something selfish, like to do their bidding to seek revenge on an enemy or something."

I shuddered at the thought of all those spirits I'd helped set free, and the thought of them being tortured. I began to pace the carpeted floor, filled with anxiety.

"Gwen, you aren't evil. *They* didn't respect the spirits, treat them with kindness, or try to help them, like you did. It may all be considered Witchcraft by outsiders, but there are two very distinct moral differences between Wiccans and Sorcerers."

Tink, tink, tink, tink.

The Tibetan bell on the front door jingled. Russell turned to say his usual store greeting, when he realized it was just Cat and Kevin.

"Hey, HEY, hey," Kevin called out.

"Whaaat's happenin'?" Cat asked, as they strutted further into the store.

"Just reading up on stuff. Whaaat's happenin' with you?" I answered.

"Just walking in the store," Kevin replied.

"Cool," Russell nodded.

"So hey, Russell, do you get a lunch break?" Kevin asked. "Do you want to come hang out with us at the Deli?"

"Nope. Working solo the whole day. My mom wanted a day off. But you're more than welcome to pick me up a sandwich if you want. I won't say no."

"You won't, huh?" Kevin grinned.

My stomach rumbled at the thought of sliced turkey and jack cheese. "Dang it! Why didn't you tell me before we left that we'd get lunch while we were out?"

"Duh. How else do you think we were going to eat?" Kevin asked with a snarky expression on his face.

"Duh, yourself," I replied making the same face back at him. I scrounged through my purse. "I didn't bring enough money."

I glanced beseechingly over at Cat, pouted, and tilted my head.

She laughed, and shrugged. "Sorry, that's not going to work, I only have enough for a bag of chips and drink, if that!"

Kevin nudged her gently. "I can cover you."

Insulted, I looked at him and said, "What am I, chopped liver over here?"

Russell disappeared from behind the counter, and returned a moment later, pulling the Velcro back on his wallet. He reached in and pulled out a $20.00 bill.

"Here," he said, as he handed it to me, "you can get something for everyone. I'd love Pastrami-on-Rye with a Dr. Pepper."

"Mr. Money Bags," I leaned up and gave him a big kiss. "Thanks." I turned around waving the crisp bill in the air.

"Right on!" Kevin cheered. "Thanks dude!"

Cat, Kevin, and I were heading to the door, and as we were passing by the watercolor paintings that lined the wall shelves, I called back over my shoulder, "We'll be back before you can say…"

I stopped mid-sentence, noticing something from the corner of my eye. Leaning in closer, to make sure it was what I thought it was, I exclaimed, "Oh, daaammnn," and pointed. "Russell, did you know this was here?"

Chapter Twenty-Three
Moon Phases

Cat stood in the threshold while Kevin held the door open for us. "What is it?" she asked as she trotted over to see. She leaned over inspecting the painting in question. "Okay, yeah, it's another painting of a place in town." She flipped her hands open, "What's the big deal?"

Russell walked up and joined us. Kevin then came back inside letting the door shut behind him. The jingling of the Tibetan bell didn't mask the loud gasp that erupted from Russell's mouth.

"Holy crap!"

"What? I don't get it, what are you two spazzing out about?" Cat asked.

I tapped the spot on the painting, "Remember the witness statements about the carvings on Amy's skin?" I gazed expectantly from one to the other, eyes wide. "We were just looking at a book of symbols..." I tapped the canvas again, "see there, in that tree?"

Cat squinted closer. "Yeah, okay... it looks like a circle with a maze in it."

"Hecate's wheel," Russell whispered in amazement.

"Exactly as the witness described," I added. "And look at this other painting... see that rock?" I turned to Russell and asked, "Which one is that?"

"Earth." He ran back to the counter and retrieved the book. "See how it is an upside-down triangle with a line through it?"

"Yeah! Okay, everyone," I said pointing to the symbols, "look at the paintings and find as many of these as you can."

Cat and Kevin each took a painting, leaning in real close to inspect every detail, and then referring back to the book. Russell inspected another, as well.

Leaning into his ear, I whispered, "Is this artist in the coven?"

"You know we can hear you, right?" Kevin asked. "We get it. Russell and his family are part of a coven."

The room went quiet, while Kevin continued to stare at the painting he was inspecting. Finally, he realized that all eyes were on him. He stood up, throwing his hands out. "What?" He raised an eyebrow as he looked directly at Russell, "Don't look at me like that. It's not like we're telling anyone." He looked at us, nodding and gesturing, waiting for us to agree with him. "You swore us to secrecy months ago. So, dude, you've got to let us in on what's going on!"

Nobody said anything for a few long seconds, waiting to see how Russell would respond. After a long sigh of resignation, he relaxed. "Okay, fine." He motioned back to the paintings. "No, Ewan Blackwood is not part of my coven."

"Blackwood?" Kevin asked with peaked interest. "As in Blackwood Estates?"

"Yeah, the Blackwoods used to be the biggest of three land holders in Douglas, but they sold it all off a long time ago."

"And you know this because?" Cat asked.

"I just hear things when everyone gets to talking, that's all."

"Who's the second?" Kevin asked.

Cat leaned over to me and whispered. "Second what?"

"That would be the MacDonalds," Russell answered.

"Landowners," I whispered back.

MacDonald... MacDonald...

Kevin nodded, "That makes sense. You can't go anywhere without seeing their name plastered on something. The MacDonald Construction Company drives around with those giant white vans."

Cat and I shrugged in confusion.

"Okay, I can tell by the looks on your faces that you don't know what I'm talking about. How about this one... all the housing developments along the freeway leading up to the Zoo..."

"So?" Cat asked.

"The MacDonalds own *all* that land! And get this, for the kicker, they're the ones getting paid to turn the Victorian into a museum. They're rolling in money."

Didn't my mom mention that was her grandmother's maiden name? Or was it her married name?

"Are *they* part of your coven?" Cat asked. I could see her wheels turning, trying to connect these details back to Blackwood's symbols.

Russell shook his head, "No."

"Who's the third?" I asked.

"Third what? Oh, largest landowner, you mean. The MacGregors."

"Huh?" The name meant nothing to me, so I turned back to the paintings, and immediately noticed a cloud that had shadows shaped as curved lines with dots just like the symbols from the moon glyph page. This made me more curious as to why he hid all these symbols within his paintings. What significance did they hold? What was he trying to say?

"Is your mother friends with Ewan?" I pointed to the artwork. "Is that why this stuff is here?" I asked.

"I don't know if they're friends. I mean, we've never had him or his family over for dinner or anything. But they used to come by the store with their son, Toby, a long time ago. He was still young enough, back then, to want to play with me."

"Hold on. Toby... like, Ciara's boyfriend, Toby?"

"Yep."

"But if they're hardly ever around, how'd he and Ciara end up dating? Did he go to Carmichael?"

"No," Russell shook his head. "He went to Glenview, it's closer to their farm."

"Blackwood has a farm?" Cat interjected.

"Do they go to college together?" I continued with my line of questioning.

"Cat, to answer your question, it's his wife's farm. And no, Toby doesn't go to school with her. She works here on and off, it's possible he came by the store. I'm really not sure how they hooked up, they just did, and obviously really hit it off."

Kevin was shaking his head in confusion over the whole Toby thing. "Okay, so going back to the paintings, why are these images the same ones found on Amy's dead body? Does that mean Blackwood is somehow involved in the murders?" he asked.

I picked up the one that had the Hecate's Wheel, turned it over, and looked at the details on the 3x5 card on the back. "This was painted over two years ago!"

"We should probably show these paintings to the police. It might help," Kevin suggested.

Russell looked concerned at the prospect. "I really don't want to get my mom's shop, and… well all of… well, everything, involved. Let me talk to her first. She has a lot of connections, and can do her own divining on the situation, to get to some answers. I'll get back to you, okay?" Russell asked of him, holding Kevin's eyes.

Kevin nodded his understanding. "Yeah, I get it. I don't want anything bad to fall on your family, and all this," he stated, waving his hand around the shop. "Brighid's cool. I trust her."

"Good! Thank you!" Russell clapped his hands together. "Now, how about that lunch? I'll cross reference the symbols in the paintings while you're gone."

With that, Cat, Kevin, and I headed to the deli, throwing back and forth ideas over what all these new discoveries meant, if they meant anything at all, until our heads were spinning. We finally gave up and simply focused on getting lunch.

Half an hour later – sandwiches in hand - we returned to the shop. As luck would have it, a couple of people milled about in the front of the store, and I could hear Russell's voice in the back, behind the blue beaded curtain, with several more.

We chose to wait outside until everyone cleared out, but after it was apparent he wasn't going to be free any time soon, I brought Russell his food.

"Thank you," he responded, after sucking down most of the Dr. Pepper in one long swig. He smiled at the bag of corn chips and grinned even wider at the giant chocolate chip cookie. "This looks sooo good."

"Are you going to have time to eat?"

"Eventually. I told you it would pick up after lunch. Guess we kinda lost our window, ya know? I'll just have to call you later, after I get home, okay?"

"Yeah, sure," I answered in disappointment. I handed him his $9.00 in change. "Thanks again for buying us lunch."

"No biggie! I'm just sad we couldn't keep hanging out," he frowned. A customer called out a question. "Okay, that's my cue." He gave me a quick peck on the cheek. "Bye."

"Bye."

∽

Later that night, Russell called. After exchanging pleasantries, I cut right to the chase. "So? What did your mom say?"

"Well, obviously, she knew there were symbols in Ewan's paintings. He'd told her 'Art is subjective. It's up to the viewer to interpret as they wish'."

"Did she find that weird?"

"What *weird*? What he said?"

"No, that he inserted a bunch of Wiccan symbols in all these paintings of the town."

"She didn't say anything about it, but she did say she will do some divining, and see if she can find what's going on."

"You said that word again… *divining*. What does that mean?"

"The easy explanation?"

"Okay, sure."

"When she needs to find something out, she uses candles to focus her psychic abilities to find the answer."

"Why a candle?"

"Well, she *could* also use water or mirrors - anything with a reflective surface - but she finds that staring into the flame and smoke works better to help relax her mind... to open up her inner eye."

I tried to picture it, and immediately images popped up of old, black and white movies... wrinkled old ladies wrapped in veils, hunkered over little tables – reading some poor sap's future. "Like the crystal ball gazing kind of thing?"

"Yeah, like that. Some people use a crystal ball, some people cast runes, some people use tarot cards. Each person who has this ability uses whatever tool works best for them."

"So, she's going to focus on why these symbols are being used on the murder victims and whether or not they relate to those paintings?"

"Well," he stammered a bit, "she didn't say all that specifically. I mean, I told her everything we discussed. She said she'd look into it."

The line went quiet for a moment, I was about to jump in, when Russell continued, "Although, there *was* something she said that hadn't occurred to me before."

"What's that?"

"The four murders fell in between a new moon cycle."

"What's the significance in that?"

He paused again, "Let's just say... we might be on the right track. If these murders are tied into the lunar cycle, it *could* be some sort of black magic and not just some random whacko trying to scare everyone."

"Why?" I inquired further.

"Because new moon ceremonies are about planting the seeds of unlimited possibility, you know, like the beginning of something meaningful. My mom feels these deaths have purposeful intent."

"And when was the last new moon?"

"The fifteenth."

"Amy was found on the eleventh..." I let it sink in, trying to piece it all together. After a quiet bit of silence, I continued, "Is it possible there's another coven out there... a bad one?"

"Honestly, I don't know, I mean my mom didn't exactly answer the question outright, but I sensed something new... anxiety. I suspect something significant is happening and it has her shaken."

I suddenly had a thought. "Okay, this might sound random, but there was mention of a farm earlier, right?"

"Yeah, that's Ewan and Maggie's place. The MacGregor Tree Farm."

"MacGregor? I thought it was Ewan's farm.

"No, it's Maggie's family property."

"And Toby is their son?"

"Right."

"Hmmm... tree farm... as in Christmas trees?"

"Yes, they do Christmas trees. That's where we get ours for Yule. They also have a pumpkin patch, a corn maze, and do a harvest festival type thing this time of year."

"Can we go this weekend?"

"This weekend?" He paused a bit too long. "What about your parents? Are they going to be okay with us going?"

"I guess I just won't tell them."

"Why the rush?"

"Remember when you said to trust my intuition?"

"Yeah."

"Well, ever since this afternoon it's been like a… a siren… or some sort of alarm with flashing lights, going off in my head. It started as soon as we talked about the farm. We have to check it out!"

The line went quiet for a moment, and I could tell Russell was struggling between two immoveable walls… please my parents' wishes or please me.

"I said I'd never second guess that again, didn't I?"

"You did."

"Okay, but then I need you to put on the amulet my mother gave you. I've noticed you haven't been wearing it. This is definitely a time to reconsider that. As my mom always says, 'ward up'."

"And what does that mean?"

"Easy answer?"

"Yes."

"Put on your armor."

I glanced over to my nightstand where I kept it handy.

"Okay, I will. When do they open, and where are you picking me up?"

Chapter Twenty-Four
Tree Hunting

Russell and I drove across the Douglas River, meandered along a winding road that stretched through MacLean's fields, and headed up into the forested foothills towards MacGregor's Tree Farm.

"How long did you say it would take?"

"It's probably another fifteen minutes from here," he answered. "And you're sure you've got the whole thing worked out at home? You won't get grounded again?"

"For the millionth time, yes!" I shook my head, a bit exasperated. "As far as my mom knows, Cat, Kevin and I took the bus downtown again to hang. Just like on Friday. Cat will cover."

"Okay, cool."

I'd never been anywhere where you got to cut down your own tree. It sounded like a fun tradition to ring in the holidays. My family tradition consisted of going down to a tree stand set up in some random parking lot near a store, where we tried to find the least expensive one that didn't look like it would last two weeks – usually a Balsam Fir. It never ended up being very big, those were too expensive.

Not a very festive tradition.

I did always look forward to going to the mall though. I'd tag along with my mom while she bought presents for the in-laws. I loved all the extravagant decorations hanging everywhere, and the Christmas music being piped through overhead loudspeakers.

The previous year, Cat, Andrea, Erin and I paid a visit to the mall to sit on Santa's lap for a photo. Despite the fact that we were too old to believe in Santa, and too big to fit, we sat two per knee, laughing so hard that the photo turned out horrible. It was a great time!

A bump in the road brought me out of my Christmas memories, and I stared ahead as we began a gradual climb up into the forest. Along the increasingly winding road, - every mile or so - was a painted wood sign with an arrow pointing towards the farm. A countdown of how much further it was to go.

I could see snowcapped mountains off in the distance, occasionally peeking through breaks in the tree line as we drove. It seemed like we were really far from home. The fact that it was just the two of us, off on an adventure, was exhilarating. These were the moments you wish you could bottle up and keep forever.

"Okay, cool," Russell, stated, "we're here."

Finally, a sign had come up that read, *MacGregor's Tree Farm - Next Right*. Russell slowed down. I kept my eyes peeled, thinking it would be some little dirt road, cut through the trees that we might miss if we blinked.

I was surprised when the tree line ended and a wide-open expanse of land opened up before us. A giant banner hung from the main sign welcoming everyone to the Harvest Festival: November 25th through the 30th. On the other side, a second one announced: Christmas Festivities every weekend starting December 5th through the 20th.

A small sign near the entrance led us down a small, bumpy dirt track, riddled with divots and potholes, along a fence line towards a large farmhouse with an adjacent barn.

"Anything coming to you?" he asked.

"Nothing yet."

On the right side were open fields with unworthy pumpkins left to die on the vine, spreading out to a line of corn stalks. Lined up along the left were rows of Christmas trees.

Cars slogged to a crawl in front of us, as they waited their turn to maneuver into a graveled parking area. We moved forward slowly. Then the crunch of tiny rocks, grinding against the tires, echoed throughout the interior of the car as we rolled into position, and came to a stop.

I could tell by the way the other people in the lot were acting that it was really cold. So, I took my hat, scarf, and gloves off my lap, and put them on before exiting the car.

Russell looked me up and down, inspecting. He pointed to my feet. "Are you sure the boots fit okay? Rose insisted you two were the same size."

"Yes, they fit great," I answered, pulling my fingers into the second glove. "Okay, ready. Let's go."

Despite the sun cresting to its highest point amidst clear skies, the brisk mountain air was chilling. Russell saw me shiver, and wrapped his arm around my shoulders as we walked from the lot onto the muddy road leading to the barn.

A tractor trundled along between the rows of trees, towing a big flatbed trailer piled high with bales of hay. Giggling children bounced and rolled on them, yipping with delight at every lurch and bump in the ground beneath.

"A tractor hayride?" I asked in astonishment. "It's so... so..."

"Farm like?"

"Smart ass."

Sloshing through the trampled mud puddles, we made our way to the barn. The outside was decorated with pumpkins, left over from Halloween, and Thanksgiving wreaths made from cornhusks, dried berries, and small gourds, as well as giant plastic maple leaves stapled to the open barn doors.

When we stepped inside, one side was a small market of harvest related crafts, pies, and jars of preserves made from the farm's orchards. Apparently, there was more to MacGregor's farm than just its trees. On the other side, was everything Christmas. There were homemade ornaments, frosted sugar cookies wrapped in cellophane, Christmas candles that smelled like candy cane or gingerbread cookies, wreaths made with boughs from their Fir trees, and handmade quilted stockings. You name it, it was there. My heart was swelling with joy from the sights, and the plethora of smells, taking me back to happy childhood memories.

Russell pointed to a giant urn perched atop a small table in the corner. A hand lettered sign in front of it read: *Free Hot Chocolate. Help yourself.*

"We'll come back in here before we leave. I'm sure we'll need to warm up for the ride home."

"Sounds like a plan."

"What would you like to do first? We could go wander through the tree lot," he suggested.

"Isn't it too early to get a Christmas tree?"

"No."

"Are you actually thinking of getting one?"

"Maybe… we'll see."

"How come you don't just cut a tree down on your own property? You're surrounded by them."

"This is more fun."

"True."

We walked outside, past the farmhouse, down the same muddy road the tractor hayride had just taken. In front of each row of Fir trees, there was a beam of wood with rusty handsaws dangling from equally rusty nails.

"My dad always called this part 'hunting'."

"Why?"

"It's just a way to entertain us kids I suppose. He'd grab the saw and say he was going to go out into the wilderness to hunt us down a tree. After that, everything became a game. When we agreed on which one was the best, he'd pretend to wrangle it into submission, then start sawing away at the trunk pretending it was fighting back."

He noticed the look on my face. "It does sound kind of morbid, now that I say it out loud."

"Yes, it really does. Poor trees. They never stood a chance."

"And yet, here we are, contemplating another murder."

"It is a festive time of year after all."

"Very festive, with, you know, all the hacking and sawing."

"Nothing says Christmas like a dead tree in your living room."

"Although my dad may have been guilty of hunting down the tree and killing it, we do acknowledge its sacrifice through ritual, burning, and saving pieces of it to include in the next year's Yule fire."

"What's that?"

"Yule is the time before and after the Winter Solstice on the 21st."

"Why is the *tree* used in a ritual?"

"Well, the tree holds a pretty deep significance. I don't think most people who celebrate Christmas even understand why they have a tree in their living room, or why they decorate it."

"Yeah, I've always wondered what a tree had to do with Jesus' birthday."

"It doesn't. The tree tradition comes from pre-Christian Germanic and northern European people, you know, like Celtic Druids... Pagans. To celebrate Yule, the ancient people would cut down a carefully chosen tree, and bring it into the house with great ceremony. Sprigs, holly berries, and wreaths of evergreen were used as decorations throughout the home, and mistletoe was strung up over the doorways to protect against evil. The tree gets decorated with candles and berries, and small gifts are placed on the branches as offerings to the Gods. Then on the Solstice, the largest end of the tree, the Yule Log, would be placed into the fire hearth, and lit with the remains of the previous year's log. In Celtic tradition, a continual fire was kept burning to prevent evil spirits from entering the home. They also believed that the longer the Yule log burned, the faster the sun would come to warm the earth. During this time, they would bring out their stored food and feast. There'd be dancing and singing to celebrate the coming longer days, knowing the dark days were almost behind them."

"Wow!" I turned and gazed admiringly up to Russell's face. "You're a fountain of knowledge!"

"Thank you."

I craned up on tippy-toes and gave him a kiss on his cold cheek. He grinned and gave my hand a quick squeeze.

"So," I turned and motioned across the procession of aligned trees. "How do you know which is the *right* one, if it has to be so carefully chosen?"

"It just happens. Somehow, as a family, we always ended up gravitating to the right one," he answered. "Come on, we'll just meander. Maybe one will speak to *you*."

"And volunteer for the slaughter?" I quipped. "Right!"

"Ah, but it will be revered and honored. So perhaps it won't put up too much of a fight after we capture it."

We continued to slosh down the muddy paths between the rows of trees, in search of the chosen one.

"I hope it's not a gory mess."

"Just makes it all the more festive."

"Ho, ho, ho."

Chapter Twenty-Five
The Barn

Grumbling, as we made our way back from the tree hunt, "Maybe we should have taken the hayride back. That was a lot of walking. That hot chocolate sounds awfully nice right about now."

"Why are *you* complaining?" Russell scoffed. "You aren't the one the dragging the tree!"

"Hey, I'm helping!" I held out the murder weapon, still covered in bits of sappy sticky gore. "I'm carrying the saw!"

He turned to scowl at me, and I batted my eyes innocently in return. He shook his head, determined to not grin.

"And, did I mention that you look so rugged and manly? It's kinda hot."

"Stop it! That won't work. You're on the naughty list."

"Me? You told me you could do it by yourself. You said it was no problem."

"I lied."

"NOW who's on the naughty list?"

"Okay, finally. We're here." He dropped the tree down in front of a makeshift checkout table, where one of the farm helpers measured the tree, referred to the chart hanging on the wall of the barn behind them, and asked for payment.

Russell got out his wallet, handed over a few bills, and waited for the guy to figure out the change from a metal cash box.

"Can I just leave this leaning here while we go inside to get some hot chocolate?" Russell asked.

"Sure thing." He produced a plastic ribbon, and a black marker. "Name?"

"Russell."

He wrote "Russell" on it in big block letters, and then tied it to a branch on the tree. "Keep your receipt with you."

"Cool," Russell responded, and then turned back to me as we walked. "Well, we've been here for a while now, how's that intuition thing going? Did you figure out why you're being drawn here?"

"Not yet. I've been enjoying myself too much! I sort of forgot what brought us here in the first place."

"Well, focus. See what comes to you."

We were just about to enter back into the craft barn when I heard clucking and braying coming from off to the right.

"Do you hear that?" I exclaimed, dragging him away from the entrance. "Let's go find them."

"Find who?"

I followed the sounds to the right side of the barn. Down at the furthest end, I saw three small poorly sheltered pens, and a coop.

My heart sank. "Oh, this is sad!"

There was one muddy area with two small pigs, a cramped cow in straw strewn quarters, one dirty dread-locked sheep housed with a couple of skinny goats, and a dirty chicken coup.

When I approached, one of the goats came to the fence and tried to stick its head through, drawing attention to a clump of green grass just out of its reach.

"Here, let me help you out little buddy." I plucked the grass, and gently brought it to its mouth. Immediately it chomped and tore away at the clump, chewing contentedly at the sudden bounty.

"Why, Doctor Doolittle, you're much prettier than I remember!" Russell chuckled.

The other goat got jealous, tried to shove its way in to steal the grass. "Hey, you, be nice. He was here first."

Russell watched, snickering as they pushed at each other, until the second one, victoriously grabbed the remaining grass from my hand.

"That wasn't very nice!" I admonished. "But I get it, you're hungry. Hold on."

I searched around to pluck another handful.

Behind me, a woman snidely remarked, "If you want to feed the animals, you need to buy feed inside."

I turned to see an elderly woman bundled against the cold. Her small fists were planted against her hips, with one thin eyebrow lifted and an impatient frown stretched across her mouth.

"Um, okay, I didn't know," I replied, and smiled politely. "Sorry."

She turned back around, and walked away.

I looked up at Russell, surprised by the lady's rude manner. "I get the impression she wanted me to pay to feed them, huh?"

"Yeah. Everything helps, right?"

"I guess. But they're miserable! They're cold, and aren't getting fed enough."

"Speaking of cold, let's go inside, we'll buy some feed, but we'll also get that hot chocolate," Russell insisted. "My hands are still pretty numb, and I could do with some warm sugary liquids."

"Alright, hang on."

I turned to grab one more handful of grass for the two goats, now joined by the sheep, up on their hind legs beseeching their newfound friend.

Suddenly I noticed another barn further away. Lights flickered in the forefront of my brain – as if I'd been staring at a light bulb too long - and a faint ringing began behind my eardrums.

"What's wrong?" Russell asked, just as I lifted my hand, pointing in its direction.

"That strange sensation is back," I answered. "I need to go and check that barn out."

Russell glanced around, made sure nobody was watching, and grabbed my hand. "Okay, let's go."

We strolled down the dirt road that led to the barn - trying to look inconspicuous as possible - the area pretty obviously not for public access. At the entrance, we were greeted by a big, shiny padlock holding the two big sliding barn doors together.

"Shoot! It's locked," I groaned.

"It makes sense you would lock up places that you don't want customers wandering into. It is someone's home after all."

"True," I relented. Looking at the structure, then back at the locked entrance, I said, "Maybe there's another way in."

"The feeling is that strong, huh?"

"Can't you feel it too?"

"No, but I can feel *your* emotional response to whatever it is."

I crept around the right side, peering around the corner... nothing. I tried the left. Nothing there, either. "I guess we'll just have to see what's around back."

"I think this is a bad idea," Russell said as he stepped ahead of me, and took my hand, "but we've come this far, so we might as well find out why this place is calling to you."

"Thanks."

We moved down the length of the barn flanked on our left by a row labeled Fraser Firs. Rounding the rear corner, that single row spread out into a sea of 4 to 6-foot-tall trees.

Set in the middle of the building's backside was a single door. After again glancing around and checking we weren't drawing attention, Russell twisted at the knob, but it wouldn't turn. "Locked," he stated.

"No, try again. We need to get inside."

"I'm telling you it's locked."

"Then unlock it!" I urged. "You know, like you did with Erin. *Make* it open."

"Gwen, come on," he sighed. "I'd be breaking in. And even though I know Ewan and Maggie, I don't think they'd be too happy about that."

Every hair on my body was standing on end, and a weird sensation went up my spine. I'd say my spider senses were tingling if I were a superhero, but I wasn't.

"We need to get inside," I insisted, a sense of immediacy washing over me.

"Okay, okay. Give me a second." He dropped my hand, took a deep breath, and then closed his eyes.

Amazingly, I heard a crack in the doorframe, followed by a metallic click.

Wow, he just did that.

He opened his eyes, reached out, and went to twist the knob... this time it turned. As he pushed the squeaking door inward, a little of the old decaying wood gave way around the metal plate.

"Are you sure?" he asked. "I don't have a good feeling about *any* of this."

"I have to get inside," I motioned to the opening, resolute and determined.

"Okay, just hold on." He crept in ahead of me and looked around for a source of light.

I stood in the doorframe with daylight spilling across the dirty wood floor - the feeling of déjà vu intense. The aroma of wet dog lingered in the air.

Russell finally found a string hanging from the ceiling and yanked down on it. One single bulb lit up the room.

I moved cautiously, brain in a hazy fog, my body moving in slow motion. My feet, moving forward of their own volition, ceased shuffling. I turned back around to face the door, then sat down, bathed in the light streaming in from outside.

I closed my eyes, felt the sun's warmth, and let my fingers rest on the wood planking. I felt something hard, yet soft – sticky, but not. I glanced down to see what was beneath my fingertips.

Wax?

"What are you doing?" Russell asked.

"THIS is where it happened!" I gasped in astonishment.

"Where what happened?"

"This is right where the girls were lying when they first woke up."

"Are you sure?"

"Yeah!" I lay down on my side. "Hold on..." The smell of earth rose from the floorboards, followed by a whiff of hay. I lifted my head, looked around, and sure enough, in the corner lay bales of hay.

I closed my eyes, again, trying to concentrate on every one of my senses.

"Gwen, you need to see this!"

"Shhhh. Give me a minute."

I listened.

At first, I could hear the sounds from the farm, but I blocked them out, and focused closer – to sounds in the room.

There. There it was.

I opened my eyes, searching for the source. A wooden bucket lay beneath a spigot attached against a beam of wood. Water dripped intermittently from the faucet head. The wood around the old bucket had rotted, a section of board actually missing.

I got up and walked over to it. Picking it up and moving it to the side, I saw exposed ground underneath.

"Russell! This IS the place!" I exclaimed in amazement. Everything was making sense.

"Okay, then you *really* need to see this!" he insisted.

Russell stood across the room, pointing up to a series of symbols and images on the wall.

I gasped.

Just like the dream.

"Russell, those girls were *here!*"

I walked towards him to get a better look at the wall, but got distracted by a workbench running along its length. On it sat a white marble mortar and pestle, alongside a row of various flowers - none of which, I recognized.

A scent caught my attention, however. It was faint, and hidden beneath the more prevalent odors of decaying wood, mold, and hay.

I leaned closer, sniffing around, until I found it. Although I didn't recognize the scent from anything in my daily life, I knew this was the floral scent Suzie and Amy had experienced.

"What kind of flower is this, do you know?"

"Lily of the Valley," he answered, coming over to inspect the array of items on the bench top.

There was a paper bag, off to one side, which also caught my attention. The top of the bag had been twisted and tied up. I pulled at the string, and, as I untwisted the bag, out crawled a horrible stench - like the smell of people's feet in a locker room.

"Ewwww! Oh my god, what is it?" I exclaimed, tossing the bag aside.

Russell picked it back up, and hesitantly peeked inside. "Oh, that's interesting. It's Valerian."

"Is it rotten?"

"No, that's just how its flower smells. Phew!" He held it back away from his face. "The oil, if ingested, affects the brain and nervous system. That stuff can knock you right out... like a sedative."

He looked around at the other flowers. "Hmmm, this isn't good. This one is Foxglove. That's Belladonna and Hemlock."

"Besides being stinky, what do they do?"

"Well, Foxglove is so poisonous, even eating just a little can kill you. Belladonna can cause blurred vision, hallucinations, and convulsions. Hemlock can also be used as sedative, but too much of either of these can also kill you."

"Well, that's not good!" I moved down the bench, pointed to some others. "What about these over here? They smell better."

"Uhhh, be careful! They may smell great, but they can be just as nasty. From paralyses to coma if ingested," he warned. "They grow everywhere around here." He pointed to each in turn, "That one's Rhododendron, that's Laurel, and that's Azalea."

"So, I'll bet, whatever they injected those girls with was made right here," I concluded. "That's how they knocked them out!"

"I'd put my money on it!" Russell agreed.

I began to pace, working the scenarios out in my head. "They must have brought the girls back here... but then what happened?" I asked, looking around the room for more clues.

Just then, I heard a voice in my head, yelling, *"You need to leave!"*

I practically jumped out of my skin. The voice yelled again. *"It isn't safe. Hurry, leave now!"*

Whirling around, I searched frantically for the source - expecting someone to be there.

"What is it?" Russell asked.

"You didn't hear that?" I asked, wheeling around finding no one.

"GWEN! You aren't safe!"

"Ugh!" I doubled over, next to the workbench, damping my hands against my head. The intensity of the voice booming in my head hurt worse than a migraine.

"What do you hear?" Russell asked, bending over me, his back to the door.

"A girl is yelling at me to leave. She's saying it isn't safe!"

"And right you are!" the eerily familiar male voice confirmed.

"Wha-" Russell yelled, right before he uttered a painful grunt. I felt his body fall away from me, followed by a loud thump as his body hit the floor.

I spun around to help him, but a sudden sharp pain prickled the back of my neck. Immediately a burning radiated from the spot and began to spread throughout my entire body.

Oh my god! I just got injected with...

Everything swirled... darkened... nothingness.

Chapter Twenty-Six
Waking Nightmare

My eyes fluttered open, but everything was blurry. The light was very dim, and it hurt to try and focus. My face felt like a block of ice crusted in dirt.

I tried rolling my head, to get a better look around but recoiled immediately from a horrible ache in my neck. My muscles were tight, and something was pinching a cluster of nerves. Wave after wave, the pain shot straight from my shoulder, through my neck, right to my temples.

I stopped moving long enough for the pain to ebb, and cautiously opened my eyes slow enough to allow them to adjust. I glanced over to my right, searching for the familiar glow of my bedroom window illuminated by streetlamps or the rising sun.

Nothing - only unfamiliar shadows.

Am I having another dream?

I focused on wanting to turn my head the other way, albeit slower, to get a better look at my surroundings. The response was immediate. I had control over the body I was in.

"Wow, this is more real than it's ever been," I whispered.

That's my voice.

"Hello?"

Yep, that's me. Oh, crap. This is actually happening!

With widening eyes, I stared down at my unmoving self. The pain, again flared through my head, and I fought a brief wave of nausea. When it passed, I took inventory.

Where's my jacket? No wonder I'm so cold. At least I still had my shirt and jeans. That's something, at least.

"Hello? Where am I?" I screamed out. The pain in my temples screamed back.

Aggh!

Closing my eyes, I took deep breaths, in and out, waiting for the pain subside. Once it did, I took a few minutes to assess my situation. Then it came back to me.

Russell!

I called out, "RUSSELL?" I recoiled from the stab of pain, waiting, and listened for a response. Nothing.

I tried again softer, "Russell? Are you okay? Talk to me!"

What little light there was didn't illuminate the space around me enough to tell if it was a small or large room, only a faint rectangular shape against a far wall.

I focused intently on the floor.

Wait… dirt?

I was lying on the ground. Wherever I was, it had no floor.

My imagination went into overdrive with memories of scenes from horror movies, where someone was buried alive.

Breathe. Breathe. Don't freak out.

I willed myself to sit up, to get a better look around the room. I realized, I *couldn't* move.

Oh, no!

I tried to roll over and relived the dream experience - everything was numb from the neck down. Each girl's final moments flew past my frontal lobe in quick succession.

Crap!

Get up! Get up!

In frustration and fear, I continued to fight my body. *Cooperate! Cooperate, damn you!*

As my anxiety rose, I got lightheaded. I clenched my eyes against the swishing blood pumping through my veins, muffling out all external sound.

Something was building… growing. I recognized it - *the spark.*

I focused on lesson Russell gave me.

Visualize a bubble.

Visualize the bubble getting bigger, filling with air.

I took a deep breath, envisioning the bubble expanding.

No, not air. Something more powerful.

Fire.

My body suddenly felt hot, as if I were running a fever, or had been sitting too close to the heater.

The bubble is filling with fire!

With all my will, I visualized the bubble swelling and pulsing with fire, just getting ready to burst.

What happens when the fire gets too hot to contain?

"IT EXPLODES!" I yelled into the night, giving my vision all the energy I had to give.

A deep bass *WHOOSH* reverberated through the room all around me. I felt a weight release from my core. The rattle of wood against wood echoed throughout the room. A hail of dirt rained down from every direction, sounding like heavy rain during a windstorm.

I winced as bits of debris hit my face, and I could hear what sounded like shelves falling, and the breaking of glass.

The surge of energy left my body, and with it, all the air in my lungs. I was left gasping for breath. The lingering scent of struck matches hung in the air.

I had imagined fire... Is that really fire that I smell?

Tentatively I opened my eyes and was able to discern more light coming from the rectangle than before. This turned out to be a small depression in a wall.

Where the hell am I?

"Russell, can you hear me?" I yelled out.

Nothing.

I tried to sit up, and this time, felt a scratchy irritation on my wrists, layered beneath an unpleasant but welcome sensation - pins and needle going up from my fingertips to my elbow. I pulled at my arm, and after some resistance, was able to bring it around underneath me.

I pushed up to a sitting position.

The room swirled for a second, and I closed my eyes, and drew a deep breath. The world steadied. I brought my other arm around, and slowly shook each hand until I had control of all my fingers.

I leaned forward and pulled the ropes from my ankles. Apparently, the blast frayed the ropes enough to loosen them. I brought them close. The burnt smell came from those as well. I tossed them aside, and looked all around, stopping at the illuminated depression in the wall until my eyes fully adjusted. I recognized the faintly lit object, and gasped.

No, it can't be!

It was the leather suitcase. The one Kevin had cut open with his Swiss Army Knife. It still had the white candle wax on it.

That's from when we did the cleansing of...

No!

I blinked hard several times. Instead of going away, the details only grew clearer.

The depression in the wall, I realized, was the entryway to the small stairwell leading up to ground level.

I'm in the cellar... I'm in the CELLAR!

Panic began to set in. I maneuvered my head around trying to pick out anything - anything at all – that could either validate or repute this assertion. There just wasn't enough light to verify anything.

The smell of burnt wood lingered.

Why the cellar?

It doesn't even look like it has been touched. If the house was still under renovation, why would the murderer bring me here?

My temples began to scream again. I tried relaxing the muscles in my neck and shoulders and waited for the painful nerves to quiet so I could think clearly.

The talisman. I'm wearing the talisman.

I brought it out from beneath my shirt, and began to repeat the mantra, "I am protected. Nothing here can harm me!"

This worked against angry spirits.

"I am...

Wait, but these aren't ghosts...

"...protected. Nothing here..."

...these are murderers.

"...can harm me!"

"I can't believe I'm going to die, lying here in the GOD DAMN CELLAR!" I yelled. "Talking! To! Myself!"

Shit! Shit! Shit!

I brought my legs up from underneath me, the nerves retaliating back with sharp stabs as blood began to pump again. Parts of my legs were still numb, and I almost fell back over as I tried my first couple steps.

All my attention was now on getting to the dirt steps leading to the surface. I stumbled a few more steps and got my hands on the wall to lean against for support.

The burning wood smell intensified.

Where is that coming from?

Another couple steps and I was in the stairwell, about to take my first steps up towards the shut cellar doors. Light gleamed through the cracks and knotholes.

I wonder why these doors haven't been replaced. Will there be workers on site? Will there be people in the park?

I pressed my cold hands on the wood doors, ready to shove them up and out of the way, when I heard footsteps coming down the steps from the inside the house. I glanced over my shoulder to see a large swath of light flood the ground below.

"What have you done?" a male voice screamed, as he descended the interior steps from the first floor.

I recognized the voice as familiar - from my dreams, and from the farm. I was absolutely confused as to why he'd taken me from the farm to the cellar, but I didn't want to wait to find out why.

With all my strength, I shoved against the cellar doors. Thankfully, they gave, and I nearly threw each one off to the side in my attempt to scramble up the steps.

The frigid air of the clear night rushed in - the familiar landscape lit before me by a nearly full moon.

Chapter Twenty-Seven
Nowhere to Run

Once my mind accepted that I was back there again - and that it was night, no less - I realized my only salvation lay in finding the park's security guard.

I moved away from the house, fully intent on dashing right, across the grass, through the parking lot, down the hill, and to the entrance gate.

I heard the male abductor yell from within the cellar, "Hey, where'd you go?"

I tried to run, but my legs were still wobbly and uncooperative. My knees buckled, and I stumbled down onto my hands. I didn't care if I had to crawl, as long as I kept forward momentum.

"SHIT!" he yelled, in frustration, once he discovered I'd escaped. "Get back here!"

Hearing him, from the bowels of the cellar, fueled me. I climbed back to my feet, and somehow, ran. Being pursued by a human was far more terrifying than facing down the twisted spirits within the Briggs' home behind me.

It occurred to me, if I headed out across the grass for the parking lot, I would be out in the open. My abductor would see me, and there was no question about it, I would never be able to outrun him.

Instinctively, I veered to the left, heading for the same embankment we'd fled to before, when hiding from the security guard.

I ran blind under the shadowed canopy of the trees, and knew I was headed for the cliff's edge. I hoped I would spot it before I fell over.

"Where'd you go?" he yelled into the night.

He was out of the cellar.

Staring ahead, thankfully I saw the darkness thicken, like a wall. The drop-off was close. I knew the dense forest was just beyond, and I could hide! Screeching to a halt, I dropped down on all fours, feeling along the ground for the edge.

Maybe I can just hide here.

All night though?

No, I've got to get help.

I decided to follow the edge to the right, in the direction of the path leading down to the tracks. From there I could run towards the zoo.

Memories of Chris and I, huddled down below on a ledge, popped into my mind. I used that memory like a map, to imagine the terrain in daylight, and guide me to the path.

"Come out, come out wherever you are!"

He was taunting me - getting closer.

Dropping down to my stomach, my heart pounding out of my chest, I held still and waited. If he was close, I couldn't tell. Maybe he couldn't either.

What does he want with me?

Closing my eyes, I tried to even my breathing, and focus my mind. I thought, maybe, if Russell was somewhere close, we could communicate.

Russell? Russell, can you hear me?

I waited… willing a response, but nothing came.

I tried again, with more force, more intent. I thought of Rose and Aileen's sweet faces and the connection we had, sending out thoughts to them as well.

Can anyone hear me?

The only response was that of heavy footsteps crunching in the dirt somewhere back near the house.

Looking back, I could see the beam of a flashlight panning back and forth. I also saw a flickering light coming from inside the house. I quickly searched my memory… the library, above the cellar.

Is that fire?

"Gwen? Oh, Gweeeennnn? I know you're out here! It's only a matter of time before I find you. And if I don't… she will!"

She? She, who?

"We're not done with you yet!"

Please, please… Rose, Aileen, Russell… Brighid… someone, please hear me!

"Oh, I hear you loud and clear, Gwen. Don't you worry, I'll be there soon enough."

Not quite the friendly response I was hoping for.

Who is this?

The footsteps, and the beam of his flashlight, got closer. I had to move, and I only had two options: over the edge and hope not to fall, or run its length until I found the path to the tracks.

Run.

I stood up and began to run as fast as my shivering cold body was able.

Once I cleared the shadow of the trees, it was easier to see the ground in the moonlight. However, that meant, I was also easier to see.

It was worth the risk, because I knew, if I could just make it to the tracks, I could hide myself anywhere in the forest.

But, what about my mind? How do I hide my mind?

If I'm being hunted by Witches, then even my thoughts and feelings will give me away.

I fought the rising panic.

Don't think! Just run!

A cut-away between the shrubs marked the makeshift path down to the tracks. I threw myself through it and found myself sliding down the gravely incline on my butt.

The faintly lit metal railings lay ahead, heading off into the impenetrable darkness of the park forest.

Pushing myself up off the dirt, winded, and ignoring the painful bruising of my tailbone, I stepped over the rail onto the ties, and jogged in the direction of the zoo.

Concentrating on moving as quickly as I could, without stumbling across the gaps between the heavy timbers, I assured myself that there would be security on duty roaming the zoo grounds. All I had to do was find someone, and then I could get home safely.

A beam of light hitting the tops of the trees above me forced me to quicken my pace.

Hurry, damnit!

Get to the zoo. Find someone. Get to a phone.

I repeated this mantra over and over again with each stride to help me focus on my steps and regulate my breathing.

I felt I was making progress until…

"Good to know."

Startled, I stopped dead. Breathing heavily, I hunched down in the darkness, making myself as small as possible.

No. No. No.

I tried to recall how Russell described the mental fortress he constructed in his mind, to protect himself when going into social settings.

I got my breathing under control, as I closed my eyes trying to visualize…

Walls… like castle walls.

No! Taller than that. A tower. One that no one can use a ladder to climb over.

A metal tower - not wood. Indestructible.

One that no battering ram can break through! No fire can burn it down!

Behind the walls of the tower, build a metal room.

Go inside the room. Shut the metal door behind yourself.
LOCK IT!
Stay small. Stay hidden. Stay quiet. Stay safe.

I inhaled deeply, exhaled slowly, and then opened my eyes. I felt empowered.

Allowing only the image of the metal room in my mind, my body rose and continued running.

Chapter Twenty-Eight
Predators Come out at Night

A bellowing off in the distance echoed through the dark night. It might have struck fear into many a heart, but to me it sounded like a choir of angels.

The elephants.

As I tumbled out of the forest, the tracks forked off to either side of the exhibit. Exterior lamps glowed above the doors of all the outbuildings, where I assumed they housed food and supplies for the elephants.

I had no idea if the doors would be locked, nor if there'd be phones inside. But, I also didn't feel comfortable leaving the tracks. If I stayed on them, I had to choose which track to follow. Either route skirted the exterior of the grounds and met up at the train station in the center of the zoo.

Stick to the tracks.

Don't think. Just go.

I chose the right, slowing down to a walk, feeling as if I might drop from exhaustion at any moment.

Don't stop.

From my memories of this route, I knew it meandered behind the Sun Bear exhibit and circled round the Polar

Bear building, before heading straight into the heart of the zoo.

Keep going.

A loud lion growl reverberated and echoed out into the night. They were usually taking a nap whenever I'd visited during day hours, and always appeared so cute. Hearing those sounds at night though, reminded me just how dangerous a predator they were.

I thought about how bad it would suck to be out in the open, hear that sound coming from behind the tall grasses of the Savannah, not being able to see where the sound came from, but knowing full well they could see *you*… and outrun you.

What if the witches have eyes on me right now?

Stop it. Stop it.

Metal room. Focus. Metal room. Tall metal fortress.

Stay quiet. Stay safe.

A railroad crossing sign was just ahead, where the tracks crossed over a frontage road. I visualized the zoo layout, coming to realize that I could detour onto it and head straight for the food court.

Renewed hope gave me another burst of energy, and I began to run again, following the road into the heart of the zoo. Thankfully, with light coming from various sources I was able to navigate my surroundings easily.

To my left, in the food court, there was no sign of activity. To my right, beyond all the cat exhibits, lay the train station, another food court, the administration buildings, and the exit.

I chose that direction and picked up my pace.

Metal room. Metal room.

Tall metal fortress.

Nothing can penetrate.

I hit a small incline, and slowed to a walk, wearily making my way past the cougars and leopards. When I rounded the corner to the lion exhibit, I saw a flashlight beam pan by in the distance.

A security guard!

"Oh, thank God!" I exhaled. Rallying every last store of energy I could muster, I started to jog.

"Hey!" I yelled, as I got closer. "I need help!"

The flashlight stopped.

"Help!" I yelled again. I cut the distance between us in half before alarm sirens went off in my head.

Something was wrong. I stopped.

The flashlight hadn't moved, and no one responded.

I started to back pedal, again trying to picture the zoo map in my head - searching for some place safe to hide.

"You really didn't think you would get away that easy, did you?" my pursuer called out.

How? Just... how?

"I did tell you if *I* couldn't find you, *she* could!" he continued to taunt.

Who is she?

"Now there's nowhere left to go. It's a dead end," he laughed. "Dead. End. Get it? Because that's how this ends!"

"Ugh, will you just shut up already?"

*So, **this** was the she... I know that voice, but...*

"Let me handle her."

No... No! It can't be!

"Yes, it can. Now be a good girl and stop running. I've got work to do."

"Ciara," I whispered in disbelief, still backing away and staring at the flashlight, afraid to lose track of where they were.

Suddenly, it bobbed and danced, then resumed moving forward.

I stopped thinking. It was fight or flight. So I flew.

My muscle memory from years of walking those paths led me onward.

As I sped along, huffing and puffing with the effort, I started to visualize myself in a suit of armor, powered by the talisman that Brighid had given me. I said her name over and over again, thinking of nothing but her warm hug filling my heart with light. I remembered Russell's words about how Brighid and Judith had both sensed the "old blood" running through my veins, and how I was more powerful than I realized.

Brighid, guide me!

I felt a small ember of warmth spark to life deep in my core. The more I concentrated on her, the brighter it flared, pulsed, and expanded. I remembered the lightness of being I'd felt after the cleansing ritual. I remembered feeling complete.

The inner warmth continued to spread. I no longer felt the cold of the night.

I imagined this new warmth as a light, getting brighter by the second. I imagined letting the light free of my body, shooting up into the air like a signal flare.

Brighid, protect me!

I came, skidding to a halt, at my destination, exhausted, gasping for air. With no time to waste, I searched around frantically, until I found a large rock in the landscaping, and threw it through the glass door. It exploded inward! The sound of cascading glass practically screamed into the still air, "Here I am!"

Leaping through the ragged doorway, I grabbed the rock and pushed my way through a curtain of heavy cloth strips used to keep the exhibit occupants from escaping.

The temperature inside jumped at least 50 degrees and the smell was overpowering.

Gross… warm bird piss!

Between the breaking glass and my sudden intrusion of their sanctuary, a cacophony of terrified birds screeched and whizzed about the large glass-domed enclosure.

Instinctively I placed my hands over my head, as their darting and swooping silhouettes were visible against the moonlit glow overhead. I did my best to send out only calm, positive energy.

Sure enough, the fluttering settled down, and within a few minutes the dome fell silent. Flock managed, I quickly found what I'd come for - the ladder I'd always noticed through the upstairs restaurant windows. Time and time again, I wondered why there was a permanent metal ladder attached to the wall. Eventually, it occurred to me that so many of these birds stayed up on the highest branches, it just made sense for the keepers to have a means to reach their roosts.

The climb was awkward at first, until I put the rock down the back of my pants, freeing up both hands.

At the top, there was nothing to hold on to, so I couldn't stand on that highest rung, and I couldn't reach the window. I tried moving a few rungs down, but that didn't help either. There was simply too much space between the ladder and the window. I couldn't reach the rock to the glass, let alone harness enough power to break the glass, especially at that angle - I was just too short.

Glancing around, an idea struck me. I could climb up the branches and get a foothold there.

I drew a few long, slow breaths, gathered my courage, and leaned out, away from the ladder. With one hand on the top rung, and one foot on the third rung down, I got hold of a strong branch, and let go of the ladder with my other hand. With that shift over, my heart skipped a beat. I steadied myself, and then continued.

An annoyed ruffle of feathers greeted me as I pulled myself up and over, until I was seated on the branch.

"Sorry, Mr. or Mrs. Bird. I didn't mean to wake you," I whispered.

Cautiously, I rose, testing my balance - all good. Reaching around, I pulled the rock out from the back of my waistband, and gingerly stepped forward until I was flush with the wall again.

I turned sideways, and swung the rock with all my strength, towards the glass. It didn't break.

The impact merely caused the rock to bounce back. The shock of which reverberated through the bones in my arm and shoulder, nearly pitching me off the branch

I gasped, heart in my throat, forced myself to calm.

Don't think about falling. Don't think about falling.

"You can do this," I whispered to myself.

A quiet squawk and ruffle of feathers urged me on.

"Thanks for your vote of encouragement," I whispered.

I took my stance again, bringing back my right arm, and this time focusing my intention on the rock - visualizing the desired outcome. I took another deep breath, and threw every ounce of my strength behind the swing.

This time when it connected, the glass cracked. It didn't shatter, but there was a weak point. I hit it again, and again. Finally, on the third hit, the entire pane completely shattered. I threw myself backward, almost landing on the bird. Hanging on for dear life, I hoped the branch would hold me. It was, after all, a long way down to the cement flooring below.

The sound of breaking glass echoed through the entire dome, as shards cascaded dangerously down through the branches.

The whole place erupted in screeching, fluttering and flapping again, as terrified birds zipped and whirled about in panic and confusion.

I hope I didn't hurt any of them.

I closed my eyes and held tight, imploring the birds to calm down.

Relax, guys… It's okay… Just relax.

One by one, the frazzled denizens of the aviary found their way back to their roosts and settled down.

Carefully, I stood back up and steadied my weight on the branch. I eased my hands out to the window frame in front of me, avoiding the ragged edges of glass still clinging to it.

Standing on my tippy-toes, I could just see the interior of the small restaurant, lit only by its emergency lighting. The sound of the breaking glass, and the ensuing bird panic, had thankfully gone unnoticed.

Using the rock, I brushed away the remaining shards of glass and prepared to hoist myself up.

Where's my break-in gang when I need them? Kevin would especially come in handy right now.

Hanging by my arms, I scampered my feet up the wall, until I could pull by torso up through the newly opened window. Finally, inside, I picked my way through the empty dining room, and crossed the tiled lobby towards the kitchen searching for a phone.

The thought of calling for help gave me hope. The thought of the kitchen made my stomach grumble.

When was the last time I ate?

I walked around the cash register mounted atop the service counter and made my way into kitchen. The smell was one of all-things-fried. I could taste the burnt oil on the tip of my tongue. I lost my appetite, but I found a wall phone.

Picking up the receiver from its cradle, I brought it up to my ear, and pressed the numbers to my home phone. Nothing happened.

I pushed disconnect and tried again. Nothing. I could hear a ring tone, but it wasn't acknowledging the numbers I dialed.

"Damnit!" I smashed the phone back onto its cradle.

I moved from behind the counter to the main lobby. The exit sign, above the double glass doors, illuminated a series of souvenir racks. In one of them, I saw the perfect solution to help navigate the rest of the dark building in search of an office. Packages of plastic faces lined up in rows, each one a different zoo animal. Within each package was also a small children's flashlight meant to illuminate the included face. It worked like a portable nightlight, or a kid friendly lamp for camping. Something for them to use so as not to be afraid of the dark.

Grabbing the nearest one, which happened to be a monkey, I pulled apart the packaging, and checked to see if the batteries in the light worked.

"Oh, thank goodness," I sighed, as the light, sans monkey face, lit up the lobby floor. Keeping the light low, to not be seen through the windows, I made my way back to the kitchen. I made my way across wide panels of rubber flooring, panning the light along the walls in search of a doorway.

The first I came to was a heavy metal door that led into a walk-in refrigerator. The next led to a giant pantry. I couldn't help myself, and grabbed a bag of Doritos from one of the shelves. Tearing it open, I scarfed down copious mouthfuls.

With chip bag in hand, I found a third door, which opened into a tiny office.

Feeling along the wall just inside the doorframe, I searched around until I found a light switch, and flipped it up.

Glorious light flooded the room.

Inside the cramped space sat a small desk and chair, a filing cabinet, a wall safe, and a telephone.

I shut the door behind me, and locked it. For the first time in what seemed like forever, I breathed a sigh of relief. Slowly cold shivers crept in. The shivers turned to tremors that quaked through me - everything hitting me at once.

In the corner, behind the door, a man's coat hung from a wall hook. I pulled it down and put it on. It was huge, and I found myself swimming in it. I wrapped it all around me, like a big blanket, and plopped down on the chair. A half-full cup of old coffee sat near the phone, and without thinking, I chugged it, washing down the last of the Doritos.

I turned my attention to the phone.

Picking up the receiver, I listened for the dial tone, and then began to push the numbers for my home phone, just as I had before.

Again, no response.

"What IN THE HELL am I doing wrong?" I screamed, beating my fists against the desk.

I glanced around, searching for an answer, when I noticed a small card tucked under a square of cracked yellowed plastic in the center of the phone itself. It read: *Push 9 to dial out.*

"OH MY GOD!" I yelled, in frustration.

I angrily hit the 9-button then dialed the rest of my home number.

It rang.

"Hello?" my dad answered immediately, panic and worry in his voice.

"Dad! I need help."

Chapter Twenty-Nine
Never a Night So Long

Gwen! Where the hell have you been? We've been calling everywhere looking for you!" he yelled. "*All* damned day!"

"Dad, please don't be angry right now. I just need your help. I'm at the zoo..."

"The Zoo? What the hell are you doing there?" he interrupted.

"... in the restaurant above the aviary. Please call the police!"

"What's happened?"

"I was taken..."

"Taken? Like the other girls?" he interrupted. "By who? Are they there now? Jesus, Gwen!"

"Dad! Calm down, I'm safe for right now, but I don't know for how long."

"Are you hurt?"

"I'm okay. Dad, listen, write this number down. It's the number here at the Avian Eatery," I reiterated. "I'm in the restaurant office." I read the numbers slowly to him. "Got it?"

"Yeah, got it!"

"Hurry, please!"

"Okay, kiddo, you hold tight. I'll call the police, then I'll call you right back."

"Dad, wait…"

"Yeah?"

"The people who took me are *here* in the zoo looking for me. And… and I *know* who they are!"

"You do?" he gasped. "Who?"

"It's Russell's sister, Ciara, and her boyfriend, Toby. He's the son of the people who run MacGregor's Farm. That's where I was taken from."

"To where?"

"To the old Victorian house in the park. You know the one that was on the news this summer? Where they found those bodies?"

"Yes, of course I know that place. But… wait," he stammered, "Russell's sister? MacGregor's Farm? What in the hell were you even doing way out there?"

"I was with Russell…"

"God damnit, Gwen! When are you ever going to learn?" he yelled.

Tears started to fall.

"Do you know if he's okay?" I asked. "Have you heard from him?"

I tried to weep quietly, but it was impossible.

"Okay… okay. Sorry. I'm just glad you're okay. Sit tight. I'll call you right back."

"But, is he…"

Click.

Beep. Beep. Beep.

…okay?"

The sobs came in uncontrollable waves.

A couple of minutes later, after I'd completely exhausted myself crying, the phone rang out. I jumped – so loud for such a small room – and quickly scooped up the receiver.

"Hello?" I answered, wiping my nose off on the coat sleeve,

"It's me, honey. How're you doing?" my dad asked, no longer angry - just concerned.

"I'm wrecked," I admitted. "I hurt all over… I'm freezing… I just want to come home!"

"Someone will be there soon."

"And you told them who took me?"

"I did, and I assured them I'd stay on the phone with you until they arrived."

"Where's mom?"

"Out looking for you! She said she was going to drive around to all your friends' houses. We were afraid you'd run away, or worse, that you'd been…" he stopped, catching himself. I heard him clear his throat.

Is he crying?

"Well, anyways," he continued, pulling himself together, "Help's on the way. We'll get you home, don't you worry."

I noticed the time on the clock above the filing cabinet, and only then realized how long I'd been gone.

"Dad, is it really 2 in the morning?"

"Yeah, it really is."

"So that makes today Monday, the 30th?"

"It does…"

We sat in silence for a few moments, until he prodded me gently, "What was the last thing you remember before you woke up in that house?" I could hear hesitation in his voice, needing to know what happened to his little girl, but terrified to know for certain. In that short moment of hesitation, I understood his pain.

"It was mid-day at the farm. Russell and I found a Christmas tree, and he cut it down. We were going to get some hot chocolate before heading home, and I got distracted with some farm animals. Then…"

I heard his breath catch in his throat. "Gwen, that was *fourteen* hours ago."

"I think they injected me with something, and I blacked out. Russell was… oh my god… dad, have you heard from him?"

"No, honey. I haven't."

"Can you call his house? Let them know where I last saw him. Have the police check the farm!"

"Now hold on! Hold on. Okay, I know you're worried, but *you're* my priority, and I'm not getting off the phone with you until I know the police are there."

"No, dad, please! Please, call his house. Check on him!"

A silence stretched between us again as he struggled with his instincts.

"You *sure* you're safe?"

"I've locked myself in. I'm fine!"

He sighed softly then, "Okay. But then I'm calling right back! *Don't* open the door for anyone but the police. Do you hear me?"

"Yes, I hear you. I promise… thank you."

Click.

Beep. Beep. Beep.

I sat quietly, staring at the phone, urging it to ring again with news that Russell was okay.

Suddenly, I heard the clacking of footsteps on tile, and voices echo out in the lobby.

I glanced back at the clock… my heart sped up.

It's too soon for the police. Zoo security?

The footsteps became more muted as they walked across the rubber flooring in the kitchen. They were getting close.

Warning lights and alarm bells went off in my head.

I rose from the chair quietly and stepped away from the desk.

The sound of footsteps came closer, approaching the office door.

I tucked into the corner between the filing cabinet and the desk, crouched down, and wrapped the large coat around me.

They stopped outside the door.

Shink. Shink. Shink.

The doorknob rattled back and forth.

Knock. Knock. Knock.

I held my breath. Remained motionless. Foolishly hoping they wouldn't know I was there. But the bright office lights were a dead giveaway to anyone on the other side of that door.

Shink. Shink. Shink.

Knock. Knock. Knock.

"Gweeeeen... we know you're in there. Do you want to do this the easy way, or the hard way?"

NOT the zoo security!

I didn't know if I should yell at them to go away, tell them I'd called the police, or remain quiet and hope...

Oh, shit. She can probably hear me thinking.

It's impossible for you to stay quiet! You're a loud thinker!

"GO AWAY!" I screamed.

Shink. Shink. Shink.

I stared at the door, trying to assess the lock situation. It appeared sturdy enough. However, with Ciara on the other side, what could prevent her from just using her mind to either unlock the door, or just explode it into splinters.

Anything was possible... and that made it terrifying.

I hunkered down.

Suddenly the phone rang, nearly sending me into a seizure.

I stood up, quickly yanking the phone off its cradle, "Dad! Dad! They're right outside the door!" I exclaimed. "Why aren't the police here yet?"

"Okay, that's *ENOUGH!*" Ciara yelled from the other side of the door, and in a cloud of splinters and dust burst inward. She stood in the threshold, glaring through the raining debris. "Play time's over!"

"Gwen!" my father screamed through the receiver. "What was that?"

Ciara entered the room.

"Dad!" I screamed back into the phone.

Toby slinked in behind her and reached over the desk at me.

I threw myself back into the corner - phone still to my ear.

He seized my hand, snatching the phone away from my head, and pulled the cord from the wall.

He began dragging me across the desk.

"No!" I yelled. "Get away from me!" I bucked, trying to free myself from his grasp.

Ciara produced a syringe and slithered around him, preparing to inject me again. I screamed, struggling against Toby as he tried to hold me still. I managed to free one arm long enough to swat the hand with the syringe in it away.

In my growing panic, I felt that spark of kinetic energy begin to swell. I recognized it now, knew its form, and knew what it could do.

As Ciara lunged towards me again, I visualized it already full of fire, bursting at the seams, ready to explode.

She hesitated and looked at me curiously.

I screamed then, forcing all my energy outward, wanting them as far away from me as possible.

A low whoosh erupted and with shocked expressions, Ciara and Toby flew back, slamming against the farthest wall, and then dropping to the floor.

For a brief moment, the only sound was my heartbeat pulsing madly in my ears as I watched a flutter of falling papers light atop my two would-be captors lying in a motionless heap.

When I rushed past them, their eyes were closed.

I quickly shrugged off the bulky coat as I ran through the dark kitchen, across the lobby, through the exit doors, and fled out into the night.

Holy crap! I just did that.

I pictured Ciara and Toby, eyes wide in disbelief as they flew through the air, hitting the wall.

Holy crap!

I ran down a cement ramp from the restaurant, past the animal show stage and across a wide lawn. I headed to the far end where I knew I could pass over that set of tracks and hop the fence. From there I could make my way through the forest, to the on-ramp from the zoo and then to the highway.

Surely, someone on the highway will stop to help.

Gwen? It's Russell, we're here now. Where are you?

Oh my god! Russell?

I slowed down. I didn't know if I could trust voices in my head or not anymore.

How do I know this is actually Russell? I asked.

I ran to the nearest tree and hid behind it.

Tell me where you are.

I peeked around the tree and peered across the lawn to see if Ciara and Toby had come out of the restaurant yet. If I didn't get out of the park and to the freeway, quick, I'd lose my chance of escape. I couldn't trust this voice wasn't just another of Ciara's tricks.

How do I know this is Russell? I asked again.

Ask me something.

I couldn't risk it. I peeled away from the tree and continued running for the zoo perimeter where I'd attempt to jump the fence.

As me something, the voice implored.

How do I know this isn't a trick? I asked as I scrambled across the tracks and leaped up onto the tall chain-link fence.

Try me.

Huffing and puffing, fingers straining, I made it to the top, swung over and dropped to the other side. There was more of an incline than I'd expected, and I tumbled down into some shrubs. Branches pulled and poked through my shirt, puncturing my skin.

I sat up, wiped the mud, twigs, and leaves off my body and out of my hair. Finally, I thought of the perfect question.

What did we keep doing, in the car ride to the dance, which we promised never to do again?

Easy! he answered immediately. *Apologize!*

RUSSELL! It is you!

I sighed with relief, and felt a welcome warmth fill in all the dark places. However, I couldn't risk stopping. Since Ciara could read my mind, like Russell was doing, she'd find me when she woke up.

I clambered to my feet and began picking my way through the bramble, heading down the hill towards the highway.

Where are you? I asked.

> *Just outside the main gate, by the train station. Where are you?*

I desperately wanted to tell him, but I knew I just couldn't.

I can't tell you.

I picked up a stick, and started hacking my way through the undergrowth, just like Kevin once did.

> *How am I supposed to help you?* he asked.

Glancing back, one last time, just to make sure no one was following, I noticed a plume of smoke against the moonlit sky, rising from the hilltop.

I gasped.

The house!

> *What about the house?*

It's on fire!

> *I can see it from here!*

Russell... I hate to have to tell you this, but it's Ciara! Ciara and Toby are the ones that did this.

Silence.

And if I tell you...

> *She'll know!* Russell responded, finishing my thought. *Ciara... shit!*

She's been inside of my head... tracking me!

> *Where is she right now?*

Hopefully still unconscious, in the Avian Eatery back office. Toby's with her.

Unconscious?

Long story… no time!"

Okay, stay safe! he replied. *You know where I am.*

I plan on it! I asserted, as I plunged headlong into the darkness of the forest, slashing my way down the hill, listening for the sounds of cars.

Chapter Thirty
Red light, Blue light

At first, I heard the wail of police sirens from off to my right, so I veered in that direction. This was followed by the whine and weal of a fire engine, rising and falling as it continued up the freeway.

Probably headed for the house.

Following the sound of the police sirens took me horizontally through the forest, back towards the zoo entrance, instead of further down the hill to the highway itself. I didn't care, though, as long as I could find a person of authority I could trust.

As I trudged through the dense undergrowth, I noticed the flash of colored lights blinking through gaps between trees.

The closer I got, the more police cruisers I heard leaving the highway. They each silenced their sirens once parked, but kept their lights flashing. The blue and red beacons kept me on course.

As I neared, I could hear the chatter of walkie-talkies discussing a fire up at the Victorian house, and that there had been no sighting of the missing girl yet.

I'm right here!

I pressed even harder making my way to the edge of the forest, shivering uncontrollably.

Peering out, I saw a group of people gathered on the sidewalk, just outside the zoo entrance, and immediately recognized my mother.

"MOM!" I yelled, as I pushed through the last of the shrubs and onto the sidewalk. I waved my arms back and forth, hopping up and down. "MOM!"

I saw her head swivel around at the sound of my voice, but she didn't see me at first.

"MOM!" I screamed louder, trying to push through the exhaustion, and will my legs to keep moving. It wasn't much of a hill, but after the day I'd had, I didn't think I could make it much further.

"Gwen?" I heard her yell out. It seemed as if she'd tuned into my voice and narrowed down her visual search. I saw her yanking on the nearest officer's sleeve and pointing down the hill towards me.

Can they see me?

"Gwen?" This time it was Russell. I saw him push through the group facing my direction, scanning. He then leaned forward and sprinted in my direction.

I dropped to my knees, barely able to move. Tears of relief streamed down my face. I could barely speak. The tremors were uncontrollable.

Russell. I'm here!

"I'm coming!" he yelled - then only a couple strides away.

I could see my mother jogging down the hill towards me as well. She was moving faster than I'd ever seen her move before.

Russell bent down mid-stride and scooped me into his arms as if he were saving me from quicksand. Once in his arms, I held on for dear life, and sobbed against his shoulder. He slowed, turned, and began carrying me up the hill, the whole while whispering repeatedly in my ear, "I got you! I love you so much! I was so worried!"

"Gwen, thank goodness you're alright!" my mom exclaimed as she met us halfway up. "Are you hurt? Take her up to the police car so someone can make sure she's okay. Oh my. Oh my."

I couldn't remember her ever fretting over me like that before.

She put her hand on my back, trailing Russell and I as he carried me up the hill, gently rubbing it, and whispering to herself, more than to me, "You'll be okay. You'll be okay."

"Young man, you can put her in the back seat of the nearest cruiser," the police officer waved us forward, motioning towards the open door. "Here, we have a couple blankets you can wrap around her." He handed those to my mom, and she wrapped them around my shoulders.

Russell bent over, allowing me to scoot out of his embrace into the narrow space of the back seat. The interior was heated, which, along with the blankets, came as a welcome relief. However, the tremors didn't stop, and my teeth were chattering.

Russell slowly started to back away.

"NO!" I screamed, startling everyone around me. It was so instantly reactive, that I didn't really understand where the outburst came from. I just knew that I couldn't bear him letting go of me or leaving my sight.

He nodded his understanding and slid into the back seat beside me - his tall legs barely able to squeeze into the cramped space behind the front seat. He wound up turning sideways, hanging one leg out the door.

"Gwen, honey," my mom said, "It's okay, we're not going anywhere."

"Does dad know I'm okay?"

"I tried to get a hold of him before we left to come here, but the line was busy! The dispatcher is trying to get through to him right now. They'll let him know you're safe!" my mom assured. "Okay, just sit tight. The police just need you to stay in the car while they continue to search the park for Ciara and Toby."

"What?" Russell gasped. "Still?"

She nodded and continued, "You said they were in the office behind the Avian Eatery, right?"

"Yes," I quivered.

"They aren't there?" Russell asked.

"I don't know what's going on yet. Let me see what I can find out." She hustled off and peppered the clutch of officers with rapid-fire questions.

"Russell, what happened to you?" I mumbled, willing my jaw to stop trembling.

"I want to know the same thing about you," he answered. "Are you really okay? Are you hurt?"

"I have cuts and bruises all over. Muscles hurt, that I didn't even know I had. I have a pounding migraine… and I'm still terrified. No, I don't think I'm okay."

Making sure the blankets were wrapped tightly around my torso, he pulled me into his arms, and scooted a little further onto the seat. "Well, I'm *way* better now that I at least know you're safe, and in my arms. I don't know what I'd have done if something happened to you."

"She's your sister," I mumbled.

Russell visibly winced, before his face darkened. "I don't know *who* she is anymore," he replied coldly.

"*Why* would she do this? How could she have *killed* those girls?"

"My mom thinks she understands now what's been going on. That's why she and Judith went into the park before the police got here. I stayed behind with your mother."

"You came here *with* my mom?"

He nodded slowly, glancing out at my mom yammering from officer to another, and then turned back, "I'd just gotten home, after escaping the barn, when she showed up. She was distraught. Kept insisting she knew something bad had happened to you. My mom took over then and led her downstairs. When they came back up, your mom… well, something had changed. I mean, like *really* changed. Her energy… everything! She wasn't the same woman who came to the door, let's just put it that way."

"What happened downstairs?"

"Enlightenment," he responded. "She either learned about the old blood, and who she really is, or maybe she confessed what she already knew."

"That's what I've been wondering…"

"Look," he gently clutched my shoulders, "I know it's weighing pretty heavily on you, but tonight we've got bigger problems to deal with."

I nodded, fully understanding his point.

"If Brighid brought Judith for backup, that must mean she felt Ciara would be a pretty big problem."

"Yes… *especially* because of her motivations!"

"Wha-"

"Sir, I'm going to have to ask you to get out of the car." The officer motioned towards the new arrival. "The ambulance is here now, and they're going to need examine Miss Evans to evaluate whether she needs to go to the hospital or not."

"Oh, okay… um, can I go with her?" Russell asked, as he gently pushed me upright, and slid off the bench seat. I grabbed the back of his jacket, and he stopped, looking back.

"It's okay. I got you." He held my hand while he stood up, and then gently pulled me across the seat towards him. "I'm not going anywhere." He reminded me.

I heard the police remark to someone as we walked away, "The girl is clearly in shock. I wonder what they did to her!"

The EMT approached, offering to lead me the rest of the way. He took my hand, and I felt a painful shock. I recoiled back in surprise, a spike of fear coursing through me.

"No! No!" I backed away from him, pulling Russell along with me. For a split second, I had relived the moment Toby reached across the desk and pulled me from the corner.

The EMT stepped away, trying to not upset me any further, and indicated that Russell could escort me the rest of the way.

As we approached, the flashing red lights started making my migraine scream even louder.

The sounds of the walkie-talkies screeching became unbearable.

Everything became a whirling haze - a strange and surreal dreamscape.

It was like I was watching time unfold from a distance.

What's wrong with me?

"If you could just sit her on the gurney, I'll get her vitals."

Russell helped steady me as I stepped into the van. He climbed in behind, helped turn me around, as if I were brain dead, and sat me down on the gurney, as requested.

He took a seat across from me, and held my hand.

Everything moved in slow motion. Colors morphed into strange shapes.

"See, I'm right here," Russell said slowly, as if soothing a child. "I didn't go anywhere."

What's happening to me?

"Sir, can you step out of the van. I'm going to need to get in there and have room to maneuver."

"Um… well…"

What's happening to me?

"Gwen!" I heard Russell yell.

What? Why are you yelling? I'm right here.

"Sir, I'm going to need to get in there, now. I need you to step out of the van."

"What did you do to her? You touched her. I saw you touch her. What did you give her? What did you do?"

"Hey, man. I don't know what you're talking about…"

"Get away from her!" Russell yelled. "POLICE!"

What…

"I need the police. There's an EMERGENCY!" he yelled again.

… is

"Get away from her! I *swear*, if you take one step closer, you *will* regret it!"

… happening?

Chapter Thirty-One
It's Still 1982

I was watching an episode of the soap opera, General Hospital. A nurse character I didn't recognize was taking a patient's blood pressure. The rhythm of the heartbeat sounded out from a machine near the patient's bed. There was an IV drip hanging with the tube leading down into the patient's arm.

I took in the faces of the other characters in the room and didn't recognize any of them from the series.

"Do you think she can hear us?" the teenage girl that was sitting at the patient's bedside asked.

I couldn't see the actor's face - her back was to the camera – but her voice did sound familiar.

"We believe she can," the doctor answered. "Her brain waves and heartbeat have responded to certain questions, as well as to certain people's voices. Go ahead, ask her something."

They must be introducing a new plot line, I thought. *These are **all** new characters. The main actors should be coming into the scene soon.*

"Gwen? If you can hear me, it's Andrea."

Andrea?

The voice definitely sounded familiar. However, the actress didn't turn around to reveal to the audience who she was.

I wish the camera would change angles!

"We missed you at the Christmas party. It was so much fun. You know how Mom is... she decorated the whole place like a showroom or something. Of course, the teenagers were exiled to the game room, but we still had fun. Ryan played a great host. My parents adore him. Oh, and you'll never guess who showed up... Erin! I couldn't believe it. She brought Russell's friend, Erik. I don't know what she sees in him. He even hit on *me* at the party. Can you believe it?" She shook her head, her back still to the camera.

Turn around, would you?

"Ryan put him in his place, though! Erin, of course was totally offended, being a complete... you know what. They left early, which was a good thing. We all meandered upstairs eventually though, with my parents' friends. By the end of the night, we were doing the twist to some classic Christmas rock. *You* would have loved it! I really wish you could have been there."

I wonder what happened to this Gwen person she's talking to?

"Can you hear me, Gwen? I miss you. I'd really love it if you could open your eyes."

Why can't the patient open her eyes?

I couldn't quite make out the patient's face from the angle of the camera positioned high off to the right.

I saw the patient twitch though.

"That's it, Gwen. You *can* hear me, can't you? It's Andrea. Open your eyes."

*Andrea? I don't recognize that name. And who the heck is Gwen? She **definitely** must be a new cast member.*

"Is she actually moving?" another familiar voice called out from the hallway. I saw a tall attractive young man enter the frame through the open door. There were other somewhat familiar people, gathered out behind him in the hallway, but I couldn't quite place what show I'd seen them on.

The doctor leaned over, opened the patient's eyelid, and shined a small flashlight into her eye.

An intense flash of light stabbed my brain.

Hey! Ouch.

Not cool! Dang… that was weird.

"There's a pupil response! Miss, go get her mom and dad!" the doctor exclaimed excitedly.

Andrea stopped in front of the tall young man and chirped, "She moved!" He let out a huge sigh of relief and stepped aside to let Andrea out into the hall. She spoke with an older couple, and then pointed back towards the room.

Why do they look so familiar?

The pair entered the room and stood in the same spot Andrea had occupied before. The woman grabbed the patient's hand expectantly, waiting for something to happen.

"Gwen. It's Mom and Dad. We're right here! We all love you so much, honey!"

*Mom and Dad? **My** Mom and Dad?*

"Russell's here too! He hasn't left your side!"

Russell?

The tall young man approached and joined them at the side of the bed. "Please wake up!"

He turned to the doctor, "If she can hear us, why won't she wake up?"

Wake up? So, the patient is just asleep, refusing to wake up? What a stupid plot. Do you want to know how to wake up? All you need to do...

A flash of light stabbed my brain again!

is just...

"Gwen. That's it!"

...open your eyes.

Even more light, and even more intense stabbing.

Why is it so bright?

Ugh, it's making me sick. I'm going to throw up.

Please turn off the lights!

"Doctor! Can you please turn off the lights? It's hurting her."

"Young man, how could you possibly know that?"

"JUST DO IT!" a chorus of voices screamed from the hallway.

I tried to open my eyes again.

This time the room was darker, and I was able to keep them open, albeit squinting, long enough to adjust my sight. Everything was blurry. It was like trying to see through oily water.

I closed my eyes again, wishing for all the loud noises to stop.

Why is it so loud?

Too much beeping! Too much clinking and clanking! I just wanted to go back to watching the show. Make it all go away.

"Gwen? Gwen, it's Russell."

Russell?

I felt pressure on my hand as someone's fingers interlaced with mine. I could feel the texture of rough skin against my fingertips.

"I know it feels too loud," he stated. "And I know it feels too bright, but it won't feel like that if you just give it a little time. Trust me. Just open your eyes and look over at me."

A sensation, his thumb rubbing the back of my hand, drew me further towards consciousness. I *wanted* to see his face.

I slowly opened my eyes again, turning my head to his voice, squinting against the light.

This time, it didn't hurt as much, so I let them stay open long enough for the oily water to dissipate, and my vision to clear.

I no longer felt like a spectator, hovering over my body. My surroundings grew real... solid... less ethereal.

The tall, attractive young man was staring back at me, smiling. "Hiya," he sighed lovingly. "There you are."

He looks so familiar. I know him from somewhere.

His smile faded, and a shadow of concern crossed his face. He glanced aside and spoke to someone, "What's wrong? Can she see okay?"

"Well, let me give her a once over. See how she responds."

A man dressed in a plain white coat came into view and shone a small flashlight into each of my eyes, causing sharp pangs in my head.

I shut them tight, wincing, and turned away.

Don't do that anymore!

"Great pupil response. She can definitely see. Gwen, can you wiggle your fingers for me?"

Wiggle, that's a silly word.

Fingers… fingers.

"Good. Good. Okay now, how about you wiggle your toes for me?"

I thought about my toes.

"Wonderful job. Would you like me to adjust the bed so you can sit up a little? I'll do it slow. It will feel strange, at first, as the blood pumps back to your head. You might feel dizzy. Just let me know if you want to stop."

The sound of a motor purred beneath me, and the view began to change. The head of the bed lifted, leaning me forward a little. I did start to feel dizzy, and wanted him to stop.

Okay, you can stop now. That's far enough.

"Tell me if you need me to stop."

I just did. I need you to stop!

"Stop! She needs you to stop!" the young man exclaimed.

"I didn't hear her say anything."

"*I* did!"

"Um, okay."

The motor quieted, and the bed ceased tilting forward. I relaxed.

"I don't think she can speak," the young man declared, a definite sound of concern in his voice.

I can talk just fine! Can't you hear me?

"Well, she *was* intubated for a long time. Maybe her throat is too dry, or it hurts. She'll find her voice again. We just need to give her time."

What does intubated mean?

The young man, with a dejected look on his face, stepped aside for the older couple to take his place. "You're doing great, Gwen," the older man said. "Tomorrow you'll be better than new."

"Maybe we should bring a chalk board, or a note pad," the woman proposed. "She can write notes until she feels like talking."

"That's a great idea!" he responded. "Oh, hey look who else is glad to see you up! Come on over, Cat."

Cat?

One of those familiar faces, from the hallway, appeared in front of me. "Hey, stupid. I'm sick of waiting around for you to get of bed. The concert was super awesome, by the way! Adam Ant is so hot, even Kevin enjoyed it too, didn't you?"

Kevin?

A different young man, just as tall, but with darker hair, slid into view, and leaned over. "Well, I didn't think he was hot, but the show was pretty great. Gwen, you would have loved it. I bought his newest record, so, ya know, maybe I'll let you borrow it when you get home. Heck, I'll even let you have it. Consider it a Christmas present. But you have to get out of bed before I'll give it to you."

"That's right. Get up already!" Cat insisted. "I don't think I can stand another day of seeing Russell mope around this place. He really misses you."

"We *all* miss you!" Kevin stated

"Noooo..." I heard a hoarse whisper, as my larynx muscle flexed, and air moved up and out through my throat. It hurt.

"Did she just say something?" Kevin gasped.

Cat leaned over towards my mouth, as I continued to push past the discomfort. "...you're stupid."

She laughed.

"What did she say?" Kevin asked.

"She just called me stupid!" Cat leaned back, yelling out.

Laughter erupted in the room. I hadn't been aware of so many people gathered around, and I didn't comprehend the big deal.

Memories, from bits and pieces of conversations I'd overheard, started inching their way in.

"*You're* stupid!" Cat responded, lying across my chest, hugging me tightly. "Don't you *dare* do that to me again! I thought you'd died! Do you have any idea what you've put me through?" She sat up, tears streaming down her face.

I didn't want to try and speak again, so I just smiled the best I could to let her know I was all right.

"Okay, let's clear the room now" the doctor ordered. "I can't have everyone crowding in here at once." He motioned towards the door. "Kids, can you please wait out in the hallway? Let's give her parents a chance to be alone with her."

A chorus of disapproving groans erupted.

"Sorry. I know. But it's hospital regulations - only a couple visitors at a time. You'll all get your turn."

Cat pulled herself away from me, and I watched her and Kevin leave my line of sight. I was too tired to move my head to see who else was there.

My mom and dad came back over. They'd been crying. I still didn't understand what was going on, or what had happened to me.

"Do you know where you are?" my mom asked, searching my eyes for a sign of comprehension.

I tried to swallow, to make some noise when I tried to speak again, but my throat was dry as a bone.

"Water..." I finally managed to whisper.

"Bob, quick, pour her some water. And grab her a straw, would you?" After they fussed about for a short moment, she slipped her hand behind my head and gently guided the straw to my lips. "Okay, the straw is right here... okay, got it?"

I felt it touch my lips and immediately began to suck up the cool liquid. It was an incredible sensation, coating the interior of my mouth, flowing down my throat and soothing the pain.

"Not too much!" She pulled the straw away, and I reluctantly stopped sipping. "Wow, you really must have been thirsty."

"I'm in a hospital," I finally whispered hoarsely.

"That's right. Do you remember why?"

Nothing came to me. Only fragments from the strange dream I'd been having.

The doctor swung back into view and stood behind my parents. "Welcome back. Can you tell me what year it is?"

"1982?" I asked. It was the first year that came into my mind.

"Yes. It still is, but just barely. You've been asleep for a couple weeks. Did you know that?"

"No."

A couple weeks?

He jotted some notes on his clipboard.

"What was the last thing you remember?"

Again, I tried to bring forth something – anything. It was like trying to push through impenetrable goo encasing my brain.

"Do you understand what I'm asking you?"

"Yes, but I…"

"Doctor, obviously she can't remember anything. You're upsetting her," my mother chided, holding tighter to my hand, as if that would protect me from him.

311

I focused on that sensation, and a memory did flash into my mind of her jogging down a hill at night.

I concentrated harder. She was worried and frightened. She was calling my name as she ran towards me, but I felt safe, because…

"RUSSELL!" I whispered loudly - a huge spike of anxiety and fear hit me all at once.

The machines around me started to beep and squeak rapidly.

"What's wrong doctor. What's happening?"

I'm here, Gwen! It's okay, I'm right outside the door.

Russell!

"Bob, go get him. She needs to see that he's okay."

He looked at her, questioningly. "Who?"

"Russell. Bring him over."

I saw him hurriedly walk away, as my mother stood up. Then Russell slid into the chair next to the bed, and grasped my hand tightly.

Oh, it's you.

"Yeah, it's me," he replied, smiling brightly, relief exuding from his every pore.

"I think you were in my dream," I whispered hoarsely.

"Do you recognize me now? Do you know who I am?" he asked, hopefully.

"I was worried."

"What were you worried about?"

"I heard you get hurt. I heard you hit the floor. I couldn't turn around to save you. Are you okay?"

He looked at me in confusion.

"There was a barn…"

"Oh, yeah, there *was* a barn. We went to the farm to look at… Christmas trees. Do you remember that?"

"The goats were too skinny."

"Yes, that's right! You fed them grass through the fence, and a lady scolded you. She wanted us to buy feed."

"Did we get hot chocolate?"

"No, we never got hot chocolate," he smiled sweetly.

A nurse came around behind Russell and placed a vase of flowers on the bedside table. "These just came for you. I'm glad to see you're feeling better. You had us all very worried." She smiled and walked out of view.

The scent of the flowers hit me, and I recoiled, turning my head away from the stench.

Ick! What is that horrible smell?

"You don't like the flowers? I can move them if you want."

Why would anyone send such horrible smelling flowers?

"Do you want me to at least read the card?"

I heard him stand up and remove the card from its envelope. A second later, I heard him gasp.

I looked back, breathing through my mouth, despite the pain it caused.

What is it? What's wrong?

He just stood there staring down at the note, reading it over and over again. The color had gone from his face.

"Read it," I whispered.

"No." He was visibly shaken. "I'm going to take these away. I'll be right back."

Russell! Read it.

He wheeled around, shock across his face. "Gwen, I'm going to…"

My eyes focused on a center flower within the bouquet, a memory flooded back in - Russell and I were leaning over the workbench in the barn, and he was telling me the name of the flower… the one that the girls…

"Lily of the Valley!" I exclaimed, as loud as my hoarse voice would allow. The monitors beeped and squawked in complaint again.

"What… you mean the flowers?" he asked, clearly confused.

The doctor rushed back to my bedside, responding to the alarms. Checking the monitor readout, he proclaimed, "Okay, a little too much excitement for one day!"

My mom hurried over and took my hand.

"Gwen, listen to me. It's okay. Calm down. You're safe. I'm here."

The doctor held up the IV and injected something into the line. "I'm going to give her something to take the edge off."

"Lily of the Valley!" I repeated. She looked at me confused, and then anxiously up at the doctor.

"The girls… the girls…" I tried to explain, but then my voice started to sound far away, until it became a disjointed thing separate and apart from my being.

I saw my mom's face blur…

Chapter Thirty-Two
The Awakening

Wednesday, the week before winter break, coincidentally the day of the New Moon, I returned home from the hospital.

"It's so good to have you home. The house has been so lonely without you," my mother cooed, as she poured me some tea. "The school has been very cooperative about your homework. You'll have all of Christmas break to catch up, and when school starts up again in January, everything will go back to normal."

Normal? Will anything ever be normal again?

"Well, as normal as can be expected," she said. "I'm sure it will take awhile for the gossiping to die down. After all, your story is all over the news. The zoo was very generous not forcing us to pay for all the damage to the aviary. They were happy you survived such a horrific night, and, between you and me, I think they liked having the media attention. They'll get more people buying tickets. It's a win-win."

Win-win? Who wins from any of this?

I glanced around the kitchen, and out into the living room. My mom had everything decorated with the usual Christmas decorations, but the tree was larger this year.

315

It looked familiar.

"Yes, Russell brought it. He said it's just like the one you'd found together. He thought you would like it when you came home."

Memories of the tree farm spiked my heart rate and brought about another panic attack. I started to feel flushed and lightheaded.

"Okay, remember we talked about this. Just breathe. The doctor said this is a normal response to trauma. Just remember, you're safe. Okay? Breathe with me."

She put her hand on my face, turning it away from the tree, to look her into the eyes. "Breath in deeply. Hold it. Count to three. One. Two. Three. Good, now exhale slowly. Good. Let's do that again."

It started to work, I calmed, - my insides no longer a hive of bees being set on fire.

"Better?" she asked.

"Yeah," I nodded, continuing to inhale and exhale slowly, until my vision cleared, and only the smell of the tea was present in the forefront of my mind.

"It's only the first day, honey. It will get easier. Do you want to talk about it?"

No.

"Okay, that's fine too."

You can hear me?

"Yes, I can," she nodded. "*Now* do you want to talk about it? We're alone. Your dad is at work. We've got a lot of catching up to do."

Shocked and speechless... I didn't even know what to do with myself.

"All right," she reached out and held my hands in hers, "how about I start. Yes, I knew."

"You knew... *what*?" I asked suspiciously, the taste of stomach acid rising into my throat.

"Please don't be angry. I had to keep us safe, Gwen. I *had* to. But you started to make it impossible as your powers blossomed." She turned her face away from me. "You were so willful – so stubborn."

My shock gave way to a feeling of betrayal.

"And then you met Russell. I suppose it was meant to happen. These things always do. I'm just so sorry I didn't take Brighid up on her offer when I had the chance. We might have been able to work together to prevent all this."

The betrayal turned to resentment. I pulled my hands free.

Hurt shadowed her face, "I just didn't know if I could trust her. So, yes, I tried to keep you from going back over there!"

The resentment turned to anger.

"How could you?" I screamed. The exertion immediately exhausted me, and a river of tears streamed from my eyes.

"Like I told you, to *protect* the both of us," she sighed, looking at me with regret and sorrow. "The last thing we needed was you getting stronger. It would draw attention. But now I realize, if you'd spent time with her, you might have learned to defend yourself better. You might not have ended up in a coma for two weeks."

"I managed to survive, didn't I?" I asked glibly.

"Well, yes, but…"

"Exactly *who* were you trying to protect me from? Because that didn't exactly work out so well, did it?"

I could feel my blood pressure rising again, and my breathing becoming erratic.

"Gwen, are you sure you're feeling up to this? This might be too much."

"No, I need to know!"

"I realize that!" Tears fell from the corner of her eyes. "Again, I'm *so* sorry I made you feel like you were wrong when you saw the ghost. I was wrong when I made you stop talking to the animals. Everything that made you special, I tried to make go away."

Watching her wipe the tears from her cheek, my anger ebbed. I felt the depth of her guilt.

She slowly shook her head and again reached across the table to grasp my hands. "My grandmother fled Scotland to put everything behind her. She wanted a fresh start. But, the magic, and the bloodline, they were bigger than *her wants*. She came to Douglas thinking she would find sanctuary with the relatives who'd established a new way of life, only to find herself in the clutches of something just as repressive - The Coven of the White Oak. They married her off immediately, despite only being a child."

"How old was she?"

"Thirteen."

"That's insane!"

"I know, but times were much different back then," she frowned. "After the marriage," she continued, "her husband, Alexander MacDonald, along with *some* of the Blackwoods, MacKinnons and MacGregors, branched off to create a whole new coven, without the High Priestess' blessing. They called themselves, Keepers of the Gate. They chose to worship a different Goddess, Hecate. She was a nocturnal Goddess of magic and witchcraft, believed to be able to cross from the underworld to the physical world with ease - often referred to as the Goddess of the Dead, who presides over deserted places. Their Wiccan practices were no longer about living in harmony with nature, seeking guidance, or healing. It was about control, money, and power by any means at their disposal - including black magic."

"Black magic? And your grandmother, my great grandmother, she was caught up in this?"

She nodded, "And apparently, it was a *very* dark time for her."

"Why, what happened?"

"She suffered a lot of trauma at the hands of her husband and members of the group - losing all her sons in infancy. I think that's why she was even more protective over her first-born daughter - knowing she was special in more ways than one. She died when she was 53. I was only 2 at the time. My mother had just married Don Campbell, who later adopted me as his own. She never spoke of anything that happened prior to meeting him."

"How *did* your grandmother die?"

"I don't know! Again, my mother wouldn't talk about it."

"That's sad."

"It explains a lot, in retrospect..." she paused, gazing off towards the window as she took another sip of tea. "...you know that old Victorian House you were always so drawn to as a child - the one you..."

Just escaped from recently.

"Yeah... of course."

"That was their Covenstead!"

"Whose? The Coven of the White Oak?"

"No, the Keepers of the Gate. They took it over after the house was abandoned."

"What? Wait... that's where they *worshipped* Hecate?"

"Yes *and* where they practiced necromancy and forms of black magic as part of those rituals. They believed Hecate would bestow wealth and blessings on her followers, but only if she was honored to her satisfaction - she was known to be cruel, if displeased. All sorts of wild, nocturnal animals were her sacred animals, especially dogs. They often referred to them as *hellhounds*, because you would hear them baying and barking like mad whenever Hecate was wandering about at night. Offerings made by her zealots usually included a sacrifice of a dog at the crossroads."

"That's awful."

My mom stiffened, and an angry scowl bunched her face. "Oh... it gets worse... much worse. That's why they took *you* to the house. Sacrifices were always made at the crossroads, as a means to placate the mistress of ghosts - the crossroads, being the location of a gateway between the living and the dead. The best time to offer a sacrifice was during the festival honoring her – November 30th. The Keepers of the Gate had been practicing blood magic, using blood from the other girls, to power their spells, all in preparation to offer *you* to Hecate that night."

I shivered at the thought.

"Yeah, I kind of figured that much. I guess I'm pretty lucky."

"*Luck* had nothing to do with it. You were right, you did survive just fine, but that's because you were strong. And I'm so thankful for that!"

My mom leaned back, squeezing my hands gently from across the table, and smiled. I could barely remember the last time I felt real affection from her. I let the moment, and the warm feelings, linger. After a short pleasant silence, I motioned toward the television.

"The other night on the news, they showed a picture of the Victorian. I couldn't believe it! It's amazing... nothing but ashes and rubble now. I'm kind of glad I was the one to bring it down, even if it *was* by accident. Good riddance!"

"Maybe it wasn't an accident. You just weren't aware that it was your deepest intent to be rid of that place! But, yes, good riddance! You know, the renovation was nothing but a ruse, anyways. The Keepers hoped that by opening that door again, between worlds, they could keep the site intact. That's why they were *not* happy with your interference in the slightest!"

How did she find out about that?

"I had some suspicions, late last summer, but… Brighid filled me in on all the rest."

"So, I don't get it… why Ciara? Why was she involved with them? Isn't she the next in line to be the High Priestess of the Circle? I mean… isn't she?"

"She would have been. This was a devastating blow for Brighid!"

"I can't even imagine! Does anyone know what happened to her, or to that jerk, Toby?"

"They found Toby unconscious in the Avian Eatery that night, but Ciara was nowhere to be found."

"Is she the one who sent the bouquet? Russell won't tell me."

"I suspect so," she nodded. Then tilted her head and pursed her brow. "I'd been meaning to ask you, why did you react so strongly to the smell? Russell said you told him it had a horrible odor, but it just smelled like flowers to us."

"It was confusing. I imagined I was picking up the stench of Valerian. I guess it's because the scent of the Lily was used to *mask* the Valerian oil she injected us with. To me… it was the smell of death."

She gazed at me in silence for a long time, a sad, worried crease in her brow. Finally, she said, "Let me warm up your tea." She retreated to the kitchen, and a moment later returned with the teakettle and box of Scottish shortbread.

The sight made me smile. A happy memory of the day Russell sat in the kitchen and convinced my mom to come to dinner.

"I've always wondered who sends these to you."

"When I was very little, some *friends* of my grandmother, from Scotland, came to visit me and my mom. I didn't know anything about our bloodline then. I loved their accents, loved their smiles, and especially their sense of humor. After they returned to Scotland, and literally every year since, they've sent a Christmas tin, just like this - even after my mother died. It's just a special reminder of those people."

"Did you ever see them again? Are they relatives?"

"No, I never saw them again, and yes, they're relatives. They would be very old by now, I'd imagine, so I'm surprised they still keep it up." She tapped the tin. "Unless... they passed the tradition on to someone else."

"Do you think it's because they knew you were the heiress?"

She took a sip of tea. "Oh my, I never thought of it that way before."

"Russell said if you were indeed the granddaughter of the missing heiress, and one of the 'first daughters' of the old blood line, then there would be a pretty big shake up in the coven hierarchy, both here and in Scotland." I shrugged, "I told him if it were true, I didn't think you'd want anything to do with it."

"Well, you're right about that. I'm a wife and mother, that's all."

"Hardly."

She frowned. "What's that supposed to mean?"

"That's *not* all. If Brighid sensed the old blood line in both of us, and if Russell told me that I was more powerful than his sisters, even with them training their whole lives, then that would mean *you* would be the most powerful one of all."

She scoffed, dipping her shortbread into the tea, "I don't think so."

"Why? You're just rusty! After all, you've been reading my thoughts this whole time, and dad said you had a gifted green thumb, which means you're probably intuitive about medicinal herbs and healing remedies. Heck, I bet you even talk to animals, just I like me."

"You're not wrong. But my mother did to me exactly what I tried to do to you."

"Why?"

She ignored the question, lost in a memory. "I was forbidden to use my gifts. I was *never* to show them... not ever. We had to suppress our powers to stay hidden!"

Exasperated, I asked, "Hidden from *who*?"

"When she met my dad, the man who raised me that is, she hid my biological father's identity from both of us. She just wanted to be a normal housewife, and raise me without any knowledge of our coven history."

"Did you ever find out who he is?"

"Yes, while you were in the coma, I had divining sessions with Brighid daily. She was able to determine that it was, Joseph Blackwood, the son of James Blackwood and

Catherine MacGregor. Catherine was the daughter of the man who owned all the land out where MacGregor's farm was built. Her husband, James Blackwood, was the heir of the Blackwood fortune, and the builder of the Blackwood Estates."

"Wow! Mom, that's nuts!" I exclaimed. My brain started spinning, trying to connect it all. "That makes us related to the founding families of Douglas. That's so cool! Dang, if you can prove it, do you get an inheritance or something? That would be awesome!"

She laughed uncomfortably, shaking her head, "I don't know about any of that."

"Does Dad know?"

"Oh, but hold on, Maggie MacGregor owns the farm now, and she's married to Ewan Blackwood. Were they part of the Hecate coven? The Gate Keepers?"

"Keepers of the Gate," she corrected. "The gate is in reference to the crossroads, Hecate being its guardian."

"Okay. But it was their son, Toby, who came after me. Why?"

"Ciara shared the news about you being the one to close the portal at the Victorian, and that you were of the old blood line. This alerted the Blackwood and MacGregor families. Ciara was next in line to be the High Priestess of the Circle, sure, and she desperately wanted that power. However, by taking over the Circle, she meant to *dissolve* it, and focus all her attention on worshiping Hecate. The Keepers of the Gate would become the most powerful people in Douglas. They'd have control over the politics of the town, and reap the benefits, with Ciara in charge. She didn't want to wait around for that day though, she had been corrupted, to put it nicely, and *you* were in the way."

"Me?"

"I think she felt threatened by your acceptance into the family. And being of the old blood would mean you would be considered above her to take over the coven. She *couldn't* let that happen. So she empowered herself through blood magic, with the intent of offering you up to Hecate on the full moon, and the day of her observance."

Shaking my head in disbelief, I responded, "I can't believe I was going to be a sacrifice..."

I could have died.

I let the words settle upon me again - a cold shiver running up my spine.

"It would get you out of the way so she could still pursue her plans."

"What about you?" I asked her. "Does that mean they could still come after you, too?"

"I don't know," she shrugged.

"And she's still out there?"

She nodded, "Yeah, but Toby's in custody, and the police are looking into it!"

"Do you know what will become of the Circle? To Russell's family?"

"Brighid mentioned several key members of the community were in the coven, so I have a feeling they'll be able to keep this all under wraps and divert attention where it's needed - the MacGregor's farm, and the Keepers of the

Gate." She then pulled her face up tight, squinting her eyes at me, "*You* need to *let this go* now, and leave it up to the authorities to track her down. Do you hear me? Your private detective days are over!" She wagged her finger at me. "No more trying to take on the world by yourself."

"I know. I know," I responded, holding my hands up in surrender. "Trust me, I'm hanging up my Sherlock Holmes cap."

As I said that, another flashback - Russell screamed at the EMT while I was in the ambulance.

The flush returned, and my heart sped up.

"Russell yelled something at the ambulance guy, didn't he? He was trying to get him away... he was shouting for the police, and..."

"Okay, so it's starting to come back to you."

"Whoa... that guy, the EMT, he was one of... them, right?"

"Yes, he injected you with something, probably meant to kill you, but put you in a coma instead. You should have seen Russell. He just went crazy! One of the cops, who by the way, according to Brighid, is part of the coven..."

I gasped.

"No... no... relax, part of the Circle, not the Gate. Brighid made sure he was there."

I sighed in relief.

"Anyway," she continued, "the officer pulled Russell off the guy. In that state, who knows what Russell might have done! They took the EMT away, and left Russell's name completely out of their reports. After all, he was just protecting *you*."

."What happened to that guy?"

"Brighid assured me he'd be taken care of."

"So, *both* covens have people in positions of power? How can we be sure that *more* of them aren't just waiting around the corner for the next chance to come get us?"

A fresh wave of panic rapidly set in. I couldn't breathe. My chest felt tight.

In my mind, I found myself back in that corner of the office again - Toby grabbing my arms, yanking me across the desk. I was hitting, kicking, and screaming, as he tried to hold me still. I could see Ciara's face contorted by hate as she held the syringe above me.

"GWEN! Snap out of it! Look at me!" my mom yelled.

I opened my eyes, to see her holding my face in her hands again, yelling my name, urging me to breathe.

When will this nightmare be over?

"Gwen, it *is*. It's over now."

Chapter Thirty-Three
Yuletide

Russell stopped by for a visit Thursday after school. We didn't discuss the coven, or Ciara, choosing to keep our conversation light, just relishing one another's company.

Friday afternoon, he came by again, but this time when I opened the door, he stood proudly, extending his hand to present me with a giant candy cane wrapped in a red satin bow.

"They delivered Secret Santa Candy Canes to all the classes today." He blushed, and winked, "I figured I'd deliver yours in person."

Just the sight of him always brightened my day, but the surprise candy was an added bonus. Then he pulled his other hand from behind his back and produced a tin of Hershey's Cocoa powder.

"I'm going to make you the best cup of Hot Chocolate the world has ever seen!"

"Really? Well then, by all means, come in."

I stepped back and allowed him to pass, closing the door behind. "I considered not letting you in, but cocoa… how could I say no to that."

"You considered NOT letting me in?"

"I might have thought about it."

"Might?"

"Oh, fine!" I relented. "I just didn't want you to know how much I missed you or that I was counting down the minutes until you knocked at the door."

"Okay, now THAT is more like it!"

He placed the cocoa powder down on the kitchen table and turned towards me, playfully coming at me, wiggling his fingers. I ran into the living room, and jumped on the couch, picked up a pillow and threw it at him. He lunged, and fell onto the coach. I jumped off, giggling, and ran to the other side of the coffee table.

He tossed a pillow at me, hitting me on the side of the head.

"Hey! Hey, you two. No roughhousing. Gwen, I know you're bored, but stop jumping on everything."

Russell looked up guiltily from the couch - another pillow in hand ready to throw across the room. He then brought it back down with lightning speed.

"It's his fault. He had the tickle monster fingers out."

"Your dad should *never* have told him about that," she laughed, shaking her head. She gazed at us for a second, lost in a moment.

It's so nice to see you happy, she thought.

Russell and I looked at each other and smiled.

We won't be able to have any private conversations now, will we?

My mom laughed, and turned, facing the kitchen. *As if you ever did.*

"MOM!"

"Oh, look, cocoa."

"Don't pretend you didn't just hear that," I called out.

This new understanding was a welcome relief. Amazingly, the whole experience had just brought us closer.

"I brought that over to make *real* hot chocolate. Not like the watered down, wimpy stuff at school." Russell rose and followed my mom into the kitchen. "I was wondering if you had enough milk and sugar for me to make a pot. You can have some too, of course."

"Of course! And as luck would have it, I do!" she stated.

"I was also wondering if you guys wanted to join us up at the house for our Yule celebration. We'll be gathering on the 22nd for the Solstice. There's gonna be great food, *of course*, and music, aaand... we'll be lighting a big bonfire out in the field to gather round at midnight. It's one of our annual traditions, along with the lighting of the Yule log."

"How is your family doing, by the way? Is your mom okay?" she asked.

"It's been really rough the last few weeks, as you can imagine. Ciara's betrayal has shaken our family to the core."

Empathizing, she nodded then continued, "This whole thing has just been awful... for everyone!"

He turned to me. "Aileen and Rose have been especially depressed. That's why I think it'd be great if they could see you. They've been so concerned - asking about you every day. If anything, you have to come just so they'll leave me alone."

Worry shadowed my mom's face, "I don't know, Gwen. Are you up to it? Won't being around too many people bring on more panic attacks?"

I thought about it as I watched Russell heating up the milk in the saucepan, stirring slowly.

It would be nice to see Brighid and the sisters... and I'm sooo bored.

"Okay, then," he exclaimed, turning back around to smile at me. "It's decided."

"Well, hold on. I have a say in this, too," my mom quipped. Holding her hand up, she asked, "What about Bob?"

"Well, he can come too, of course. He and dad get along great."

"No, I meant... how will you explain the rituals, and the Yule Altar?"

"My dad has co-workers come each year, and they aren't part of the coven. The ritual parts happen later, around the bonfire. By then, most everyone else has gone home." Russell puffed out his bottom lip and brought his palms together pleading. "Please, my mom would be so happy."

"Okay, okay. Twist my arm already. What is it with you? I just can't say no." She shook her head, smiling. Leaving us alone in the kitchen, she went off to tend to something in the back of the house.

"It'll be good for you, in my opinion, to get out of the house," Russell stated, as he began to slowly pour cocoa into the warming milk. He concentrated on stirring, adding sugar, and the concoction began to thicken.

Yummm.

"Don't be too impressed. This is the only thing I know how to cook."

～

The front door was practically covered by an enormous fresh evergreen wreath, speckled all over with red berries and little silver bells.

When the door opened, amid the bright jingling of the bells, Cameron greeted us each with a warm hug.

I'd been nervous the entire drive up about how the rest of Russell's family would react towards me. I felt guilty, as if for some reason, I had brought about Ciara's downfall. I cost them their child. But Cameron's big warm hug assured me I was welcome... loved, even. I nearly sobbed against his soft plaid shirt.

"Gwen!" Rose squealed with delight, racing to the door, pushing away her father and wrapping me in a hug of her own. "I am so, so, sooo glad you're okay."

We held one another for a long while. Her energy, like cough syrup to a sore throat, made me feel better from the inside out. When she released, I was actually disappointed.

"Thank you, I'm glad I am, too."

"Well don't just stand there, come in, come in!" Cameron insisted.

We gathered in the foyer, hanging our coats, as we'd done before, and then made our way out into the great room.

I was awed at all the tiny white lights strewn throughout. Literally everywhere... it was, in a word, magical. Sprigs of evergreen, holly, and ivy had been tucked into every nook and cranny and across every window frame. Mistletoe dangled above the archway between the dining room and kitchen, as well as over the entrance and down the wide hallway leading into the heart of the house.

A small log with three lit candles perched atop the center of the fireplace mantel, and fresh garland draped beneath it. On either side of the big stone fireplace were two large pots filled with tall Birch branches, and at the far end of the huge space towered a giant tree covered in white candles, red berries, white berries, and small paper packages.

A help-yourself buffet steamed and glistened across the dining room table with too many dishes to identify. The combination of smells was scrumptious!

A small gathering of men clustered around Cameron's liquor cabinet toasting one another and laughing.

Cameron announced us loudly over the din of the room, and, in response, the group lifted their glasses and let out a hardy "Slàinte mhath" – which sounded like Slan ge var.

Cameron led my father over to join them, while a bustle of ladies, led by Brighid, emerged from the kitchen.

"Och, ah'm sae happy ye could join us! Come haur, my dear, I need tae hug ye." Brighid shuffled towards me in a flowing green velour dress, her arms wide, and brought me in for a squeeze.

And, just as it was with Rose, a warm healing elixir of positive energy flowed so generously from her soul. It soothed every part of me still in need of mending, and a huge weight lifted from my shoulders.

She whispered in my ear as she held me, "We watched o'er ye evert night, yer mum an' me, pullin ye fae that dark slumber. Ah'm sae glad ye heard us an' came back into the realm o' the livin. I can feel hoo, being stuck in that limbo between livin an' deid, has malafoustered sae much o' yer light! But tis still thaur... can ye feel it?"

I do.

The women had formed a loose circle around me. I hadn't even noticed them gathering. Even my mom was part of the circle, holding hands with Rose on one side, and Aileen on the other. A wonderful warmth filled me to the core.

"Aye, thaur tis. Thaur tis the light."

Yes, there it is.

As Brighid pulled away, she kept hold of my hands, smiling. "Welcome back, dear ane."

I felt dizzy for a second. "Thank you," I responded meekly. These weren't the words that expressed my feelings to any adequacy, but they were all I could think to say.

Looking to my mother, holding hands with Rose and Aileen, I felt this sense of… togetherness. A belonging I'd never experienced before.

I slid into her arms and hugged her tightly. "Thank you, too, for watching over me."

She resisted it at first, I could tell she hated the sudden spotlight, everyone watching us, but I wouldn't let go, not until I felt her relax and hug me back.

"Braw!" Brighid cheered. "Aileen, want tae turn up the music?"

A tune, reminding me of something from a medieval movie, had been playing softly in the background. Aileen disappeared, and the song abruptly changed to an up-tempo instrumental complete with bagpipes and drums.

"I ken, isnae the Christmas music ye're uised tae," Brighid smiled. "Elizabeth, come intae the kitchen an' have a wee nip o' mulled wine."

My mom smiled sheepishly and followed the women into the other room. Aileen awkwardly approached. I opened my arms. After a few long moments' hesitation, sadness filling her face, she finally moved in for a hug.

Oh, see that was what I was afraid of.

"I'm sorry," I whispered into her ear. Her body relaxed in response. I heard her sniffling. "Really, I am. I never wanted any of this."

"I know. I know, and you don't have anything to apologize for." She stepped back, wiping her eyes, her mascara running slightly. "It's just…"

"Yeah, I know. It sucks."

She nodded, and I could tell she was holding back even more tears. Finally, she straightened herself up, and shook it off. "You're probably wondering where Russell is. Right?"

"He does seem to be absent, yes."

"We teased him about how dirty his room was, and, if he was ever going to show you his inner sanctuary, he would have need to make it habitable for humans."

This made me giggle. "Oh, dear. That bad, huh?"

"You have *no* idea! Boys are gross." With this she finally smiled, and whispered, "If you go now, no one will notice you missing."

I took the hint. I slunk down the hallway, trotted down the steps to the next level. When I emerged from the stairwell, I saw his door ajar. I could hear hurried rustling and the slamming of drawers.

I peeked around the corner, and yelled, "Boo!"

"Shit!" he exclaimed, jumping and staring back at the door in confusion. "Don't! Do! That!"

I laughed.

"Gwen? What are you doing here already?"

"We're early. Sorry. I didn't mean to scare you."

He tucked in a sock that was sticking out, and pushed the drawer closed. He hurried to his closet and shut the door in haste, scanning the rest of the room in a panic for anything embarrassing.

"Sooo… whatcha doing?" I asked, completely entertained by his fussing about.

I savored the moment slowly, sniffing the air, searching for anything that screamed out for further investigating.

"Don't even think about it." Russell warned with a grin. He covered the distance between the closet and I in two long strides.

I ducked down and veered off to the left to inspect his soccer trophies, but he predicted my moves, from previous attempts, grabbed me around the waist, and pulled me into his embrace.

"Let *me* show you around, little miss nosey pants!"

He held me against him, stepping us forward together, and shared details of the many competitions he'd won.

I steered us towards the shelves of team photos.

"Oh my, look how young you were. Wow, look at that hair! I like it much better now."

"Thanks."

Then I noticed a letter open on top of his dresser drawers. It was from Princeton.

"Russell! You were accepted?"

"Yeah, about that... I'd been meaning to tell you. I applied to several places, mostly because my dad wanted me to."

I felt a lump in my chest.

Whispering to myself more than anyone, I said, "You got accepted at your dad's alma mater... he must be proud."

"Hey, that doesn't mean I have to go. It just means they'll take me. Don't worry, I'm not going anywhere. I got into Douglas as well!"

"But, this looks like a *full ride*. For soccer. Russell, this is incredible! Princeton! *And* you get to keep playing!"

"Gwen, I'm not leaving. Please, just close that up!" He gently took the letter from me and stuffed it back into the envelope. "I have something much better I'd like to show you." He scurried over to his nightstand and picked up a small wrapped box sitting in front of a framed photo. "I was gonna save this for later, but what the hell."

"Hey, where did you get that photo from?"

I saw a guilty expression pass across his face, and a blush hit his cheeks.

"I'm not mad you have a picture of me on your nightstand, I'm flattered. I just don't remember posing for this."

"Kevin's been taking candid shots all school year with his new 35mm automatic camera. He said he didn't want people to pose and look stiff, he wanted to capture moments in time. When he showed them to me, I was quite impressed. He has a great eye. But this one, well this one caught *my* eye, and I couldn't look away."

Now it was my turn to blush.

He came over and tapped the edge of his bed for me to sit, then presented me with the small gift.

He nodded to it. "Go ahead, open it."

I pulled at the tape on the wrapping, and a little wooden box fell out into my lap. There was a Celtic symbol chiseled into the lid.

"That's a *Serch Bythol* symbol."

I traced my finger over the smooth etching.

"What does it mean?"

He blushed again.

"What? Come on. You can't give this to me and not tell me what it symbolizes?"

"It represents two people joined together. Forever. Mind, body, and spirit."

"Wow…" My heart leapt into my throat. I gazed deep into his eyes.

Am I dreaming?

"Now *open* the box. The present is actually inside."

"*That* was kind of… well… I don't think anything can top that!"

"Come on… I'm dying here. Open it."

"Can't a lady just enjoy the moment?"

Russell, as impatient as a little kid on Christmas morning, leaned forward, urging me to just get on with it. It was just so cute I couldn't stop grinning.

Slowly, prolonging the drama, I lifted the lid to reveal a little crush of black velvet. Resting atop, gleaming in the soft light of his room lay a gold necklace of two intertwined hearts. My breath caught in my throat.

"Oh my god, Russell. It's sooo beautiful!"

"You like it? I really wanted you to like it."

"I *love* it." I stood up and gestured for him to place it around my neck. I pulled my hair back, so he could bring the dainty gold chain around and fasten it.

"Okay, turn around let me see."

I felt positively princess-like!

"It's beautiful, Gwen. I mean... *you* look beautiful."

"I can't thank you enough, this is so special!" I reached up to kiss him, but he backed away, a sly grin on his face.

"Hey!" I balked.

"Okay, *now* read the note."

I stepped forward, and he stepped back. "Why are you being such a weirdo? Just let me kiss you, and thank you properly."

"Nope!" He laughed, backing away again. "Read the note first."

I stepped back, grabbed the box off the bed. Tucked in between the velvet and the wood interior was a little note. Unfolding it, I read aloud, "Will you go to..."

The question was followed by a list of events with empty boxes next to each: Winter Formal; Senior Prom; Graduation Party, and Scotland. Following the long checklist, the sentence ended... "with me?"

"Is this a joke?" I looked up at him, my mouth agape. "What am I supposed to do? Am I supposed to put a check mark next to *just one*?"

He shook his head, cleared his throat. "Gwenevere Iona Evans," he began, assuming a serious and formal tone while moving closer and taking my hand, "will you, Gwenevere Iona Evans, go to..." he swept his arm in arc over his head, "*all of the above* with me?"

A smile spread across his face in response to my expression.

"*All* of them?" I asked in confusion. "You're asking me to go to *Scotland*?"

He huffed. "Really? That's the *only one* that stood out?"

I started jumping up and down, unable to contain my excitement. I was absolutely over the moon, bursting.

"Can I kiss you now?" I asked, jumping back and forth, spinning in circles.

He planted his fists to his hips, tilted his head, and raised a questioning eyebrow. "Is that a yes?"

"YES! YES! YES! YES!"

～

When we returned upstairs to join the party, I was playing with the heart pendant around my neck. Before us, the great room had filled with strangers.

Russell stopped and pointed upwards. I looked.

Mistletoe. Sly dog.

He winked at me, bent down, and gave me a modest little kiss. It couldn't have been sweeter.

Scanning over the sea of adults, I finally recognized a familiar face standing between my mom and Brighid. It was Judith.

"Oh!"

"What is it?" Russell asked, looking over to the women talking.

"Erik isn't going to show up, is he?"

"Erik? Ohhh, I forgot to tell you about that, didn't I?" He shook his head, weighing his next words carefully.

"While you were *asleep*... well, let's just say... I had a few *words* with him."

"A few words?" I asked. "And how did that go?"

"Um, yeah. So, it's like this... he came up to Mike and I, all bragging about how, after what happened with you, he was off the hook and no longer a suspect in Suzie's murder."

I gasped. "He didn't!"

"Oh, yes, he did. And, well... something just snapped."

"Oh, dear. An emotional response, huh?" I asked, knowing what that meant. "What did you do?"

"I punched him in the face."

I tried not to laugh. "Seriously? You're just kidding, right?" The look on his face confirmed his words. "*No...* you really did!"

"Yeah, I did. I thought about you lying there in a coma, and about what he put you through - cornered like that in the library - and how he treated Suzie! I couldn't stand it anymore!"

"Aaand?"

Russell tipped his head and shrugged, "Bloody nose, is all. I didn't even break it. I used a little restraint. Not much... but just enough."

"Dang. *My* hero!" I beamed. "What about Judith? Is she mad at you?"

"You actually think he'd go running to his mommy? He didn't say anything. Besides, if he did, he'd have to admit what he did to deserve it. Judith's wrath would have been far worse."

"Ahhh… well… I can't say I'm disappointed, you know, about him not being here."

"Huh, would never have guessed!" he quipped. "Come on, let's join the party!"

As we continued, I noticed the pluck and lilt of the Celtic music. Pointing up into the air I asked, "Is it weird I miss hearing traditional Christmas songs?"

He tilted his head, noticing for the first time what was being played, before responding, "No, not at all. I don't think mum would mind if we switched it up a little. Hold on."

He let go of my hand and disappeared into the crowd, leaving me standing there alone. Finally, after a minute or two, the Celtic music stopped. A second later, a series of keyboard notes rang out, followed by a few strums of a guitar, then a steady 4-4 rhythm of a drumbeat.

Cheers erupted from the grown-ups around me, but I didn't recognize the song.

Russell appeared, noting the perplexed look on my face. "You haven't heard this before? Slade!"

I shrugged. "Is that the name of the song, or something else?"

Russell looked back at me, like I was from Mars. "The band… Slade! Oh my god, they're HUGE in Scotland."

People paired up around me, breaking into dance. Russell pulled me in close, with one arm behind my back, and the other hand up. He started rocking us side to side to the rock rhythm.

When the chorus started, most everyone bellowed along, "So here it is... Merry Christmas..."

He pushed me away, spun me around under his hand, and began to guide me through a swing dance.

"You're a quick learner!" he called out with approval.

"Let me guess, years of watching your sisters at dance rehearsal?" I replied loudly over the din.

"And years of parties like this!"

The frivolity continued on, with the room breaking into song each time the chorus repeated. As the music slowed, Russell pulled me in tight. Gazing into my eyes, he sang along quietly as the music wound to an end.

The final lyrics... the future had just begun.

Epilogue

It took a couple hours, on a crowded bus, to travel the length of Mull. The driver kept us occupied with historical tales of the area. Mostly though, he obsessed over the ever-changing moods of Scottish weather. People in the UK, in general, seemed obsessed with the weather throughout our entire visit. Apparently, the previous month, Scotland had experienced one of its wettest Junes, and the most thunder they'd seen in the 20th century. The driver mentioned the rain being so torrential that "the brolly couldn'y stop yer clothes fae being drookit!" This, I was told, had something to do with an umbrella and being soaking wet.

The week we arrived though, in July, was dry. If the crowds were any indication, it seemed to be the most popular time to visit.

A ten-minute ferry ride took us from the pier at Fionnphort, Mull across the Sound of Iona to the village of Baile Mor. Atlantic Grey Seals played alongside the ferry during the crossing. As we approached the pier in Baile Mor, charming stone cottages stared back at us. If I didn't know better, I'd think we'd travelled back in time.

According to the map, the Isle was only 3 ½ miles long by 1 ½ mile wide, with only about 150 residents on average year-round. It seemed most of them lived on this side –

East, facing Mull, where they'd be sheltered from the open ocean. In the wintertime, I heard, the west side, facing the Atlantic wasn't kind.

As we exited the crowded ferry, we could see the village bustling with activity, as tourists nosed through gift shops before setting out to explore the ruins of the Nunnery, the sacred sight of the Abbey, and St. Oran's chapel where king's were buried.

All these tourist destinations were just a short walk north from the village pier, with the highest point on the little island, Dun I, being only a little further. Dun I, meaning the Hill of Iona, was part of the ancient Celtic legend of Brighid, who was said to visit Iona at midnight during the summer solstice. At a small peaty water pool, adjacent to the hill, it's claimed she blessed the waters to carry healing to those in need. This place, the Well of Eternal Youth, is where Pilgrims can often be seen washing their faces, or drinking its waters, seeking new beginnings.

We, on the other hand, were headed to the west side of the Isle, in search of a different place, sacred only to a few.

Cameron, handling his heavy backpack of camping gear with ease, led us away from the pier, past the crowded gift shop and pub, onto a road that carried us up a hill.

Brighid, Aileen, Rose and my mom followed close behind, each carrying a pack with overnight essentials. Sadly, my father missed out, not being able to take time from work. He wasn't much for adventure anyways. Russell and I lagged behind the group, taking our time, relishing every moment.

As we crested the hilltop, I soaked in the scenery of meandering green pastures spread out before us. Dotting the landscape rose rocky mounts, and flocks of grazing sheep. Oddly, there wasn't a single tree to be found. For a girl from the Pacific Northwest, that amazed me.

From the moment we'd left the pier, I'd been aware of a peculiar sensation pulsing through my body – a sensation wholly unfamiliar. With each step, it was as if the very ground I walked upon responded to my presence with surges of electrical impulses. Even the air resonated within me - sparking endorphins, and spiking serotonin levels.

"It's beautiful, isn't it?" Russell remarked quietly.

I could only nod. I had no words to describe what I was feeling.

Cameron led us across the wild-flower strewn *Machair* where furry red-haired Highland cattle grazed, and the occasional random golfer passed through when using it as a golf course.

Then the ever-expanding view of the Atlantic Ocean spread out before us. It was breathtaking. The trail marker read, *Bay at the Back*.

From our vantage point, I could make out pink and green stones, rounded and smoothed from tumbling in the sea, scattered along the shoreline. Just beyond the rocky beach, giant waves crashed against the cliffs. The occasional waterspout gushed up high into the air before dissipating in the wind sweeping back out to sea.

We turned right, heading north along a sheep trail, and walked the length of the shoreline with views of tide pools and nesting Sand Martins in the cliff's nooks and crannies. We came up to Port Ban, a sheltered cove with a stunning beach of pale gold sand. The turquoise water glittered crystal clear as far as the eye could see. If I didn't know any better, I'd swear I was on some sort of tropical island.

Sea gulls cawed from overhead, and noisy Oyster Catchers - large black and white wading birds - chased the tide in and out for food. My heart filled beyond any previous known capacity.

"You okay?" Russell asked. "You're being awful quiet."

I still had no words. The electricity was now humming continually within me. The sheer profundity of the experience made me feel as though I would weep. It was as if I knew this place, and it knew me - was speaking *to* me.

Cameron stopped to adjust his pack, and Brighid took the lead, heading up a steep incline of precarious rocks. She picked her way with sure feet, making it appear easy, and arrived at the top of the mount.

Once I made the peak, I was met with a beautiful ocean view, with an almost 360-degree view of the surrounding Hebrides Islands. Just a few yards from the edge, Brighid had set down her pack, and was laying out a picnic blanket for us all. Glancing around I realized she had settled within the rocky ruins of a cottage.

It was the cottage that once stood overlooking the Atlantic Ocean, surrounded in mist and sea spray - just as it had been depicted in the painting.

Russell squeezed my hand as we approached, and said, "Are you ready to commune with your ancestors?"

Until that moment, I never understood what that missing part of me was. I had been homesick for a land I never knew.

At last, I was home.

Thank You

To my Editors: Thank you for your wonderfully eager response, when I told you I hoped to have Book Three out in spring. "Another one? So soon?" I guess I should be especially grateful that you agreed to continue to indulge me, at all, and grumble to yourselves out my purview. ☺ In any case, I'd like you to know that this year's long difficult journey would not have been successfully navigated had you not been part of the process.

To my Cover Artist: Thank you for bringing my vision to life in the beautiful piece of art you created – yet again. I wish you nothing but success in your future artistic endeavors. The world is your oyster.

Dear Readers,

Thank you for your kind reception of this nostalgic series, and for your positive responses to my characters and the world they live in. I enjoyed getting messages from readers, who were mid-way through a book, with their thoughts and feelings about what was happening. Truly gratifying.

I'm glad it offered up some laughs, had you a little scared, and maybe even pulled at a heartstring or two, along the way.

Love,
Ginger